# *Shadows in our View*

By

Lj Ryan

Published in Ireland.

Publisher Lj Ryan. All Rights Reserved.

First printed 2023

Cover by – BGS, Books Go Social

With thanks to my editor:

Eamon Ó Cléirigh - http://clearviewfictionediting.com/

Contact - clearviewediting@gmail.com

Learn more about Lj Ryan –

Twitter: @authorljryan

Instagram: lj_ryan07

Facebook: facebook.com/authorlj.ryan

# *Prologue*

∞

The body lay across the train tracks, with Declan, hidden behind some tree growth, watching to ensure there was no movement. Having placed it in that exact position, he knew it would be too late for the train to stop once it came around the bend. He checked his watch, hoping Irish Rail was as fastidious as he about time. Then an air horn blasted to his right.

'Yes!'

He glanced at the body. It was a shame really – the man about to be shredded had been a good asset, even a colleague. *But once his actions detrimentally affected my world, my business, then his fate was decided – his death inevitable. Good old Peter. When the drug took effect, your eyes lit up as your life flashed before you. Then the terror showed at the realisation that this was your end, you weren't getting out, your body unable to fight back, with only your brain left unaffected. Such a good choice of drug on my part. Good old Peter. When I placed you across the tracks, you were like a rag doll, spent and still. Only your eyes showed the truth.*

'You just lie here, like a good boy.' He'd patted his victim's head and laughed as he walked away.

*These days, I need to be judge and jury. Never too lenient – never show weakness. I have control. I'm the man with the power. You wronged me, Peter, and I can't have that. Now you are an example for those in the future – a calculated decision. Yes, you're a sacrifice but this is the best choice. No one will cross me once word gets out to those who need to know.*

*For everyone else, it's important to make this look like a suicide. It's a risk – people who knew Peter will be shocked, but they are stupid. It's revenge, pure, unadulterated, delightful revenge. The only disappointment is no one outside my world will know.*

He wanted to take a video on his cell phone, then remembered he'd left it in the bar where he and Peter met that evening. With modern technology, the Gardaí, if they showed any aptitude, could easily trace his whereabouts by tracking it. Such a slip-up wasn't going to happen on his watch. The bar didn't even have CCTV. No, the clientele would never allow that. Peter hadn't a clue when he met up for drinks and a goodbye chat. Slipping the tab into his beer was too easy.

He'd toyed with hiring someone to do the work but that would be too risky. They could blab to the Gardaí if caught, boast to their friends, get the cover-up wrong – too many scenarios that could see him locked up, or worse. The best option was to take care of his own issues. A calculated risk but the right option. His international colleagues would expect nothing less. Their respect would grow – their fear too. Besides, he enjoyed this kind of work. That look of terror on another victim – nothing like it.

When the train shot around the bend, the screeching started but it was too late, its wheels ripping through the motionless body. Declan almost climaxed as Peter was torn to pieces, his torso bobbing around under the carriages. Even with its diminishing speed, the freight train took nearly a half mile to come to a full stop.

'Nice.' He smiled as he moved out from the bushes to get a better look at the remains, ensuring first the coast was clear.

*This will show all that there's more to me than meets the eye. It will shut up my enemies once and for all.* He couldn't hold back a snort as he chuckled. Peter always thought they were partners. *Partners! Don't make me laugh.*

After nearly four years, the whole arrangement turned out to be one pathetic let-down – there was no other way to describe the situation. *Yes, it was mutually beneficial when we first started up but that was it – nothing more – and that train has now left the station.*

He chuckled again at his little joke. When Peter said he was stepping back from the operation, outrage surged through his veins as he listened to the idiotic reasons. Peter was being overly dramatic under the circumstances. *So what if his marriage was failing. Being married to that bitch, who wouldn't expect that?*

At first, his response was silence – impassive – showing no emotion. Peter's nervousness radiated from him. He thought fast and reset his tone, keeping his voice cool, friendly but authoritative. Peter was out of his depth, not the asset he'd hoped for. Pathetic. They'd shared secrets – not all of them but enough to justify silencing a threat. As he'd responded, he kept it all laughter and smiles, hiding his true intentions.

He picked up the pace as he walked away from the scene, his thoughts somewhat agitated, spoiling his earlier sense of achievement. The cause was clear. *That bitch, who, unfortunately, is my sister! However, this will shut her up. No one will get in my way.*

Ten minutes later, he was back in the pub, looking around the floor area.

'You looking for this?' the barman called out, loud enough for nearby punters to hear.

Declan raised his gaze, acting surprised. 'Fuck's sake, where was it? I got my friend to call it but it's offline.'

'Yeah, looks like the battery's dead. You left it where you were drinking, buddy. Lucky I found it and no one else.'

A knowing look passed between them – he'd paid him well.

# *Chapter 1*

∞

## Eight Years Later

David watched from their small office window. The sun was beaming down on the hill, with the children enjoying games of chasing while Laurel and Veronique tended to the younger ones on the picnic blanket. *What a wonderful life we've created here, mon amie.*

He turned to the three letters received earlier in the post, all sent from his solicitor, Jacques, in Paris. The first explained the details of the other two. 'A wonderful request and honour,' Jacques called it – an invitation from the committee of the Cannes Film Festival to be president of the jury that would choose the winner of the prestigious Palme d'Or and Grand Prix. He couldn't believe they wanted him to be a member of the jury – never mind actual president.

The second letter was worrying. The Columbian film project finally raised sufficient finance to complete the movie that fell apart in such a disastrous way nearly seven years ago. They now wanted him to go to Los Angeles to complete voice-over editing and then hit the movie trail of promotions and interviews when it premiered. That meant he could be gone for six months or more. He sighed. No way did he want to go, but he would need advice from Jacques about any existing contractual difficulties that may arise.

*Surely, after all this time, they can't force me to work for them again. Why can't they just leave it on the shelf where it belongs?*

He closed his eyes and thought back to that time in Columbia. While he rarely experienced nightmares now, sometimes certain events hit him like a ton of bricks, like when Jacqueline had seduced him. He'd tried everything to scrub the previous night away, his shower lasting longer than any restriction on the water would allow, washing and scrubbing almost beyond his skin's endurance. The hangover wasn't receding, and he didn't want it to. He deserved to suffer for what he'd done.

'How could I?' he roared, not caring if anybody heard him.

What did she want to achieve from this? Revenge? He'd found it so easy to stay faithful to Laurel, and this was the last week – the shoot was almost over – and now Jacqueline. *Bitch!*

If any member of the crew found out about this, they'd see it as a quick way to make some money through their so-called journalistic contacts. The French gossip columns would jump all over it.

When he stepped out of the shower and towelled down, he still didn't feel clean. Staring into the bathroom mirror, he felt nothing but disgust at himself. Yes, he'd had an affair and a few one-night stands but he'd never felt this guilty or this used before. He'd need to phone home, warn Papa, and prepare Laurel. He couldn't hide this, because there was no doubt about Jacqueline's objective.

Somebody was shouting in the corridor, along with what sounded like doors being barged open. *What the hell is happening now?*

People were running about. As he walked towards the door, it burst open and the Colombian police screamed at him, their machine guns pointing to the floor. He knew not to disagree with their orders. This was a drugs raid…

'There you are,' Laurel said, walking into the room.

He smiled and opened his eyes, his soulmate's sweet voice bringing him back from that horrible time. 'Yep, here I am.'

'Well, are you going to tell me what your mood is all about? As soon as you got that letter from Jacques, you disappeared, but I could see you through the window. You can't hide that tense look behind your sexy smile.'

He held out his hand and she took it as a full invitation to sit on his lap.

'Sexy smile, eh?'

'You know it.' She giggled. 'So, are you going to tell me?'

'Why don't you read them?'

She curled up with him in the chair and started reading. He helped when she struggled with a few of the complicated French sentences in Jacques' letter. As she read it, he closed his eyes, inhaling the calming lavender scent from her hair. Then her warm lips met his.

'President of the jury at the Cannes Film Festival? Wow, David, that's wonderful! Will you do it?'

'Would you mind?'

'No way! Shite, David, that's such an honour, I would never try to stop you from doing something you love.'

He felt such pride for the woman he held in his arms. 'Thank you, mon amie.' He kissed her, loving the sound of her pet-name, perfect for the woman he loved – his soulmate.

'So what's the other letter about?'

He tensed inside, though only for a moment, but knew she got the vibe straight away.

'Ahh, so this is the problem.' She read the last letter – no difficulty there for her, it was all in English. He watched her face as she made her way through it. Then she sat up from her comfortable, loving position. She looked at him, then turned to stare out the window, and all he could comprehend from her expression was that she was remembering something, or trying to.

'What is it, Laurel?'

'I don't know, it's just something I seem to… Ahh, it's nothing.'

'They want me to go to L.A. I don't. What do you think?'

'Now, that's a decision you need to discuss with Jacques. I wouldn't like you to go, either. It's such a distance, and for months, I'd say.'

He smiled once more. *Sometimes you know my thoughts and actions before I do, mon amie.*

She curled up on his lap and rested her head on his shoulder as he wrapped his arms around her, certain their thoughts were the same. *L.A. Los Angeles – It's such a different world over there...*

## *Chapter 2*

∞

Laurel paced the waiting area of Marseille Provence airport. She hated delays. Between her starting out to the airport and parking the car, Paul and Marc's flight arrival changed, with a twenty-five-minute delay – something about an aborted landing. Now, with the plane safe on the ground, baggage collection was her next annoyance.

When she turned back towards the arrivals' door, she recognised the familiar and welcome sight of her two friends coming through. As Marc checked his cell phone, Paul spotted her and smiled, and she ran to him and jumped into his open arms, wrapping herself around his well-defined body. She admired how he kept himself in such good shape with his regular gym workouts.

'You know I should be jealous,' Marc said, laughing as she pulled him into a group hug.

'But you know better. Welcome back to Marseille!'

By the time they got to Aix-en-Esperance, she'd informed them of all the news regarding the children since their last visit. Paul was quiet. Marc, on the other hand, chatted and responded in all the right places. Something was up – she knew it.

As soon as they exited the car, Emma and Jack ran towards them, calling their names. Group hugs and kisses ensued.

Laurel laughed at her children's excitement, knowing teenagers don't tend to act this way. Then again, few teenagers had wonderful uncles like Paul and Marc.

Marc looked around. 'Where's David and the rest of your brood?'

'He's probably inside, sending yet another argumentative email to the other Cannes' judges.' She shrugged. 'Pierre and Chantal were visiting their mother's family in the north but they're travelling home now and should be back for dinner. And the last of my *brood*, as you so eloquently put it, are hopefully taking their afternoon nap. If not, there'll be hell to pay later.'

Dinner went well, with all the adults taking time to recover from the delights they'd just savoured. The aroma of coffee and Cognac filled the room, adding to their culinary satisfaction. Laurel noticed that Paul was quieter than normal throughout.

'Right so, the kids are happily playing and reading, and Emma is gone to the cinema with Pierre. Are you going to tell me the real reason for this sudden visit? You were both here less than two months ago.'

'Laurel!' David looked surprised but then noticed both men's reactions and the deafening silence which ensued.

Marc shrugged. 'Tell them.'

'Declan is applying for parole.' Paul sounded defeated as he said it. 'And it's looking likely he's going to get it.'

Laurel snorted. 'The criminal justice system at its best.' She shook her head. 'Well, it's nearly six years, what did he originally get?'

'Ten,' Marc answered.

'So why so early?' David's furrowed brows showed his bafflement.

'Because he is proving to be the perfect reformed prisoner,' Laurel explained without hesitation. 'Besides, a prison year is not the normal twelve months. Am I right? I bet he's doing everything by the book, volunteering and helping others. Shite, I'd say he's even applied for a degree in psychology, or something close to that.' She glared at

Marc. 'Why the hell didn't you charge him with Peter's murder instead of just manslaughter?'

She knew why, and she'd been so angry when Paul first told her of the deal they'd made with her brother after his arrest. They'd no choice, really, with him threatening to go public with everything – the government couldn't take the risk. In the end, it got noticed by an investigative journalist and all hell broke loose, with the government collapsing. How could a drug baron and diamond smuggler use the government like he did, right under their noses, exploiting diplomatic bags and the transport of all new government cash into the country? Maguire Logistics & Transport had all the contracts, with Declan using every part of them for his smuggling and to facilitate his money laundering. Of course, it was with their mother's help. After all, Patricia was the CEO of the company.

A new and bitter election ensued. Paul and many other outgoing TDs lost their seats to upcoming promises, who swore they would clean out all the secrecy and corruption, and *guaranteed* a government with full transparency. The people were still waiting for that to happen. Life went on but the media didn't let them forget, constantly using the headlines: *Same old, same old.*

Paul decided not to continue in politics, returning to the legal trade and taking over his father's practice. He told

Laurel he was more drained from politics than defeated. Marc continued to work undercover but that proved difficult once their relationship was exposed in the press. *Underhanded,* the media opined about one of the lead investigating officers in a trial that brought down a government while being in a relationship with the then Minister for Justice. For months, the media wouldn't let up, with Marc losing his temper publicly when a particular investigative journalist interfered with an investigation, leading to him deciding to leave the force.

It was tough going at times, made worse by Paul's concern for his parents, whose Christian views left him anxious that he would lose them to their faith. His worries proved baseless when his dad unexpectedly called to their home one evening.

'So this is where you two are hiding out?' he stated with a smile. 'Don't worry, son, the media will soon tire of you and Marc and then we'll all get on with our lives.'

Paul nearly burst out crying and hugged his dad for ages.

'Easy now, son. When you're popping over for next Sunday's dinner, just make sure Marc is with you this time, and he brings both flowers and chocolates for your mam.

And a decent whiskey for me – you two have a lot to make up for with all this hiding from us.'

For Marc, life after service in the police force proved somewhat tougher. Over time, Paul and Laurel assisted him with setting up a private security firm. It was a struggle at the start but, within four years, it developed into one of the most successful in Ireland, with serious expansion into the UK, and now he was looking to develop contacts in the US. The company specialised in providing bodyguards and security for the Irish rich list, high-end special events, and famous visitors to both countries. However, parallel with that was its top-notch team of private investigators.

It had been a long journey, for everyone involved, and now Laurel saw that both men looked exhausted. Whatever they were involved in, it was as if the past two months had drained their energy from them. *Is there more to what they're telling me?*

Paul sat forward, his discomfort obvious. 'I'm sorry, Laurel, but your mam called to see me in my office last week.'

She let out a choked cry, and David wasted no time in moving to her side. 'She… She's free from prison?'

'Yes, everyone concerned felt it was best under the circumstances.'

'Circumstances? What about our feelings? Why didn't anyone inform us?' She leaned into David as he wrapped her tighter in his arms.

'As your solicitor for any affairs you have in Ireland, it was left to me to inform you. I'm sorry but she has cancer, and…it's terminal.'

Her eyes burned as the tears came. 'H-how long does she have left?'

'Six months, maybe a bit more, maybe a bit less.' He glanced at Marc. 'Laurel, she wants to meet with you.' He raised a hand to hold off her reaction. 'She said she needs to make amends. She's asked me to contact all of you, including your dad and Carl in L.A.'

Silence reigned for a long minute, interrupted by the soft vibrating hum of David's mobile. He ignored it but Laurel told him to answer it, in case it was family.

He looked at the screen. 'It's just one of the Cannes' judges. I'll phone them back.'

'No, go answer it. I'm ok, honest.'

She didn't feel ok, with her stomach churning, but she needed to show strength at this moment. Her mother was dying. Was it too late to make amends? Should she give Patricia one more chance, before it was too late?

'They can leave a voicemail,' he said, placing the phone in his trouser pocket.

She loved him so much for that small gesture. Yes, his life was now engrossed with the Cannes Film Festival but things were different – he'd changed from his old ways of placing his career first and family second. At first, she feared he would revert to the public life he had before they were together, but her confidence grew every time he opted to take the children to school, or helped her with daily chores before disappearing to the office to answer emails and make calls.

Now, his actions helped with her decision. She fixed her focus on Paul. 'Where does she want to meet?'

Marc shot up from his seat. 'Laurel, you can't honestly be considering the idea.'

David and Paul smiled, and she knew they'd expected her response. She dabbed her wet cheeks with a tissue. 'I can't carry hatred on my shoulders, Marc. She's my mother, she gave me life and now she's losing hers. I can't leave her with that lost opportunity of actually reconnecting with her family. It won't make up for what happened in the past – she really was a money-mad, power-hungry bitch – but we can make the present, and what little future she has left, a little easier for her.'

She felt David's heat as he kissed the top of her head.

Marc shrugged once, then nodded. 'Well, all I can say is more power to you. I honestly don't think I could.'

'You owe me a fiver, Marc.' Paul smiled. 'He was convinced you would say no.'

Laurel laughed as her tears continued to flow. 'Typical! I couldn't expect anything less from you two.'

Even so, she understood Marc's reasons, after all that had happened. Her mother had been a hateful, manipulative woman. She leaned back against David and allowed her thoughts to take her back seven years…

'Nice new offices, Patricia,' she said to her mother, then stopped in her tracks, her mouth falling open. 'Declan?'

'Are you surprised, my dear?' Patricia asked, a triumphant sneer plastered across her face.

She resisted the urge to snap back – not with so much at stake – and turned to her brother. 'What on earth are you doing here?'

He didn't respond, just nodded to Patricia.

'We're waiting for a call,' Patricia said.

The last thing Laurel had expected was this partial family reunion. *Declan? No. Pull yourself together, girl! It can't be him. It can't be!*

'Where are the documents?' Patricia asked, breaking the heavy silence.

Laurel watched Declan's face contort with rage, his gaze burning into Patricia, who reacted as if slapped. *What hold has he got on you, Mother?*

Knowing the meeting was to be acted out as a social visit, she gained a little confidence from this deviation from the agreed set-piece. If Declan was *Red Key*, she could build on this in the hope he'd expose himself.

'When will your call come through?' she asked, directing the question at Declan. 'Nothing will be handed over until I know David is safe.'

Her brother remained silent, giving no reaction. He just poured tea and offered it to her with a wry smile.

She looked away, disgusted but aware that she had work to do. 'You bastard.' She turned back to him. 'Why? What did I ever do on you?'

The tension only grew as he refused to answer any of her questions. She looked at her mother, sitting behind her desk. The woman kept her gaze lowered, but she was shaking.

*Why are you so nervous? Do you know?*

Declan slurped his tea, and the clinking of his cup returning to its saucer made her want a cigarette. She walked across the room to open a window and light one up.

Declan stepped in front of her. 'What are you doing?'

She kept her calm. 'I fancy a cigarette. I'm opening a window.' She sidestepped him and sniggered, knowing how much he hated smoking. He'd always argued when he came into the sitting room as she and Dad sat smoking and chatting into the night. *See how much you like this.* As she smoked, his eyebrows knitted together as he struggled to control his temper, his face reddening from the effort.

Nearly fifteen minutes later, his mobile started playing Bach's Fifth Symphony. He answered and, for the first time, Laurel heard him speak in Spanish – one-word answers each time, which may as well have been Swedish for all she understood. He hung up and looked hard at her. 'It's done.'

*It's done?* Her energy drained from her and she had to lean on the window frame to prevent collapse. *It's done.* All she wanted to do was ask about David but she needed to gain more from Declan. She pulled herself together and took a leaf from Patricia's direct-approach book.

'Declan, did you kill Peter?'

Patricia gasped. 'You bitch, what the hell are you doing?'

Declan raised his hand to stop Patricia from speaking further. 'We've done what we promised. I don't know what individuals are free. Mam told you we couldn't guarantee his safety once he left the police station. Where's the file?'

Laurel sensed his anger radiating through the room. Her dear brother was revealing a little too much of himself.

'Why did you do it, Declan?'

He didn't move or say a word, just stared at her, his mouth worked into a thin line with his lips pulled back against his teeth.

'Answer me, Declan,' she said, stepping forward. 'Why did you do it?'

She'd hardly finished her sentence when he exploded towards her and smashed her against the open window. He held her as he closed it, then shoved her face into the glass, holding it there while he frisked her, his hands rough against her skin as he ran them from her ankles up to her head, even tracing his fingers through her hair. When he took the three USB sticks from her pocket, he weighed them in his hand, smiled, then laid them on the desk. Laurel held her breath until he finished, only pushing away when his hand left her neck.

'Get away from me!' she snapped. 'What the hell did you think you'd find?'

He shoved her back, glaring into her face. She didn't know where she got the strength but she held her ground and maintained direct eye contact. *Are you enjoying this, Brother?* She attempted to get past him but he grabbed her hair and pushed her against the window, his breath hot on her ear.

'Yes, I killed him,' he whispered, so low she hardly heard him.' His grip tightened and she was sure she'd lose clumps of hair. 'Do you want the details?' he asked, his voice dripping with venom. 'Choo, choo!'

Patricia stood. 'Declan, no! That's enough.'

Laurel slapped him across the face but he just smiled and pulled her up by the hair.

'You and your spoilt little world,' he hissed, his words still so low she had to strain to catch them, wondering as she did if Marc could hear. 'I found Peter, and he was perfect for my needs.'

She had to swallow back for fear she'd vomit. 'Wha-what are you talking about?'

'He knew from the beginning, Laurel. It's why he worked for us. The suave, sophisticated Peter. Businessman, my bollox! He was mine. I placed him, right in the middle – right where I could use him best.' He jerked her head back and pressed against her. 'I had all the contacts, Sister, and your so-loyal hubby did all the leg work.'

She caught the glare of madness in his eyes. The man was pumped with adrenalin and there was no knowing what he'd do. Even with her head held back, she was able to see Patricia, who looked shocked at the turn of events. *Did she hear his confession? Would it have any effect? Did she already know?*

'But then you came along,' Declan roared, frightening the life out of her and Patricia. 'You couldn't be happy with your little desk job, could you? You had to use your slutty charm on him. But our Peter knew how to handle you, and I knew he would.' He leaned back and produced a knowing smile that sent shivers through her. 'Promised you wouldn't get in the way. Said he just wanted a little wifey by his side to make everything look kosher.' His smile disappeared and his eyes went cold. 'But then you did get in the way and tried to change him, and it might have worked only I got there first.' He laughed into her face, his spit splashing off her skin. 'You killed Peter, Laurel, just as much as I did.'

She tried to push him away. 'No!'

'Yes, Laurel, you got in the way, and—'

'In the way of what?' she screamed, slapping his face again. 'What did I get in the way of? I don't even know what's in those files you want so badly.'

She fought back the terror, knowing she needed to lie like she'd never done before. This was way beyond the scene practiced with Marc. She grabbed up the three USB sticks from the desk and threw them at Patricia.

'Peter destroyed all the paperwork, but he told me to scan everything before he did.' She continued with the practiced lie. 'He told me it would be back-up to protect our children, but I never understood until now what he meant. It's all there, whatever *it* is.'

'Once again, Laurel, you show me how stupid you are. You've no idea what you've just given us. It's everything—'

'No, No, Declan, I don't want to know.' She struggled to fight back the tears but refused to show any weakness. 'Peter was changing before he died, and it was for me and our children. Even with Emma not being his biological child, he fully accepted her and proudly let everyone know he was her dad.'

'Yeah, whatever,' Declan said, meeting her words with a sneer that was a mirror of the one she'd seen on Patricia's face earlier. 'Check those sticks, Mam. She's going nowhere before they're verified.'

Laurel waited, unable to pass him, anyway, while Patricia checked each stick's contents on her laptop. She looked up. 'It's all here.'

'Now you have your files,' Laurel said, 'tell me if you've kept your side of the deal? Is David going to be released?

He laughed out loud. 'Oh, don't worry about Frenchy, he'll be released all right.'

Her heart skipped a beat. Something about his eyes spread horror through her. 'What have you done, you bastard?' She punched him, straight in the jaw. 'What have you done?'

He rubbed his jaw, his face red and his eyes on fire. 'You'll see, little sister. You wanted him released? He'll be released. You'll both be together before you know it. Now get the fuck out of our lives.' He grabbed her and shoved her out the door but not before she caught a glimpse of a horrified Patricia.

# *Chapter 3*

∞

Laurel relaxed back into her pillows as she watched David pack and unpack his suitcases. 'Are you sure I can't help?'

He smiled. 'I'm okay. Lie back there and enjoy the show.'

Her heart swelled with love and admiration as she looked him up and down. 'Yep, I'm enjoying the show, all right.'

Wearing just his trainer pants, every part of his toned body was more apt to a twenty-five-year-old than a man in his mid-forties. She wished her own body could stand the test of time as well as his but, after the twins, she was still fighting to regain what she called her *pre-twins'* physique. As she stretched over to get some chocolates and her glass of wine, she acknowledged how real the struggle was.

Recently, she was losing out in her efforts to sleep at night, with so much running through her mind like a movie on repeat. It was so unfair. All had been going great in their lives but then the news from Ireland threw a right spanner in the works. Should she tell the children about their grandmother? They deserved to know she was dying. Would they show indifference? Patricia was a subject rarely raised in conversation. It wasn't that they refused to talk about her – the woman's existence simply didn't come up, with never a question asked. A thought occurred to her: *Are Emma and Jack afraid to ask questions? Surely they remember her. They have access to all the family photos from when they lived in Ireland, only they never ask who the woman in the background is. The woman who gave birth to their own mother and Uncle Carl. Who married their grandad. They must remember her.*

The photos were there to see in the wedding album sitting in the same box as her one. When their Grandad Gerard visited last year, they never asked where his wife was – their grandmother. Maybe it was something she should chat to them about. They were mature kids, both old enough to tell her how they felt. Knowing why they never asked might be a good indication of their readiness to hear of her impending death. She'd talk to them tomorrow before including Pierre and Chantal.

And then there remained the question of going to meet Patricia. When asked, she automatically said yes, with no hesitation. Why? Did she still have hope of reconciliation, or just wanted to know why the woman wasn't a mother to her? When she thought of her now, there was no hatred or resentment – nothing. She had no feelings towards her mother.

Initially, she'd admitted to herself that there was a lot of hatred – a lot of anger – especially during the trial. The details that emerged, in particular the evidence she hadn't known about, made her feel inadequate and guilty – that she was to blame as much as those on trial. But, over time, and with the help of both David and Jean-Pierre, the resentment faded into the distant past, though it didn't disappear altogether.

Paul and Marc's news about her release had evoked only slight shock until the reason was given. It was then she understood that if her mother wanted to make amends, why couldn't she? Someone once said to her, or maybe she'd read it in a book – either way, the meaning held true to her at this moment in time: the best apology is changed behaviour. Maybe, just maybe, her mother had changed. She would know in four days' time. There was no turning back now, flights were booked, arrangements made, and David's family were only too happy to help out with taking care of the children.

'What do you think?'

David came out from the walk-in wardrobe with another Armani black-tie tux. She couldn't work out how it was any different to the last one he'd shown her but she didn't want to insult him by asking, so she tried another tactic.

'It's going to be pretty hot. Are you just packing tux suits? Why can't you go for more casual options, too?'

'Mais oui, mon amie. But I need many options. Simplicity can be the most powerful weapon in terms of style. So, daytime, it will be uncomplicated, timeless, and cool. For evening events, the tux fit must be perfect, sobriety inspiring. You understand, no?'

She knew to just nod in agreement and laugh inside when his eccentric characteristics showed up, especially when it came to his career.

The Cannes Film Festival took place over eleven days, with the judges expected to attend all the major feature films being shown, dividing their attendance then at the *Cinefondation* and *Short Films* presentations, along with the other two sections of the festival. During those eleven days, the president – normally a famous actor or director – along with the chosen jury, would meet at the historic *Villa Domergue* for the selection of the winners. David had told her on many occasions how chaotic the whole event was.

She tried to show interest but when he repeated some of his stories, it proved difficult to give them her full attention. However, her current addiction to high-end celebrity magazines helped, with her ears pricking up when he mentioned the famous actors and directors attending.

Jacques hired two PAs to assist with the preparations, and they soon proved to be experts in their field. Top designers clambered to dress David, and new gadgets arrived nearly every week in the hope he would use some during red-carpet events. The French media were delighted to hear about his return from self-imposed retirement but were miffed when he refused to partake in interviews and photo shoots in his family home. Hotel meetings were arranged by the PAs, and all that remained was for David to pack, and re-pack, with only one week to the festival.

She sipped her wine and smiled as he paced from their wardrobe to the temporary clothes' rail, taking outfits off the bar only to return them yet again.

'David.'

'Oui?' He studied a lightweight jacket, matching it with slim-fit denim jeans and sneakers, all provided by the designer Tom Ford.

'You know I love you, right?'

Straight away, he stopped what he was doing and looked towards her, his smile lighting up his eyes. 'But, of course, mon amie.' He placed the clothes back on the rail. 'Will you miss me too?'

'Hmm,'—she placed her wine glass on the bedside table—'that depends. Give me a reason to miss you.'

Within seconds, he was on their bed, crawling towards her. 'Now this, I will miss.' He kissed her inner thighs, then her tummy, moving up to brush his lips over her breasts.

## *Chapter 4*

∞

The next day, Laurel paced the patio area again and sensed Jean-Pierre watching her. She was overdue a long, comforting chat with him. He always knew when she needed him, never pushing, just waiting for her to initiate the troubling topic. She loved his gift of patience and was even envious of it at times, or maybe she just couldn't comprehend how someone could possess such an ability. *Who do you talk to, Jean-Pierre?*

She stopped pacing and sat opposite him. 'I need to talk to Emma and Jack about Patricia.'

As she waited for his response, she knew full well he was waiting for her to get to her own resolution.

'They can handle it, yeah? I know they probably don't remember her but I think it's important they know what's happening. No secrets – no whispering – in our family. That's how it all started in my past life. The dishonesty and betrayal wasn't just in big lies but in small secrets. It kills relationships.' She shrugged. 'I don't want that for or with my children.'

Jean-Pierre nodded. 'It is always good to know and be disappointed than to not know and always wonder.'

'The worst thing for me, Jean-Pierre, was thinking that I wasn't worth the truth. Not from my mother, my brother, and not from my husband. I don't want Emma or Jack to feel that way. They can't feel the betrayal I experienced.' She sat up. 'What if I sound biased to them? Bitter?'

'You don't have it in you to be bitter, Laurel.'

She leaned back. 'I don't? I've never sounded acrimonious about all that happened? I doubt that.'

'You were angry, yes. But spiteful? Bitter? No, that was never expressed in any words or actions from you. You never wished any ill towards your brother and Patricia – you wanted justice. There is a difference. The justice served on them both was a type of soul cleansing for you, and you found peace from hearing about their wrongdoings and the punishment they received.'

She sighed. 'David said the same. I think he's learned so much from you.'

His laugh was soft, which made her realise that perhaps her husband had the exact same conversation with his father as she'd just had.

'Have you two been talking about me behind my back? No wonder David sounds so sensible sometimes.'

'It's how we all learn. I hope my sons will not only follow my example in life but also my advice. It makes me smile when I see they are doing exactly that.'

The perfect response. She looked around her, allowing the sounds of a working farm to envelop them for a while. In the distance, Joel, Paul, and Marc were walking towards them from the far fields. What an unusual combination of friends – of acceptance. Joel, your typical farmer, masculine and strong in both frame and character. Sometimes he gave the impression of being a full alpha-male heterosexual and, yet, both he and her two gay friends had formed a deep bond. And as close as she was with them, even she didn't know how or why. Was it Jean-Pierre's influence at work again? Did Joel show initial signs of being unable to accept that two people of the same sex could fall in love just as easily as two of the opposite sex? Jean-Pierre's guidance and advice would be to just talk to them and see, learn that they were no different to anyone else. Of course, their shared love of rugby helped, with the Six Nations being their time to meet up and share celebrations and commiserations.

She closed her eyes, facing up to the sky as she took a deep breath, allowing the surrounding influence of this tranquil life seep into her heart and soul.

'You want to bring Patricia here, yes?'

She laughed as she looked at him. 'Now that is something I haven't discussed with anyone. How on earth do you know these things about me?'

'Because I understand you. I know the woman my son loves so much he would give up his life for you. I know you are the woman I trust with my heart, and my heart is my family. You are stronger than you think, Laurel, and you will bring her to us so we can care for her.'

She got up and sat beside him, clasping her hands tight. 'I'm unsure if I can trust her.'

He nodded in agreement. 'You are concerned for your children. The trust of the innocent is a liar's most useful tool. You fear she may say things that are not entirely the way events happened.'

'I'm also unsure how David will react, especially as he will be away at Cannes, and then L.A, if Hollywood gets its way. But, yes, my main concern is what she could say to

Emma and Jack.' She remembered how manipulative her mother could be, and had always got a sense from her that she was an enemy – the person in her way – unwanted. Trying to work out why had left her feeling lost. Why did her mother hate her so much? Did she not know how low Declan would go? At the trial, Patricia pleaded she had no knowledge that Declan had set up Peter's murder, and even admitted how shocked she felt when she found out he'd hired an assassin to murder her daughter. Was she telling the truth or was it just one of her many lies to have the charge of being an accessory to murder dropped? Whatever the truth was, she'd convinced the jury, receiving a guilty verdict on the smuggling and fraud charges only.

She squeezed her hands. *And now she has cancer.*

Jean-Pierre placed his hand over hers. 'This is an opportunity for you to make peace with your mother, Laurel. Grab it while you can. Don't have regrets in your life.'

*Have no regrets? Easier said than done.* She trusted him, followed his advice on many occasions, but still searched his face for doubts in his words.

'David will understand. I'd say he is waiting for you to talk to him about it. Then both of you should talk to all of your children. Be careful to speak with them all. Well, at least the older four.'

She laughed. 'Yes, it might be a bit too complicated for the twins.'

They smiled as footsteps heralded the three men approaching the house.

She turned to her friends. 'So, is the issue of who will win the Six Nations sorted? Time for lunch?'

'I think the discussion is more about what dates we can attend certain matches,' Paul replied. 'Ireland will win again.'

Jean-Pierre got to his feet. 'Yes, time to discuss this further over some wine, cheese, and bread, I think.'

## *Chapter 5*

∞

'She's alive?' Emma sat wide-eyed at the revelation.

'Yes, Sweetpea. Did you really not know?' Laurel was a little taken aback at her daughter's reaction.

'No.' She turned to Jack. 'Did you think she was alive?'

'I didn't think about it, to be honest. I just thought… Actually, I didn't think anything. I kind of remember her, but then I don't. The photos are there in some of the albums so I remember what she looked like but, anything else…' He shrugged.

'She was a bitch.'

'Emma!' Laurel snapped, louder than intended.

'Well, she was, Mam,' she cried out, matching her mother's tone. 'Especially to you.'

Laurel glanced at David, who was trying to stop himself from laughing at Emma's outburst. She gave him one of her *We need to be parents now* looks and he straightened up.

'Your grandmother made many mistakes in her life, which she now regrets.' He sounded convincing. 'Now she needs our help and we…'—he looked at Laurel—'we would like to be there for her in her final months.'

'Are you happy to bring her here, Maman?' Jack's tone – the voice of reason – was a lot calmer than his sister's.

'Yes, Jack.' She smiled. 'Would you both be comfortable with having Patricia here?'

Brother and sister looked at each other but neither responded. Laurel took that as a no, and felt for them. Perhaps the memories of their grandmother's behaviour towards them and her were too hurtful.

'I don't remember her that much. Honestly.' Jack looked to his sister for support. 'I do feel something, and it's not a great feeling.'

'What if we get to know her again?' Emma looked close to tears. 'What if she's not how we…how I remember her, and she's actually a nice person now?'

'I think what Emma is trying to say, Maman, is, what if we grow to like her and then she's gone? Dead.'

'Ohh.' Laurel put her hand to her mouth. It wasn't a scenario she'd thought about. *Emma and Jack may actually get to know their grandmother, grow to love her, and then she'll be taken away from them again.* Her concern had been all about how Patricia might influence her children, even turn them against her. Having good and happy memories of her mother didn't enter her head. *I can't believe how selfish I've been.*

David put his arm across her shoulder. 'We didn't think this through properly, did we? Our children are teaching us a little lesson here, mon amie.'

'I'm so sorry, guys,' she said. 'I know it's asking a lot, and we need to talk to Pierre and Chantel too. But we thought it best to speak privately to you both first and then as a family.'

'I don't know, Mam.' Emma glanced at Jack, then lowered her gaze. 'I don't know if I want to meet her again.'

'We might as well find out what she's like now,' Jack said. 'Let's give her a chance. And Maman wants her here.'

Emma looked at her. 'Well, I'll be calling her Patricia too. She won't be Grandmother or Nanny or Granny to me. Not like Gabrielle. Not like Nana Anne.'

Jack and Emma often visited Peter's mother in Dublin, with Nana Anne being their memory base to their deceased father. They would return, asking her questions about their dad, and she answered in the best way she could, without tainting his memory.

'Ok, so let's think over this a little more, shall we?' She tried to sound optimistic. 'We have time, there's no rush, and Paul needs to find out if Patricia can leave Ireland under her release conditions.'

'How long has she left?' Emma asked.

'A few months, maybe.' She knew her teenage daughter would want to make a decision now.

'Then she hasn't got much time, has she?'

Laurel and David glanced at each other, knowing what they were each thinking. It was going to be difficult for Emma and Jack, and David being away for the beginning of Patricia's stay, if it happened, would put pressure on her. *Thankfully, he'll be here when I fly to Dublin to meet with Patricia and, hopefully, both of us will return to France together.* They were banking on their maturity to help with the transition.

'What do Jean-Pierre and Gabrielle think about Patricia coming here?' Emma looked to David for an answer.

'They are compassionate about her illness and have offered to help if needed. They trust us. They trust our decision. When I say *our*, I mean us all as a family.'

Emma looked to Jack, who shrugged in response.

'Ok, Mam, let us talk to Pierre and Chantal and then I'll give my final decision.' She sounded calmer and more confident. 'But, what if it's a no? What will you do?'

'If it's no, then Patricia stays in Ireland and I'll ensure she's as comfortable as possible and that she has all she needs for her time left. Listen, she may not want to come here, and then all plans are out the window.'

Emma stood up, tying her blonde hair back, the look elongating her slim body. 'She'll want to come here. Let's talk to the others.'

Laurel smiled. Her daughter meant business and knew Pierre would be the obstacle.

## *Chapter 6*

∞

Unable to sit still all morning, Laurel now waited in a hotel room in Dublin, not looking forward to the meeting set up with her mother. Five more minutes and there would be a knock on the door, then Paul would bring Patricia into an already tense atmosphere, and that was just with herself present. She'd hoped a room with some afternoon tea in The Shelbourne Hotel would create an ambiance of calm and help diffuse what might be an awkward first few minutes of greetings and niceties.

The last time she saw her mother was when the woman walked down from the courtroom to start her prison sentence. While she'd been unable to stop staring at Patricia, the look wasn't returned. Her mother kept her head down, her body lacking its once-confident gait. At the time, she felt no pity for her, only anger, but like in previous days since the decision was made to offer her a chance to live with them, she wondered how she would feel now when she walked into the room. *Has she regained that sense of superiority I hated so much? Her self-reliance?* That was difficult to forget, and she couldn't stop herself being brought back ten years.

'Hello, Laurel.'

The skin around her temples prickled at the sound of Patricia's voice. 'Oh, hello, Patricia.' Her heart thundered. *What the hell?* 'Is there something wrong?' She nearly gagged as she swallowed back a ball of nerves. 'Is it…Daddy?'

Patricia laughed, that false cackle that made Laurel wince. She assured her that everybody was fit and healthy. 'I'm surprised you care. Imagine your own daughter visiting Dublin for a week and not even a call or a visit.'

Laurel ignored the barb. 'Why are you calling?'

'Oh, it's the annual audit, my dear, and there seems to be some data missing from the first quarter of last year's records.' She went silent, and Laurel waited, knowing what was coming. 'Any help would be greatly appreciated.'

'Well, it might help if I knew what files you're talking about.' *The annual audit, my eye.* It was done every November, not September. She noticed the conversation was on speakerphone. *Who has she got with her?*

'Just some work Peter and I did together,' Patricia said. 'It's important that we locate it, if you understand me? We can't have important files like that going missing. It's in everybody's interest to…find them.'

'I don't have any files from that period. Have you checked Peter's office or computer?' She put her hand over the phone and took a deep breath, not wanting to give away how much of a mess she was.

'That's gone, my dear. Didn't you know we'd moved to larger premises? I'm surprised at that. It was a case of having to, what with the increases in both imports and exports – our business is booming. Shame you couldn't hang in.'

Laurel flushed with rage, fighting back the urge to scream down the phone. She pinched the bridge of her nose and exhaled, visualising the wonderful view from her window. *I'm so better off here.* 'Well, Patricia, there's your answer. You obviously lost them in the move. Listen, I have to go. Emma and Jack have just arrived back from school.'

'Oh, how are they, my dear?'

'Thriving. Things have never been better. We're a true family at last. Goodbye, Patricia.' She hung up, shaking. 'Bitch!'

Three gentle knocks on the door snapped her back to her present. She shook herself clear of the past and walked towards it but hesitated, her heart thundering, sending heat rushing into her face. *Ohh God. Pull yourself together, Laurel!*

Her walk became more determined and she got to the door and opened it. Paul stood there, his eyes shadowed with concern, which worried her. Then he moved aside and there she stood. Laurel took a sharp intake of breath, not expecting to see this small woman in front of her. Where was her tall, slim, and arrogant mother?

'Hello, Laurel.'

She glanced at Paul, then looked at this woman. 'Patricia?'

The person standing in front of her looked like Patricia but it wasn't the one she remembered. Her cancer seemed to have taken everything away, leaving nothing but skin and bone on what was once a tall, confident frame. This reality – this shadow of the woman she'd known – shook her.

'Can we come in?' Paul shrugged his brows just enough not to make it blatant, the action cutting through her emotional strain.

'Shite, yes! I'm sorry. Please, come in.'

It was then she noticed the walking stick, and the seriousness of her mother's illness hit her like a truck. Her life was now turning into every grown child's nightmare: the impending death of a parent. The thought sent a shiver through her. Every month now – every day – left to Patricia had so much more significance, giving the woman the chance to make amends.

Her face seemed calmer, though tired. Never a smiley person at the best of times, the harsh furrows on her forehead and around her eyes seemed softer than she remembered.

'Please, Patricia, sit down. I ordered some afternoon tea with cakes and sandwiches.' She tried to keep her voice calm and stop her hands from shaking but neither would obey.

'I'll pour, shall I?' Paul volunteered.

'Thanks,' both women replied.

'Beautiful room,' Patricia said, looking around. 'They've still kept its rich heritage in this latest refurbishment. It's pure luxury, don't you think?'

'Em…yes.' Laurel grimaced inside at her struggle to string a sentence together. Her mother's voice sounded weak and croaky.

Patricia looked at her, then at Paul. 'Maybe this wasn't such a good idea. I'm sorry if I'm upsetting you, Laurel. This isn't what I wanted.'

Paul took Laurel's hand. 'Are you ok? Do you want us to leave?'

His gentle touch was all she needed to gather her senses and reply. 'No, no, I'm sorry. It's just… Christ, Patricia, you look ill but, then again, you seem so calm and…'—she floundered as she searched for the right word—'and happy…ish, I think. Am I making any sense here?' She looked from one to the other for help.

Her mother's laugh was gentle. 'I never felt happier, to be honest with you both. As soon as Paul told me you would meet with me, I felt stronger than I have in a long time. Especially since I got the…news.'

Laurel noticed her face, although ashen, showed a slight blush in her cheeks. 'Are you receiving any treatment?'

'Only painkillers. I don't want to prolong my situation – my illness – especially as the treatment won't cure the cancer. So I decided to let another poor soul take my place in the treatment centre. They may have a better chance.'

Silence surrounded them for a while. Paul placed some sandwiches and cakes on each plate and poured more tea.

'I'm sorry, Laurel.' Patricia looked at her. 'I truly am sorry for all that happened.'

Laurel grew rigid as those words sank in. It was something she never thought she would hear from her mother. Like a young teen, her defences shot up and she wanted to scream back *Now you say it? Now, when we've so little time left?*

'Do you know how many times I sat down and wrote a letter to you? Some just said *I'm sorry*, but each time I wrote it down, and believe me, it took time to get the words from pen to paper, I stupidly tore up the letter and threw it in the bin.' She looked at Paul. 'Would you have sent them to her? I doubted you would, and then I figured that even if you did, she'd throw them in the bin.' She looked at Laurel. 'I felt unworthy of contact with you. It just felt like the wrong time or the wrong words.' She turned a small bun with her thin fingers. 'I doubted if an apology was enough. I'm sorry.'

Paul straightened in his chair. 'Yes, although it would feel wrong, I am obliged to send any correspondence to Laurel. She is my client as well as my friend.'

'And, yes, Patricia, I would've thrown them in the bin.' While her words came soft, she knew they'd hit hard, but she had to be honest.

Her mother's head bowed as she took a small bite of a sandwich. Silence ensued again.

Laurel didn't know where to take it. It was like time had slowed to a standstill, upping the surreal feel of being here with her mother. So strange, with no raised voices or animosity between them. Patricia's no-nonsense attitude was gone, replaced by a calm demeanour, as if she's accepted her fate and had made her plans, cleaning out her closet of any cobwebs or skeletons.

*Should I just accept her apology and not ask questions? Why she made my life so difficult? Why we didn't have even a notion of a mother-daughter relationship?*

She straightened in her seat. 'Where are you staying at the moment?'

'I have a small flat Paul kindly found for me. I was in a hostel when I first approached him asking to meet with you.'

'A hostel?'

The corner of her mouth lifted. 'I had to start somewhere.'

'And money? How are you paying the rent, food, even your medication?'

'Social welfare covers most of it. But your dad is sending an allowance over to me too. It helps. Every little helps. Didn't think you'd ever see your mam on welfare, did you?' She laughed to herself, the sound as soft as before.

Laurel looked at Paul. 'Have you proposed the move to her and her parole officer?'

'What move?' her mother asked.

'Not to Patricia but her parole officer said it was approved.'

'What move?'

She looked at her mother again. 'Will you come to France and live with us for a while? Both Emma and Jack want to see you before…'—a flurry of words and phrases flew behind her eyes—'you know, before you go.'

Patricia's mouth fell open. 'Ohh.'

## *Chapter 7*

∞

'Et violà! They are confirming flight time for Laurel and Patricia now.' David read the message on his phone, then looked to those around the table. 'They should be here tomorrow.'

All were gathered for dinner in the family farmhouse. Silence fell among the adults, each looking at their neighbouring diner before turning to him. Pierre attempted to get up to leave but Emma grabbed his arm and gave him a pleading eye.

David sensed the atmosphere and looked to Jean-Pierre for some guidance on the group's reaction. Gabrielle came in from the kitchen, unaware of his announcement.

'Ohh la la! But what is the problem?' She looked to everyone. 'You will all turn the wine sour with this ill air.'

'No-one wants Patricia here,' Pierre stated.

'No!' they all chorused in response.

'Pierre, you have no right to speak for others without consulting us first,' Joel said.

'Then why is everyone so hesitant,' David asked. 'Both Laurel and myself discussed this with you all. You didn't object then, so what's changed?'

'Nothing has changed,' Jean-Pierre replied, 'and I think I speak for everyone when I say that.' He looked at Pierre. 'But as Patricia's arrival draws closer, we have a growing concern for you all.'

David sighed. *Of course, it is concern from my family, not objection.*

'We all understand,' Joel said, his tone soft and kind, 'and are so happy Laurel can reconcile with her mother before she is lost from this world. But do we trust her?' He looked around the table. 'That must be no.'

David chose his response with care. This was not the time for anger, and he needed to show example to Pierre.

'Mais oui! I fully understand and I'm sorry for not acknowledging this concern. But Paul and Marc have assured us that Patricia has not contacted nor wants any interaction with her son.'

Declan's impending early release from prison was a growing, constant worry in his own home without it being a burden in his parent's home too.

'But what of Patricia herself?' Gabrielle asked. 'Is she to be trusted? Will she say unhappy things to the children?'

'Maman, we have concerns, yes, but those worries are not of Patricia's actions. Laurel has assured me of that. Last night we spoke for quite a while, and she is happy that her mother is of a different mindset now. She has accepted that her life is ending and has no ill-feeling towards Laurel or anyone.'

His mother nodded once, her hand on her husband's. 'She just wants to make amends with Laurel, with all of her family?'

'Yes, Maman, it will be a peaceful time for Patricia,'—he looked at Pierre—'and a time to reconcile. Gerard and Carl have agreed to come here too. It will be a sad but wonderful time for all of Laurel's family.'

A reflective silence settled around the table for a while, a rare occurrence in the Rousseau family home.

'This is what Laurel and David want,' Jean-Pierre said, his voice always reassuring for everyone. 'And it is a good thing. A family environment is supposed to be a safe haven, but, very often, it's the place people find the deepest sadness.

Laurel found her haven with us, but that unhappiness is sometimes still in her eyes. Would you not agree, David?'

He nodded his agreement, content to see that everyone was captivated by his father's sage words.

'Everybody's family has problems,' Jean-Pierre continued. 'Are we not fixing ours now?' Everyone nodded. 'Good, so let us help, let us support Laurel in the next few months. She will need it. A dying woman needs it.' As he looked around at each member of his family, Gabrielle rubbed the back of his hand.

He kissed her temple. 'We are the ones who support each other in the things we do, and no matter what, we are here for each other. Now we must be here for Laurel. Her wounds never show on her body but, believe me, if she doesn't get this chance with her mother, then that hidden wound will be more hurtful and grow deeper than anything that bleeds.'

David thought he should say something, but how could he follow what his father had just said? Jean-Pierre hit the nail on the head with his description of Laurel's sadness. No matter what he did to make her life as perfect and happy as was humanly possible, he would sometimes catch her looking into space, her thoughts her own, and could see the sadness in her eyes. If she caught him watching her, she snapped out of it and smiled. It saddened him that he could not fix that wound.

'Do you all understand what must be done, what we must do for our family member who needs us?' Jean-Pierre asked.

Everyone nodded as they muttered their response.

'Good. Now, ma chère, ma famille, let us eat!'

An amiable chattering erupted around the table as Gabrielle returned to the kitchen to get their food. David opened more wine, nodding in gratitude to his father. No more words were needed. The deep-rooted ritual of a French family enjoying their food, their social gathering, continued much later than normal that evening.

# *Chapter 8*

∞

A song kept repeating in Emma's head as she walked up the hill with everyone. Songbird by Fleetwood Mac. She didn't know why it kept reverberating around her brain because it didn't match what she was feeling or thinking. *Or did it?*

It didn't really relate to anyone in particular, but to everyone. She remembered reading Christine McVie say that it was 'a universal song, about you and nobody, about you and everybody'.

She looked back at Pierre straggling behind their little group, the distance growing with each step. Dinner with the family proved difficult for him this evening. Too many voices, too many differing opinions to his own growing ideals. He didn't agree with Patricia coming over. It was too much of a risk – a concession his family shouldn't make. She nudged David and told him she would wait for Pierre to catch up. He looked back and nodded in agreement, his eyes sad. She knew he sometimes struggled to understand his eldest son. Their personalities were so similar, yet so different on some views.

As Pierre stopped again, pretending to see something in the woods, Emma sighed and leaned back against a tree. She wasn't going to walk back to him, knowing he would get to her in his own time.

She was right. Five minutes passed before he started walking towards her.

'You ok?' she asked.

He shrugged, his demeanour forlorn, his dark, brooding eyes looking everywhere but at her.

'It's ok to be annoyed, you know.' She kept her hands in her hoodie's pockets and continued to lean against the tree. While she wanted to hug him, she knew he wasn't ready for such a gesture. It saddened her when he became dark and silent like this. As usual, she would do all the talking, at first, and after a long silence where he would digest her words, his reaction would come.

From the day he defended her from a bully in school, she always wanted to be there for him during his dark phases. That period in her life was horrible and she still shivered when the memory came to her, often as she lay in bed trying to sleep. Since then, they worked well together, when he allowed her in. Pierre was the boldest and most fearless of all her friends when he wanted to be, and the best looking – all the girls wanted to date him. He showed some interest but never anything serious. His ability to talk to anyone helped bring fun to the most boring of days. But he could be so serious too. He wanted so much to right the world, and to protect the family from the horrors outside; there was no fear in him, his sense of duty intense. However, when he shared his thoughts with her, his eyes sparkled and he no longer felt like a stranger to her, unlike when he was caught in the darkness of his mood swings.

'I know what's getting you down,' she said. 'The thought of Patricia staying here and how everyone is ok with it.'

He looked everywhere except in her direction. She knew he was listening – it was like a ritual between them now.

'We haven't had a moment to chat properly about it.' He turned to her and she gave him an encouraging smile. 'Any chance we can now?'

No reaction. She tried another tactic. 'She's family.'

'Hmph.' His scowl became more pronounced.

'What would you prefer us to do? Leave her in a poky flat in Dublin, to die alone? Does anyone deserve that? She's my grandmother, Pierre. Perhaps I deserve to know her just a little bit before she dies. You're so lucky, having your grandparents around you, and your Mam's parents are just a short distance away. I get to see my Nana Anne through Facetime or Zoom.'

She sighed. 'I think I want this opportunity to meet Patricia before time runs out, perhaps get to know her a little bit. Something I didn't get the chance to do with my dad.'

'She is dangerous,' Pierre said, stepping towards her. 'Manipulative. And she tried to kill our parents. Did we deserve that?'

'Allegedly tried to kill our parents. She has denied it and a jury believed her.'

'Bah!' He threw his hands up. 'That's exactly what manipulative people can do. Imagine the hurt she could cause here. No, I won't let my guard down while she's around.'

'Oh, so you accept that she will be arriving here tomorrow then? You're not leaving us.'

He shook his head, 'You know I won't.'

'Good.' She smiled. 'Let's take it one day at a time, shall we? Remember, Mam said Patricia seems to have changed – more peaceful, it seems – maybe accepting her fate. Who wouldn't when you receive a death sentence?'

She offered her hand, which Pierre accepted. They commenced their walk uphill, their pace slow. She knew this wasn't the end of his mood, more a stepping stone across a fast-flowing river. He was so sincere, so intense, and she needed to watch out for him, just as much as he felt the need to watch out for everyone. His vulnerability was sometimes disguised by his anger. Other times, he would retreat and she needed to work on pulling him out of his dark tunnel.

'I honestly feel everyone is thinking the same as you, Pierre.' She stopped walking and turned to him. 'I do, too, but I want to take a chance on her. I guess, a leap of faith that she really does want to make amends.'

She looked into his dark-brown eyes. 'Can you allow us to try? I know I sound very simple and trusting, perhaps even inexperienced, but I need to take this risk. And I need you to be here with me.'

They stood there, locked and still like statues in a garden. Then he brushed her hair from her face, his touch so soft. In that instant, her stomach swirled with butterflies and she had an overwhelming urge to get home. His gesture was so unexpected, her feelings knocking her off-centre. They were friends, that was all – nothing would come of anything else. Pierre was far too emotional now, and she needed to distract him but it was he who pulled away.

Maybe he read her face. He always said she was like an open book, her feelings showing in her facial expressions. Was her reaction that obvious to him?

As they continued to walk, she felt awkward. He still held her hand, and she didn't want him to think anything was wrong if she tried to let go. Why did she feel this way? They were friends, that's all – this was just a blip, a feeling of comradery – nothing more. When she looked at him, his scowl eased, with the hint of a smile showing through.

'So, Trinity and Dublin.' She decided a change of subject was on the cards. 'It's a definite yes to us moving there next year?'

His smile grew. 'Yes, the subjects we both want to study are perfect, don't you think?'

This was the perfect opportunity to tease him. She kept her face as neutral as possible. 'I wonder do they have college jumpers like in the US. We could get matching ones.'

His face blanched, then his eyes narrowed as he realised what she was at. She burst out laughing as he gave her a gentle shove.

He laughed with her. 'Don't even think about something like that!'

## *Chapter 9*

∞

As Laurel drove home, her apprehension grew. How were her children going to react to Patricia? Would they welcome her with open arms, hug her, or keep their distance? These questions had filled her mind since she'd phoned to let them know they were on their way. Paul kindly travelled with them in case Patricia took a turn for the worse due to the journey but, thankfully, it had gone well.

She glanced behind and saw her mother staring out the side window. From the look of her drooping eyes, she was on the verge of falling asleep.

'Won't be long now, Patricia. Are you ok?'

Her head jerked up. 'Yes, yes, I'm good. Just feeling a little drained, and I'm due to take my medication.'

Five minutes later, they arrived at the house. Jack was outside, wearing his favourite soccer team's jersey and shorts, enjoying his regular habit of bouncing a football off each foot. He ran inside as soon as he spotted the car, the ball rolling under the bench. Paul got out to organise the luggage as Laurel opened Patricia's door. Her mother edged out, with Laurel resisting the urge to assist her, having learnt from earlier when the woman struggled from her plane seat and refused to take her hand.

'I need to do this myself,' she'd explained. 'When the time is right and I need you, I promise I'll ask. Thank you, Laurel.'

She straightened herself and looked back down the hill to the forest and farm. 'My, it's hot in this country, and such a clear blue sky. Is it always like this?'

'It can get pretty cold at night during the winter.'

Nearby chatting caught her attention, and she smiled at the sound of her older children's voices. They filed out of the house.

'Ahh, hello.' Patricia smiled. 'My, you have all gotten so big.'

Pierre stood behind Emma, while Jack and Chantal waited several metres away. They'd stopped talking, and Laurel hoped this would go well but saw that Pierre had one of those moody scowls, his arms folded tight. The others just stood there, in shock at seeing the small, thin woman beside her. It was an awkward moment, made worse by the silence.

'Well, that's everything in the house,' Paul said on his return. He smiled at the sibling crew. 'So, are you lot going to say hello to Patricia?'

'Hello,' they said in unison. No one moved towards her.

She made the first move, extending her free hand before stepping forward and smiling. 'Nowadays, believe me, I don't bite. You must be Pierre and Chantal, David's children. And Emma, my, you're growing tall, and as beautiful as your mother.' She then looked to Jack and shook his hand. He produced a shy nod and stepped back beside his sister. Patricia turned to Laurel. 'There's no mistaking he's taking after Peter's side of the family.'

Laurel smiled an acknowledgment, on edge, wondering where David had got to. To answer her question, two more familiar voices shouted '*Maman'*, with David calling for them to slow down.

She hunkered down with her arms opened wide. 'Well, hello there you two!'

'More? And twins! When did this happen?' Patricia pursed her lips, her eyes wide. 'You've got your hands full here, Laurel. Are you sure it's ok for me to stay?'

'Of course, it is, Madame Maguire.' David smiled and offered her his hand. 'Laurel and I have a wonderful network of family here to help us when needed.'

Laurel kissed his cheek, her touch gentle. 'C'mon, let's all go inside and have lunch. Are you up to having some food, Patricia?'

'Yes, yes, thank you, and then, if it's ok with you, I'll take my meds and lie down for a while.'

Laurel smiled to herself. *Well, that went swimmingly awkward.*

***

Lunch was full of chatter and laughter. Laurel watched her mother, who'd stayed silent for much of the meal. Occasionally, Paul spoke to her but her expression for the most part remained one of awe at the scene before her. At one stage, a bread fight erupted between Jack and the twins, which led to David giving a light warning to the trio. Jack and Chantal then volunteered to take the younger two outside for games.

The table became quieter. She put her arm across Emma's shoulder and whispered 'Thank you', knowing her daughter had prepared the lunch with Pierre.

'Are you the person who set up the attempt on my father's life?' Pierre asked.

'Pierre, now is not the time,' David said.

Laurel straightened in her seat, her face hot. She knew something was going to happen when she'd noticed Pierre's demeanour earlier. Granted, he was entitled to an answer, even if his question was a bit extreme and direct. Unease rippled through the room, and she shivered. *Perhaps he's asking what everyone else is thinking.* The thought had popped into her head every now and then since the trial.

'No, son, and I'm sorry for everything that happened, I truly am. But, I honestly didn't know what Declan had planned.'

His stern expression didn't falter. 'I find it hard to believe you. And I am not your *son*.'

'Yes, I would find it hard to believe me too.' She shrugged. 'He used me for the finance and logistics of his little enterprise. I knew little else, and he wouldn't share anything with me if I asked. I was blinded by the money and blinkered when it came to his actions.'

Laurel inhaled a slow breath, trying to stay calm. 'Perhaps we can talk about this at a later stage, and not when we've just arrived home.'

'And I'll gladly answer any questions you have, Pierre, if I can. But, if you don't mind, I need to take my medication and try to get some sleep.'

With timely interruption, both Paul and David's phones rang. David looked at his and said it could go to voicemail. Paul, however, gave an apologetic shrug. 'It's the office, sorry, I need to take it.' As he left the room, Laurel didn't miss his anxious look.

'Would you like me to show you to your room, Patricia?'

'Yes, please.'

Once she ensured her mother was comfortable, she returned to the kitchen, where everyone was clearing up the remains of lunch. 'Well, that went ok, I think. But, Pierre, do you have to be so blunt?'

'I only asked what you were thinking,' he retorted.

Emma and David laughed.

'Ehh, hello! This is serious. Patricia will be here for as long as possible, so please don't make it an uncomfortable stay for any of us.'

'We won't!' both Pierre and Emma chorused.

Paul returned and nodded to her. 'Can we talk?'

She didn't like his tone. 'What's happened? Is Marc ok?'

David, Emma, and Pierre stopped what they were doing. Paul leaned on the back of a kitchen chair, taking a sharp breath.

'Jesus, Paul, what's wrong?' Laurel sat down, wondering what could be making her friend look so stressed.

'Declan's being released next week. His parole was approved. Laurel, I'm sorry but he's getting out.'

'Who's Declan?' Emma asked. 'I was going to ask earlier when Patricia mentioned him.'

David and Paul looked to Laurel.

*Oh shite* was all that came to mind.

## *Chapter 10*

∞

David refused to leave for Cannes but Laurel put her foot down, telling him life needed to continue as normal. As she waved him goodbye at the airport, she struggled to push back the fear in her gut. Was she right to insist he leave? Paul was still here and assured them Marc was setting up surveillance on Declan.

'He won't be able to buy a coffee without us knowing.'

She was already disillusioned with the Irish justice system because of his original light sentence but this early parole was taking the biscuit. As she wove through the airport crowd towards the car park, she kept her head down, self-conscious, hoping to avoid meeting anyone.

When she arrived home, she sat in the car and watched as all appeared normal around her. The children were playing, the small forest swayed in the gentle breeze, and Joel was heading from the farm to gather in the goats for the evening milking. He waved back when the twins called out to him. Paul, Gabrielle, and Patricia were sitting in the shade, enjoying the scene before them.

Everything was as it should be. And even with the slow, developing relationship with her mother, she was handling her declining health better than expected.

But her heart fluttered and she gripped the steering wheel as an immense emotional weight bore down on her. Things weren't as they should be. Far from it. Her shoulders shuddered with the impact of the sob she couldn't hold back, her tears brimming over and streaming down her cheeks. *Why is that man getting out now? It's so unfair. When everything was going great – our lives had moved on.*

She simply couldn't accept why he was successful in his parole request. For the past couple of nights, she'd lain in bed struggling to sleep, with everything and nothing running around her head, and all she could think was how unfair it was. Unfair that *he* was free, unfair that Peter was dead, and unfair that her life and the lives of her family now felt threatened, because *that man* was free. She slapped the steering wheel. *By God, you aren't going to do this to us.* She wiped her eyes, got out of the car, and walked towards her family.

The dry heat had reduced to a pleasant nineteen Celsius. Without fail, every summer, July was the hottest and driest in the Mediterranean region, with this year being no different. But she wouldn't swap it for the world, even with her psycho brother being released early.

'Well now,' she said, 'what are we up to today? With David gone to Cannes, we're free to get up to mischief.' She laughed as her children gathered around her.

'We could have ice cream,' Chantel suggested.

'Yes, we could, but what else? Will we have a big picnic? We can call everyone and ask if they can join us.'

The twins squealed with excitement. She turned to the adults. 'Are you all up for a picnic?'

Nobody said no, which brought a smile. She figured now was as good a time for a picnic as any. As she looked around, she sucked in the fresh mountain air and the joyful sounds around her. Everything felt fresher, clearer, helping to cleanse the fear of the past week and that horrible feeling she'd had in the car.

'You seem to be determined to make this a happy day for everyone,' Paul said after stepping over to her. 'I noticed you sitting in the car. Are you ok?'

'Yep, we need a pick-me-up, don't we? And what better way than a lovely picnic in the evening sunshine?'

He chuckled. 'Gabrielle is on the phone to Jean-Pierre. The word will soon spread to Joel and the others.'

'Ahh, the Rousseau grapevine.' She smiled. 'You're familiar with this form of family chat. That means even Claude and Helene will be here. With peak traffic in Marseille, they should only be an hour or so. Great! This is what we all need – food, wine, and great banter.'

But then she looked over to Patricia and Gabrielle, who were attempting to converse, using the family photos on Gabrielle's phone to overcome the language barrier. Patricia knew a few French phrases and the two grandmothers seemed to be doing fine with that. Would this be overwhelming for her mother, having so many of David's family around her? When Jean-Pierre and Gabrielle first called to meet with her, she'd become distressed, like it was all too much to comprehend that David and his family could be so nice to her, so forgiving after all that had happened.

She turned back to Paul to ask—

'Yes, she will be ok,' he said, as if reading her mind. 'She's feeling strong today, and with Gabrielle's help, more comfortable with how life is here in your home. You know, this family is so accepting, so appreciative of everything around them, it should be of no surprise to you that Patricia has just slipped into their little world as if there was no history between them. It's truly amazing. So unique.'

'You think?' She didn't wait for an answer, hugging her friend close.

He kissed her head. 'A big family picnic. I'd love Marc to be here too.'

'Only if he can get here within the next hour.' She squeezed his arm and walked into the house.

It wasn't long before the workers arrived for the meal in the garden. The evening was warm and pleasant, with the Mediterranean sun beginning to set beneath a sky tinted with slashes of purple, peach, and gold. Music played in the background, with a gentle breeze lifting the sounds of the day: children's laughter, barking dogs, and adult's chatting and joking.

'Ahh, there's nothing like a picnic,' Laurel said to Joel's wife, Veronique as they lay on the chequered rug.

'But, yes,' Veronique replied, 'this is the life.' She raised her face to the ebbing sun, relaxed.

'Do you miss working in the maternity hospital?' Laurel asked.

'Not in the slightest. With two children? You know how it is, no rest for the wicked. Work as a midwife and all its wonderful perks is satisfying, but the shift work was getting to me. I missed tucking my two girls into bed at night and reading them their bedtime stories. Even bath time and all the chaos of it.'

Laurel rolled her eyes. 'I know how that goes.'

Veronique tapped her tummy. 'Besides, I'll be busy again soon.'

Laurel jerked up into a sitting position and stared at her friend. 'Hold on, what! What did you just say?'

Veronique laughed. 'The shift work, even part-time, it wasn't working out for me. So I gave in my notice, no more midwifery for me.'

'No, not that. I mean, it's fantastic to hear you're taking time out for the kids and you, but…'—she glanced around—'you're pregnant? Did I imagine what I just heard?'

Veronique laughed again. 'Joel! I think we should tell everyone now, especially as we are all together.'

Her husband blushed and shrugged, and Claude laughed.

Laurel realised her mouth was hanging open. 'I don't believe this. Does David know yet?'

'We told him when we called to wish him safe travels last night.'

'And he didn't tell me? Hmmm, so he's keeping secrets from me. Methinks a long chat awaits him when he calls tonight.' She smiled, touched Veronique's tummy, then both women hugged each other before she got up and walked towards Paul and Patricia.

'Such wonderful news,' her mother said. 'Please give Veronique my warmest congratulations. Paul was good enough to explain.' She looked around. 'There's so much going on – it's all a little overwhelming.' She yawned. 'Would it be terribly rude if I went inside to rest for a while?'

'No, of course not, Patricia. Please, let me help you.'

'Thank you.' She struggled to rise from her chair.

Laurel couldn't believe it – this was the first time her mother had accepted her offer of assistance. She looked to Paul, who gave a slight nod as he closed his eyes. *This isn't looking good.*

As she helped Patricia into her bed, the strain showed on her face, her skin pasty and grey.

'Are you comfortable?' She sat on the edge of the bed.

'I am, thanks. Honest, I'm just tired. It's been a long day and the picnic was lovely. Everyone's so kind and…'—she looked at the ceiling—'so forgiving.'

Laurel smiled. 'Ahh, the Rousseau's uniqueness. Paul said you've just slipped into their little world.' She turned and looked out of the window, at the night drawing in, then back to her mother. 'Are you sure…?'

Patricia was asleep. She'd never seen her mother look as peaceful as she did now.

## *Chapter 11*

∞

As she looked at her reflection in her bedroom mirror, Laurel sighed, running a hand over her tummy. 'Maybe I need to start paying attention to my own body.' She turned to her friend sitting at the end of her bed. 'Nothing too drastic but I could afford to lose a few pounds from here, and tone up.'

Paul laughed, shaking his head.

'What? What's the harm in taking care of myself? You and David are the peak of physical fitness for your age.'

'David loves you. He doesn't look for anything from you. And thanks for the compliment.'

'It's not only for him, it's for me too. I truly need to get myself back into my old routine of jogging daily. Even if I start with a brisk walk every morning, you know, ease back into it.'

The Cannes Film Festival started two days ago and the TV was constantly on the entertainment channel so the children had the opportunity to see David.

Watching a red-carpet event last night, she'd become conscious that some of the actresses walking beside David had incredible figures. She tried to see if he noticed, too, but he just busied himself with reporters and photographers. The glamour, as expected, brought style and sparkle, with extra-high splits in their dresses, and tiers of tulle on some, while she wore her pyjamas with her hair tied up in a ponytail. She sat with her children and hugged her cushion, even more convinced she'd let herself go since the twins were born three years ago.

'What time is Marc's flight landing?' she asked, opting to change the subject and her clothes yet again. She picked up her dark jeans, a light knit top, dark in colour, too, as she convinced herself it would make her look slimmer.

Paul stood beside her. 'Laurel, put some light clothes on, it's twenty-five degrees outside.'

She turned to look at him. 'Bah, I can handle it!'

He laughed again. 'I'm not carrying you if you faint from the heat.'

'So…flight time? Landing?'

He looked at his watch. 'We need to leave in the next half hour. Are you sure you're happy leaving Patricia and the kids with Gabrielle?'

'Definitely, both Joel and Jean-Pierre will be working in the yard, so if anything happens, Gabrielle has them nearby.'

As they drove to the airport, they chatted about Emma's schooling. She and Pierre were now in their last year of *Lycee Baccalaureat Professionnel* and were determined to attend University together. Paul had persuaded them to go to college in Ireland – Trinity College, where he'd graduated – but Laurel was more interested in what they wanted to study. Pierre had chosen History of Art and Architecture, with Emma opting for History and Political Science.

'What jobs can they get from these degrees?'

'Their masters will determine what they'll do in life,' Paul said. 'Let them enjoy uni.'

'Hmm, neither seems a reliable career path.'

'What did you want at eighteen? Did you know?'

She remembered their shared eighteenth birthday was celebrated together before Paul's college life took over and she flitted from one job to another. When they were young, her joy of life, her free soul, helped Paul through several difficult stages in his late teens and early twenties, even when he became practically reclusive during the final years of his law studies.

Then there was that first time. 'You knew what you wanted at eighteen,' she teased.

'So did you. Well, that night you definitely did.' He smiled and raised his brows. 'But I'm talking about after school. Did you want to attend university? You never gave me that impression.'

'At that time in my life, it sounded boring. I think I went through nearly a dozen jobs before I hit my twenty-fifth birthday. Emma calmed me down.'

'And you turned out all right, didn't you? Let them enjoy their journey.'

'Like you did?'

'Ah, it worked out in the end.'

She studied his face, his expression conveying a mix of emotions.

As they waited in Arrivals, she contemplated their chat in the car. She remembered how they'd promised they would always be together, except that didn't go to plan. As Paul's law studies took over his life and she wanted to dance and drink away her home troubles, they drifted apart. Now and then, she met him when she visited his sisters, and it was like they were never apart, with no awkwardness or animosity as they chatted the night away.

And then there was the night Emma was conceived – a wonderful night, providing the drive she needed to get her life back on track. Their bodies were so responsive and alive, as if the years spent apart had never happened. From that night, she was convinced she'd fallen pregnant. Of course, Paul wanted to get married but she didn't want that – her family would ruin their relationship and their bond, using him for his political connections. In the end, he agreed to be her support and friend, always there in the background for Emma when needed –the reason she would always love and appreciate him. When Peter arrived on the scene, it was accepted that he would take over the 'father' responsibilities when they got married. It worked but she knew the time was coming when Emma would have to know the truth. Her daughter never asked why when she saw no father's name on her birth certificate. Peter intended to adopt her but, when he died, that particular plan fell apart.

Why would she answer a question that was never raised? She had prepared herself to tell her at some stage but the timing never felt right. For now, though, there was no need to upset the applecart. Teenage years could be so hormonal at the best of times – no point adding more drama to her daughter's struggle with growing up.

'Ahh, finally, they're coming.' He got to his feet, trying to see past the other passengers walking through the doorway. 'Ohh.'

Laurel didn't like the sound of that and craned her neck to see what had made Paul go pale.

## *Chapter 12*

∞

Six hours earlier, Marc had stepped inside a small bedsit once occupied by his nemesis, his nostrils and gut reacting to the strong smell of bleach. Once he got the call from his agent that Declan had slipped their watch, his stomach refused to settle, his heart beating so fast he was sure his colleagues, Mike and Steven, could hear it.

The layout of the bedsit was the same as those in any old Georgian building in Dublin city, except this one was ultra clean – not one iota of dust, with the bed stripped, the small table gleaming, and the kitchenette left without food or crumbs for his team to analyse. Steven continued to scan all surfaces with an ultra-violet light to see if anything came up.

As Marc looked around, anger surged from his gut. It was so strange standing in the space where their tormentor lived, albeit for a short period of time. He'd left no personal touches, with nothing to indicate someone had stayed here.

The room looked ready to move into, not just abandoned. It gave him the creeps. But it also gave him a sick sense of knowing. It was Declan all over – a clean-freak, psychopath's den.

He remembered reading somewhere a psychopath was egocentric, with no remorse or empathy. Declan covered every aspect of this criminal characteristic.

'Marc, look here.'

Steven nodded to a corner of the kitchenette's counter, which he held the UV light over. Marc took a few steps over, all the tiny room necessitated, and there it was, the clue they knew had to be here – a message from Declan:

*Ohh, you can't get me out of your head, boy,*

*One day, I might slip into your bed, boy.*

He gripped the counter as he stared at the couplet, his anger burning through him. It was the same type of message Declan had arranged to be sent to him and Paul over the past year or so. The communication was consistent but left no clue who it was from, so the prison service couldn't do anything and Declan denied all knowledge.

The man was beyond redemption. *Only one way to deal with this.*

'Marc? Boss, are you ok?'

Steven's voice sounded miles away but was enough to pull him out of it. He needed fresh air. His phone showed he had an hour before check-in for his flight to France. He needed to make some calls before he broke the news to Paul and Laurel.

He reassured his colleague that he was ok. 'Pack up here, there's nothing else to be found. But get Mike to take photo evidence and swabs of that message before cleaning it away. The gardaí aren't interested in checking the bedsit out, it's only a parole breach in their eyes.'

***

Laurel spotted Marc, on his phone, and his expression said it all. 'Shite. Declan must have slipped their surveillance. I knew he would!'

As Marc walked over to them, he shrugged. 'I'm sorry, we don't know where he is.'

'Did you check with his parole officer?' Paul asked. 'Did you notify the gardaí to help search for him?'

'Of course, Paul. What the hell!' His face was like thunder. 'I know my job and what had to be done!'

'Look, I'm not accusing you of anything, just trying to help. You're attacking the wrong person here.' Paul's face was red, his risen voice drawing unwanted attention.

'Ok, you two, calm down. C'mon, let's get to the car and talk this over.'

She drove home, seething. Marc and Paul made calls to their contacts, with no success. The atmosphere was toxic, and she tried deep breaths to calm her nerves.

The operative Marc had assigned to keep surveillance on Declan was discovered asleep by his replacement that morning. His cup of coffee, with most spilt over his clothes and the car seat, was found to contain a strong dose of Temazepam, a prescribed sleeping tablet. The man didn't know how it happened, as he'd bought it in a local late-night café. An analyst confirmed the dose was close to lethal and the guy was lucky not to have imbibed enough coffee to kill him.

Marc planned to return to Dublin as soon as possible but Laurel wanted him to stay in case Declan turned up. The tense atmosphere between her friends upset her and she pulled the car into a lay-by close to the village. She turned to them, and each man glanced at the other. It broke her heart to see them sit so far apart, the distance seeming wider than the small middle passenger seat.

'Look, this isn't your fault, Marc. And, Paul, you've got to calm it a notch or two. If the children notice your temperament when you arrive, and I know Pierre and Emma will pick it up straight away, then the house will become a prison for us all.'

She took a sharp breath. 'The question for me at the moment is, do I tell Patricia?'

'No!' both men said.

'What if Declan tries to contact her?'

'He won't,' Marc said, shaking his head. 'Declan isn't interested in his mother, and I doubt at this stage if he's interested in you or the family. Honestly, my guess is he wants to set up his network again, to get some funds together. We need to co-ordinate a plan and work with my police contacts here and in Ireland to make sure he gets nowhere near you or Patricia, just in case I'm wrong. Does she have her own phone?'

'Not that I know of. I've never seen one so I presume no. Anytime Daddy calls, it's on our house phone. And just so you know, I think you're wrong. Declan will want his pound of flesh.'

Marc turned to Paul. 'Do you think you might have some contacts in the Department of Justice to put a bit of pressure on the Gardaí to help search for him? I know they won't be interested if we just report a parole violation.'

Laurel's face went cold. 'Jesus, what if Patricia is involved? Fooled us into thinking she'd changed? She's there with my family now.' Her gut tightened and sweat broke out on her forehead, even though the air-conditioning was set at a fresh twelve degrees.

'Hold on, Laurel,'—Paul's voice was back to his cool, practiced tone—'Declan has never tried to contact Patricia. I made sure to check that before I told you she wanted to meet with you.' He glanced at Marc. 'We both did. We took no risks in case she had other plans for you. I promise, she's genuine.'

Even so, she didn't waste time pulling the car back onto the road.

## *Chapter 13*

∞

Emma, Pierre, and Laurel sat around the kitchen table looking at accommodation options for Dublin. Although the offer to stay with family was generous, both young adults wanted a place of their own.

'Christ, the rent is ridiculous,' Laurel said. 'It's more expensive than London.' She couldn't believe some of the available city centre apartments were looking for nearly three thousand euros a month. 'Are you willing to share with another student to help with the rent?'

They looked at each other and nodded no.

'It's just the high rent will eat into the allowance we've set up for you. After food and other bills, you won't have much left for anything.' She looked from one to the other. 'No nights out, no parties.'

'It's not about the money, Mam,' Emma said. 'What if we don't get on with the person we choose to live with us? And we both want to get part-time jobs while we're there.'

Pierre tapped the screen. 'And, besides, we will be studying, with a lot of assignments to write up. I think an apartment like this one would be good for us.' He turned the laptop for Laurel to have a better view. 'The rent is lower – only two thousand.'

'Only?' She sighed. Then she copped that it was a one-bedroom apartment. She leaned back. 'Ehh, what's going on here?'

'Stop it!' Emma snapped at Pierre, who groaned as he leaned down to rub his leg under the table.

Then the normally cool, serious Pierre laughed out loud. 'Love your reaction. But, if we were together, what would be the harm? We're not related.'

Laurel looked from him to Emma. 'No, there's no harm, I know that.' Although she was relieved, she kept it hidden. *They're too young for anything like that.* She glanced at Emma once more. Did she see some flustering from her daughter or was her imagination running wild.

'Right so, let's talk about budgets and accommodation more when David gets back. Thankfully, it's still nearly a year away. Paul can advise which areas are good, too. He's delighted you've both decided on Trinity.'

As they cleared up, Jack came into the room. 'Maman, Patricia is calling for you and Paul, she seems upset about something but won't tell us. She asked us all to leave the room and get you both.'

'Huh?' She didn't like the sound of that. 'Where's Paul and Marc?'

'I'll go get them now. Oh, Chantal is taking the twins upstairs.'

'I'll go check on them,' Emma said.

Pierre walked towards the TV room, his temperamental scowl replacing the smile. Laurel followed him, knowing full well he still didn't trust her mother regardless of her illness.

'Take it easy, Pierre.'

As they entered the room, she heard the heavy thump of Paul and Marc coming down the stairs.

'Laurel, Laurel, why didn't you tell me he was free?'

She froze.

'What do you mean, Madame Maguire?' Pierre asked, sounding calmer than Laurel expected him to be. 'Who? And why did you ask the kids to leave?'

Patricia glared at her. 'Declan! When were you going to tell me?'

*What the hell?* She clasped the back of the couch as the room spun, taking a deep breath to steady herself, wondering how things had shifted from happy to horrendous in such a short space of time.

'He's here!' Patricia cried, eyes wide.

'What? Has he contacted you?' Marc strode over to look out the window. 'He's here now?'

'No, no, Marc. Look!' She pointed to the TV on the wall, at the frozen image of David smiling back at them – another red-carpet event with the adoring public looking on.

'What are you talking about?' Pierre asked. 'That's David, my papa.'

As Laurel stared at the screen, scanning the background visual of the public standing behind barriers, she did a double-take. She'd almost missed him. 'Shite, he's bald. He's shaved his head and grown a beard.'

'What? Where?' Paul moved closer to the big screen. 'Christ, Marc, call your security team there.'

Marc was ahead of him, leaving the room with his phone to his ear.

Patricia sobbed, stress and fear edged on her thin face. 'Why didn't you tell me?'

'I'm sorry, Patricia, but—'

'We decided you were not well enough to know, Madame Maguire,' Pierre said.

'We were wrong, Patricia.' She tried with all her strength not to cry. 'Promise me, I beg you. Please, if he has tried to contact you, or if he does, please tell us.'

Paul hugged her, his support appreciated.

'Can we trust you, Madame Maguire?' Pierre asked, his face dark beneath his frown.

Patricia tried to rise from her chair but failed, shaking her head in annoyance at her weakness. 'I know what sort of person I was but I have said this to you before and I'll say it again: I'm sorry.' Her breath rasped. 'I know my apology sounds petty in your eyes, perhaps to all of you, but my only wish is to make amends with my daughter and the rest of my family.'

Pierre's eyes widened, and he was about to respond but Patricia jabbed her forefinger at the TV.

'If that thing I, unfortunately, have to call my son tries to contact me, believe me, Paul and Marc will be the first to know, then Laurel and David. She held a hand to her chest as she took time to steady her breathing. ‘Not because your parents are second to Paul and Marc but because I know *they* will be able to put a stop to Declan, as they did before.’

Laurel shook her head and sat on the couch opposite her mother before she collapsed. *How much more of this can I take?*

Paul touched her shoulder and leaned down. ‘I’m just going to check with Marc and make sure the other children are ok.’

Pierre stepped over to her. ‘Are you ok, Laurel?’

She looked up at him. *What a fine young man you’ve become.* ‘I don’t know what to think, it’s weird. I don’t feel angry or anxious, just…numb. I think I’m in shock.’

‘We need to let Papa know.’

‘Yes, but I need to talk to Paul and Marc first.’

‘But Papa is in danger!’ The muscles in his jaw rippled.

She didn’t want to have a shouting match with him. ‘Pierre, I’m not a fool. This was deliberate.’ Her mind was now racing.

‘Huh?’

‘Declan exposing himself like that.’ She looked over to Patricia. ‘You know him, do you think he would make a mistake like that? He's planning something, all right, but at the moment, he's chipping away at our lives bit by bit, opening up old wounds.'

'My God, Laurel!' Patricia wailed. 'I think you're right.'

A gnawing fear chewed at Laurel. She realised her fists were clenched so she stretched out her fingers, trying to ease the tension. *Pull yourself together, woman.*

Marc and Paul returned to the room. Both looked stressed. She took a slow, calm breath. *The best thing is to take action and face this head-on.* 'Declan is playing a game with us, with me, and perhaps Patricia too.'

Marc sat beside her. 'My security team are on alert and will notify David as soon as his latest event is finished.'

'He's playing a game, Marc, don't you see it?'

He looked at her for a long moment. 'I think it's best we stay here, notify the local police, and keep security vigilant in Cannes.'

'I'd say he's gone from Cannes. He could be on his way here or heading out of the country. This isn't a live event, is it?' She looked at Patricia. 'What do you think he's planning?'

'Now? Letting us know he can get around. You're right, he's playing a game. Well, what he thinks is a game.'

Marc stood and took a photo of the frozen image on the TV with his phone. 'I'll edit this to show just Declan as he looks now, and send it to my security team in Cannes.' He tapped the screen a few times. 'Paul is taking first watch, then I'll cover from three a.m. until you're all awake in the morning. Two extra bodyguards are on their way here from London as we speak.'

'I can stay with you when Paul goes to bed,' Pierre said, then walked out, leaving no room for objection.

Laurel got to her feet. 'We need to tell everyone. I'll call Jean-Pierre.' She took her phone from her pocket and walked out to the kitchen area, her legs shaking with each step.

## *Chapter 14*

∞

A week passed, with David safe in Cannes without any further incident or sighting of Declan. For Laurel, he couldn't come home soon enough. Two more days and he'd be with them, and she would know his location, what he was doing, and their lives could return to some sense of normality.

She couldn't wait to lean into his chest and listen to the regular beat of his heart. It would be so good to have him back in their home – in her bed. Missing him so much made her body tremble. She drew in a huge breath, exhaling slow and easy to help calm herself. The fact that she missed him so much scared her. Since that disastrous Columbian movie shoot, they hadn't been apart for more than a couple of days, until now. If he returned to acting full-time, would she feel like this every time he went away to work?

Curled up on her couch, she tried to read her book. Her mother, sitting opposite, was engrossed in a new Patricia

Scanlon novel. She seemed to have calmed over the past few days, especially when the two new bodyguards arrived. The house was pretty packed at the moment, which helped the family feel secure. With no further sightings of Declan at Cannes or here in Aix-en-Esperance, she and Patricia were convinced he'd left the country. How, puzzled them, as did where he got the funds from. Where would he turn up next? What was his plan? Would he just continue to tease them, to make them feel like they were living under a cloud for the rest of their lives? Under his cloud.

All she could do was count the hours down until her man was here safe and by her side.

'Stop thinking of David.' Her mother's gaze didn't shift from her book.

'I'm not.'

'Yes, you are. You probably don't realise it but your hands tremble and your cheeks change to dark pink when you think of him.'

Laurel laughed. 'It's a tropical moment.'

'I always called them power surges. They sounded better with that name, and besides, you're too young.'

'Hmm, they say to go by your mother. So, what age where you?'

'When I hit the big five-oh mark, so you've a couple of years to go, and that's why I know it's David you're thinking about.' She put her book aside. 'You work so well together. I never saw that with you and Peter, or even with me and your dad – we were always so professional. It's truly something special to see.'

Laurel shifted onto her back. 'Thanks.'

Patricia laughed again. 'I'm sorry, am I embarrassing you? I don't mean to.'

'No, it's ok. I'll admit you're right, just this once, mind.' She smiled. 'I didn't realise it was so obvious.'

'Only to a new observer. You know…you deserved a normal, real mother. It's my biggest regret before I die.'

'Patricia, don't, please.'

'No, I need to say this. It's human nature to want to fix what's broken, and I broke my maternal part of the bargain as you grew up. I'm sorry. I know I keep saying it but, with us here, together, I hope it's helping to fix our relationship a little.'

'Yeah, we're in the same house and we haven't had a fight yet.' She laughed but it was tinged with sadness, and regret.

'We won't, I promise we won't.'

Laurel closed her book, deciding it was best to give her mother time to talk, about the past, and to ease the regret in her heart. This was her mother now, and she acknowledged that, for the short time they had left together, giving peace to her was crucial.

Patricia looked out the window, then back to Laurel. 'When you were younger and learning to do anything, you were so determined to get it right. I remember one time watching you learning to ride your first bike. You insisted on having no stabilisers, wanting to be like your big brothers.'

She sighed. 'Of course, Carl was so helpful and patient. The other one, bah!' She gasped in a big breath. 'He was gone down the road to his friends, having no time for others. The stupid thing is, I looked on *his*…behaviour as being strong and independent, and Carl's help to you, his little sister, as being weak – a soft-hearted sod.' She held her hand to her chest. 'How wrong I was.'

Her upset was obvious as she struggled with her breathing.

'It's ok, you don't have to tell me this.'

'Ohh, but I do. I want you to know that, yes, I know I failed you as a mother but knowing and understanding are two different things. I want you to understand, too.'

Laurel nodded – it was all she could do to let her mother know it was ok to continue.

'You kept falling off the bike, and Carl would run over to help you up. Sometimes you let him, sometimes you got up before he reached you. But you kept trying to ride that bike,'—she gawped in a short breath—'and it was so obvious that you weren't afraid to fall off. You just brushed off your scrapes and bruises and got right back up on that saddle again.'

She stopped to gather herself, taking a few shallow breaths. 'The magical thing I saw in you was that you had no fear of that bike, or of hurting yourself. You were determined to achieve what you wanted and nothing was stopping you. You cared so much about achieving your goal, but you weren't afraid of it.' She leaned over to get some water and a tissue.

'My mistake was I took that as a sign that you would accomplish so much, and you have! Just not in the direction I thought was right for you. I had these brilliant ideas that you would be a strong businesswoman. A top CEO in a major global company. My own dreams were then transferred to you and I was determined you would get there with my guidance.'

Laurel couldn't believe this was her mother telling this story. She never remembered her being at home, never mind watching or caring for her children, taking note of what they did in their playtime. 'Well, I did go into business, anyhow. It was a decent job, even if it was with the family.'

'Ahh, of course, I wasn't happy with that, was I? I felt you'd wasted your opportunity, the fool I was. Now I see you with David, with your children, and I know this is what you were made to do.' She coughed into her tissue, then sipped the water. 'This, everything here, is your triumph in your life. I should never have tried to make my dreams your dreams – your life. That was wrong of me, and the bitterness I felt was because I thought I'd failed with my career and then with my daughter's. Stupid.' She wiped away her tears and sipped more water.

'Perhaps your mistakes with me are why I'm here now,' Laurel said, doing her best to think of something to console the woman. 'You know, if you hadn't acted in the way you did, I may still be in Ireland, a top CEO, or whatever, and our relationship may have been better but I wouldn't have all I have now.'

*What would Jean-Pierre say in this situation?* 'Life never works out the way we want it to, Patricia, but we get there in the end. I don't worry about any failures in my life. Yes, it's upsetting and regretful that we didn't have any sort of a relationship, but look at us now. If you hadn't taken the chance to contact Paul, look at what we could've missed.'

A faint smile showed on Patricia's face, and Laurel hoped her words were helping her come to terms with her life. Jean-Pierre had advised her that proper apologies had three parts in life: to admit what you did was wrong; to feel bad for the hurt you caused; and to make things right. At first, she didn't understand what he'd been saying to her but, as the weeks passed, with her mother staying here, she felt she was freeing not only her own soul but that of her mother's too.

'Apologies are not meant to change the past, Patricia, so stop thinking or looking back, they can only change the future, and you have.'

'You know, I once read, the best kind of relationship is the one in which a sorry and a smile can bring everything back to normal.' The tears were flowing down her face, yet she didn't try to wipe them away. 'I know this isn't normal but I hope it's better than it was.'

Laurel wiped her own tears, then got up, walked over to her mother, and sat beside her. 'It is, believe me, it is, and with Daddy coming from L.A next week, you'll see how good it is. Thank you for being so open and honest with me, it really means a lot.'

She hugged her mother, and Patricia softened in her arms and cried some more.

## *Chapter 15*

∞

'Morning, Patricia!'

'Ohh, hello you two. Your mam said you would be popping in today to bring me for a little jaunt around.' She tried to sit up but stopped, not wanting to look feeble in front of the teenagers. 'Tell me, do you think it's safe?'

'Of course, Madam Maguire.' Pierre unfolded the wheelchair. 'We won't be going too far from the house.'

'And the height of this guy?' Emma laughed, giving a sideways nod at him. 'No-one will come near us.'

'Oh, no, I didn't mean it that way. Just, can I go closer to the little forest?' She pointed at the window. 'It looks beautiful.'

Emma and Pierre looked at each other and shrugged.

'It is a bit steep,' Pierre said, 'but I think if we're careful,'—he nudged Emma—'and you allow me to push the chair, I'm sure we could manage a bit of it.'

'Do you want to bring the small oxygen canister?' Emma asked. 'It'll need to sit on your lap, if that's ok?'

'Yes, please, just in case. To be honest, I was a bit breathless the last time and couldn't wait to get back here.' She didn't want to make an issue of it but the oxygen would help. 'I want to enjoy this little trip, especially if we can get close to the forest.'

Emma lifted the canister. 'Why are you so interested in visiting the forest? It's not much really.'

'Ohh, but the view from here, Emma, it looks beautiful. Reminds me of the small forest where I lived as a young child on the family farm.'

'Wait, what? Your family had a farm when you were small?'

'Ohh, yes, it was a small dairy farm.' *Maybe I've said too much. But then, what's the harm in it?* 'I didn't mind it, and it was hard work back in those days, believe me. Still is, I'd say.'

The teenagers helped her out of the bed and into the wheelchair, and they carried it off with a compassion and care she was thankful for.

'So, how many brothers and sisters did you have?' Emma asked, her curiosity seeming to get the better of her. 'Where are they now?' She ignored another nudge from Pierre. 'Is the farm still there? Where exactly are you from?'

Patricia laughed. 'I don't think your mother even knows this. It's not something I spoke about, to be honest.'

'Why?' Pierre asked. 'There's no shame in living on a farm.'

'When I left the farm, I swore I'd never go back. As a teenager, I hated it. I just had one brother, Seamus, and when my parents died, he took over. The son always inherited everything from the parents in those days. He married quickly. I was just seventeen at the time and me and the new wife didn't get on.' She sighed. 'I don't blame her, I was an ambitious cow. Wanted more for the farm, always badgering Seamus to buy bigger, get more land and stock. Arguments were constant in the evenings as she tried to establish herself as the woman of the house.'

Silence fell as they digested that information. She contemplated what she should tell them next. *How will*

*Laurel feel about me divulging such details when she never knew any of it herself?*

'Go on, tell us,' Emma said, full of encouragement. 'It's great to learn all this.'

'My brother took me aside one night. "Patricia," he said, "it's time you moved on and found yerself a husband. I think yer best shot is in Dublin. You'd be happier there," he said. And he shoved one hundred and fifty pounds, which was a lot in those days, into my hand and gave me my suitcase and a train ticket.'

Emma knelt beside her, her arm warm where it touched Patricia's. 'Are they still alive?'

'Honestly, I don't know. I hope they were happy and had a large family. I hope the place is still in the family – my great-grandparents were one of the first Irish Catholic landowners after some Act was passed around the 1880s.'

'So who walked you down the aisle?'

'I did. We just had a small ceremony, to be honest – your grandad's immediate family and a couple of friends. Nothing like the big parties nowadays. And then a wedding breakfast in The Gresham.' She sighed, nodding to herself. 'Richard Burton and Elizabeth Taylor stayed there, it was so fashionable at the time.'

Emma smiled. 'I read somewhere they were early morning weddings in churches, is that right? Part of the early morning mass. I must pull out your wedding album, I know Mam has it somewhere.'

'You could do some genealogy, Emma,' Pierre suggested, 'and make it part of your year-end project.'

With Patricia set, they pushed the chair out of her room – Emma letting Pierre take control.

'Would you mind if I did a little more digging, Patricia? I'll need names and dates. Where did you say you were from?'

Patricia laughed. *What have I started?* 'A small area just outside Carlow town. As you head towards Tullow.'

Pierre and Emma glanced at each other and shrugged.

She rolled her eyes on seeing their blank faces. 'You two need to explore Ireland a bit now you're going to live there for a while.'

Emma rubbed her hands together, her eyes wide. 'I'm going to start searching tonight – I love family history.'

'See what you've done now, Patricia.' Pierre laughed, 'You've started her on a mission to find your family.'

'Her family.' She touched Emma's hand, something she would never have done in her other life. But things were different now. She was different, even if it was too late. 'It really would be lovely to know what happened to the farm, and to Seamus.'

As they headed down the hilly pathway, they stopped so Emma could help fix the oxygen mask over Patricia's mouth, evoking a thumbs-up from her.

'Ohh, Emma,' Pierre said, holding a finger up, 'I forgot to tell you there's a letter in the hall for you. I left it there when the post was delivered.'

'Hmm, not expecting anything but, thanks, I'll get it later.'

## *Chapter 16*

∞

Emma stood at the kitchen door clutching the sheet of paper. Her mam and Jack were joking as they cooked lunch for everyone. The scene looked so happy to her, so normal, but the words on that page confused and hurt her. *Is it true?* She never felt she was different or the odd one out. There was never anything *wrong* in her life. It was simple and uncomplicated, exactly how she liked it. But now that had changed – it was like her mam had betrayed her, lied to her. Did she and Peter just never find the time or opportunity to tell her the truth? *Where's Pierre when I need him?*

Jack laughed at something their mam said, then noticed her standing in the doorway, his eyes widening when he saw she was about to cry. He nudged their mother. Emma looked at her mam, her nails digging into her palm as she scrunched the page into a ball. She wanted it to disappear, to not be true. A shudder ran through her. *I am the odd one out. I'm not a part of this family.*

'Sweetpea?' Her mother walked towards her, arms out. 'What's wrong?'

Emma stepped back – she wanted that hug so much but just couldn't stop her body from moving away when her mam's warm embrace was offered.

The confusion in her mother's face was clear.

*Time to get some answers.* 'Is…Dad not my dad?' Tears welled and she blinked to clear her vision.

Her mam's face turned pale and she knew the letter and its horrible vindictive words were true. The strength went from her and she collapsed into a ball on the floor.

'Jack, turn off the cooker and go to the kids for a few minutes.' Her mother knelt beside her.

'What's going on, Maman?'

'Jack, just do as I ask and make sure no-one comes in here.'

'But, I—'

'Please, just do this now and I'll explain all later, I promise.'

Emma felt her mother's arms around her.

'C'mon, Sweetpea, let's sit up and tell me what this is all about.' Her soft tone helped calm Emma a bit, her arms like a security blanket as they walked over to sit at the table.

Her mam gave her some serviettes and kissed her forehead, placing a strand of her hair behind her ear, just like Pierre had done. Every little motion gave her much needed solace and strength.

'Are you going to tell me what this is all about? Did something happen? Did someone say something to you?'

Emma placed the scrunched-up letter on the table. 'Your brother decided to write to me.'

Her mam didn't pick up the letter, and seemed to remain calm, which wasn't the reaction she's expected or hoped for.

'Is it true, Mam?' Her shoulders shook as the sobs escaped. 'Is Dad not my true father?'

'He is…was your father in every sense of the word. Just like David is now.'

'Ohh, Christ, Mam! Why didn't you tell me?'

Her mam sat back, her shoulders up. 'You…never asked. You knew his name wasn't on your birth certificate. I just…presumed you would ask when you were ready.'

'What?' She couldn't believe she was being so blasé about it. 'I thought this family never had secrets?'

'It wasn't a secret, as such.'

'No? And what do you think not telling me such an incredibly important detail made it?'

She folded her arms when her mother reached out, knowing the action would hurt but unable to stop herself. The hurt was too much and she wanted her to feel some of it.

Her mam sighed. 'That piece of scum really knows how to hurt, doesn't he? He's an expert at getting under your skin.'

In the ensuing silence, so much raced through Emma's brain. *Who else knows? Am I the only person not given this important piece of information? Why didn't anyone tell me? Why did Declan pick on me to hurt?* Her mam's betrayal dug right into her heart. How could she leave her daughter so open to attack like this?

'The letter says you had a *brilliant* time before meeting Dad – I mean, Peter.'

Her mam laughed. 'I wouldn't call it that but, yes, I had some fun going out with friends, in between drinking myself into oblivion because of my troubles at home.'

'He said he doubts you know who my father is.'

'That's a lie!'

Emma flinched at the retort, and also at the sight of her mam's reddened face.

'Ohh, I'm so sorry, Sweetpea.'

Her mother reached out to take her hands once more but she couldn't help refuse her attempt at reassurance.

'Why did you never ask when you saw your birth cert? You knew your surname was my maiden name.' Her mam touched her arm, her voice soft. 'Did you not think of asking?'

Emma shrugged. 'I just presumed you and Dad, I mean, Peter, never got around to changing it after you got married.'

'It's still ok to call him Dad, nothing has changed. He loved you so much and was always there for you.'

'Nothing? Then why do I suddenly feel so different?' She sobbed the words. 'Did you think I was too immature to understand?'

'I'm so, so sorry, I should've known this would happen. Perhaps I was too casual about how it may affect you. When I found out I was pregnant, even though we planned you, life for me and your biological dad was extremely complicated. But your birth matured me, and you made me grow into the woman I am now, giving me the courage to leave home again and make a life for myself. I'm so proud of what we created with our love for each other.'

Emma watched as her mam struggled to control her own emotions, tears brimming in her bright-blue eyes. She was being genuine, as always. Feeling relaxed a little, she took her hands in hers.

Her mam let out a sigh, long and slow, like she was exhaling some pent-up apprehension.

'We dated each other when we were teenagers, and we loved each other but just couldn't be together. Life was too complicated. Then, a couple of years later, we had a reunion of sorts when we met at a conference in Waterford. It was just meant to be. And those wonderful three nights gave us you.'

'A conference? So, if you loved him so much, why isn't he here? Why didn't he stick around and fight for you when…Peter proposed?'

'I told you, it was complicated.'

Emma scoffed at her mother's words. 'Complicated enough not to tell me, ever!'

'I'm sorry, I need to talk to him first before I say anything else.'

Doubt slipped in again. *Need to talk to him? Why? To get your stories straight?* 'So he's still alive? Who the hell is he and, after all these years, why the hell hasn't he contacted me?'

'Ohh, Emma, honey, I've always been here.'

She snapped around to see Paul standing in the doorway. For a long moment, she stared at him, then at her mam, now sitting upright, her whole demeanour changed – on edge. She looked at Paul again, then at her mam. Now it all made sense. Paul. He'd always been in her life, always close, within easy reach – a bastion of security and advice. Paul. Her real father had never been far away. Her life's jigsaw wasn't missing a piece, it had just been misplaced. But yet, she still felt overwhelmed. *I need to talk to Pierre.*

At least now she knew why they couldn't be together when she was born. The old Patricia and psycho Declan would've taken full advantage of Paul's political connections. *But why didn't they tell me after Peter died? Why did they leave it so long?* Anger still burned in her, tempered now, though, by relief that it was Paul.

She turned to him then back to her mam, who shrugged, her eyebrows raised. *This is going to be a long night.* 'You two have a lot of explaining to do.'

***

*18 years before* – Paul was at a business conference in Waterford, and to his surprise and delight, discovered Laurel was attending too. With it being a three-day event, invited speakers and attendees filled the rooms of the large hotel for that weekend.

At the time, she was 30, still single and sounded happy, acting as sharp and as business-like as ever. But he knew her, and after dinner his concern grew as she downed her drinks quicker than the others in their company. Determined to get to the root of the problem, he asked her to dance with him. Everyone knew they were old friends, so nothing more was thought of it.

They moved around the floor and, as much as he tried, small talk was the only mode of conversation she would tolerate; he couldn't get behind the veil she'd drawn across her truth. Knowing she liked to get to the point in her life and business, he asked the question he thought might be at the root of the problem: 'So how is living back with your parents going after your travels?'

He saw it in her eyes that he'd hit the bull's-eye. 'Oh, that good?' He hugged her to him. 'How about having a cup of coffee with me in the foyer?'

'You're being overly discreet, Paul. How about your room?'

With her voice so toneless, he knew she wouldn't take no for an answer. 'Let the night finish with some coffee and we'll talk. Is that okay?'

Agreeing with a soft nod, she lay her head on his shoulder and they returned to the dance. 'My only friend at this moment in time.'

Nearly two hours later, the guests started retiring for the night, off to recover for the next tedious day.

Laurel got up from her chair. 'I'm afraid I must leave your wonderful company.' She smiled and nodded to all at the table, then turned to him. 'Paul, as we're placed on the same floor, could you kindly escort me to my room?'

He didn't hesitate. That night they made wonderful, passionate love – something he could never achieve with other women in his life. As she lay in his arms, pouring her heart out to him, he wanted so much to help her, protect her, and never let her go. But they both knew and accepted that it wasn't to be. He'd just finished his law studies and his political career was taking off. To have an on-off relationship with a woman who financially supported him would not help his ambitions.

'You can never do that to yourself, Paul. Not for me. I'm not worth ruining your career and your life for.'

He knew her father was drinking himself into an early grave, and everyone was aware of it. Her mother was ambitious, to put it mildly – she'd thrive on their relationship but only to further her own goals for the company, regardless of what damage it caused to his career. Laurel, he knew, couldn't stay in that house. It would destroy her. One of her brothers had already made the escape and moved to the US but, selfishly, he didn't want to lose her to another country.

On their second night together, they made a pact. He didn't know where his personal life was taking him – there was something missing in all his relationships; he just never felt complete. Laurel, he knew, understood his mixed feelings whenever he dated someone. She would always be there for him when the eventual break-up happened. Even if they didn't see each other for months on end, when they did meet up it felt like they'd only spoken yesterday. It was a connection they'd have until their end, and he'd do anything to keep her safe, but most of all he longed for her to remain the Laurel he knew and loved.

With his head on her abdomen, he was confident they had just created something wonderful. He looked up at her as she cupped his face in her hands. 'I know something beautiful will come from this, because I know how beautiful and strong the mother is.'

When she announced she was pregnant to her family, he felt a surge of pride at the way it returned her strength, and how her apathy faded to the background where it belonged. She never told them who the father was, and Paul played his part as the concerned friend, reining in her small circle of friends to help with her move to her own apartment and a return to the Laurel he knew so well.

## *Chapter 17*

∞

David arrived home much to Laurel and the family's relief. With a full house, Paul and Marc decided it was best to return to Ireland and their work. Although they could do the majority of their work remotely, it proved difficult with active children, noise, and a house overflowing with adults. One more would join the teaming house tomorrow with the arrival of Laurel's father, Gerard.

'Why do you have to go?' A flutter of panic at the thought of losing her reliable safety blanket had goosebumps popping up across her shoulders and arms. She hugged herself, leaning against the kitchen table.

'We're only a phone call away,' Paul said.

'Yeah, and a two-hour plane journey.'

Marc laughed at that but one look from Paul wiped the smile off his face. 'Ahem…right, our guards will ensure everyone's safety. I trust them, and they are the elite of my team. You have nothing to fear, Laurel.'

'Ohh, I know, but they're not you and Paul.'

It was Paul's turn to laugh now. 'Thankfully, they're not! They are highly trained operatives,'—he flicked a look at Marc—'and not an ex-garda who could do with some re-training in that field.' Marc rolled his eyes and smiled. 'And I'm a solicitor. Honestly, Laurel, we would be of no help if anything were to happen.'

'Hey, speak for yourself!' Marc retorted.

'Sorry, but when was the last time you worked in the field?'

Their banter delighted Laurel, reminding her of days before this *Declan* nightmare began.

David joined them. 'So have you broken the news to her yet?'

'Yes, they have, and I'm not taking it well.' She pouted in a joking way but it did miff her that they'd told him their news first.

He hugged her. 'We need to return to our everyday lives, Laurel. Declan will not win this war. Yes, mon amie, I would prefer if they stayed, too, but we are playing into his hands by turning our home and our lives into this prison.

We can't live like this, and it's not fair to ask Paul and Marc to stop their lives to protect ours.'

In her heart, she knew this day would come but still fought the urge to burst out crying and beg them to stay. David was right, it was unfair, but as he was going to L.A in less than two weeks, she felt alone and vulnerable, even with his family around her, the security guards, and the local police aware of the situation.

'Maybe we should get some guard dogs.'

'You're replacing us with dogs.' Paul laughed again. 'You have a dog and he's great with the children, and protective. There's no need for more. I honestly believe Declan's gone back to Ireland, or the UK. Marc, back me up here, please.'

'Yeah, the dog bit, not a nice feeling.' They all burst out laughing. 'But, seriously, Laurel, he's not in France anymore. I'm certain, and my sources are reliable. He may have played his little mocking game with you but he needs to get his network together again. The man needs money. It's likely his visit was financed by one of his partners-in-crime because he kept silent on some of the people he worked with. They would owe him big-time for that.'

She chewed over what was being said to her. *Get a grip, girl.* Since Declan's release, her stress levels had hit a high note and showed no hint of falling. While she was snappy with the adults around her, she did her utmost to play it calm in front of the children. But they weren't blind or deaf, and she knew they felt it too. Perhaps she was overreacting – out of touch with the real world in her cocoon of domesticity. Trying to make time for her family and the Rousseaus, the speed of the outside world sometimes seemed daunting. *Maybe I should get a part-time job, ease myself back to the way I was before I lived here. I was sharp, I took care of business, and knew how to handle difficult situations. I should've kept myself busy instead of sitting back and letting the world pass me by. God, was I wrong to live this life?*

'Mon amie.' David took her hand, his touch warm and soft. 'We have no room for Gerard to sleep here so he's staying at the farm. When Carl and his family arrive, they will have to stay with Maman and Papa too. Let's make these visits as comfortable as possible for everyone.'

She sighed, though it came out more like a groan. 'When are you guys leaving?'

Paul sat back in his chair, relief in his eyes. 'We'll book the flights and let you know, probably tomorrow.'

'Tomorrow!' She couldn't believe they wanted to leave so soon. 'But you won't get to meet up with Gerard.'

'Laurel, Declan's gone. There's no need for us to be in the way here.'

Light rain peppered the kitchen window, and the youngest children came running in from the back garden. Laurel and David stood to greet them and get warm towels to wipe them down.

As she sorted the twins, she felt at peace with what she'd just decided. Julia, the youngest twin by five minutes, smiled and brushed her hand across Laurel's cheek, her sky-blue eyes providing warmth and an innocent love to her mother's soul. She patted the child's fair hair. *No way is Declan going to get the better of me, or my family. My life has been too easy, too smooth, and relying on everyone else is wrong of me. That's it, out speed-walking tomorrow morning. It'll help get my brain and my body working again, and then I'll work out a plan to get my life back on track.*

Once finished with the children, she walked over to the window to look out at the rain, aware that the three men at the table were waiting for her response. She turned to them. 'Ok, so, a few things need to change around here. Starting with the tension in this house, which is probably being caused by me more than anyone.'

'No, No!' they chorused in reply, Marc laughing until Paul elbowed his ribs.

'Lads!' It came out louder than expected. She stared them down until they focused on her. 'Stop trying to wrap me in cotton wool. I know I've become a burden these past few weeks, and I'm sorry you felt you had to discuss how to approach me about going home.' She sighed again. 'About everything, to be honest.'

She chuckled. 'See, my snappiness just now is a classic example of how much I've been on edge. You're all correct – I need to get a grip on this situation and on me. I'm scared, yes, I'll admit that fact to you. Declan tried to kill me – you too, David – and now he's messing with my family. That letter to Emma is a clear example. So please allow me to be afraid.' She tugged at the hem of her top. 'You're right, we need to get on with our lives, not let this nightmare that is my brother control us and turn our home into a prison.' She took a sharp breath. 'I want two of the guards here at night only. Let's find them somewhere to live, close by and quiet so they can have the daytime to sleep. The third operative can stay here during the day. The local police are exactly that, local, and can be here in less than ten minutes if the need arises. Thankfully, it's the summertime so the children are here. If they want to go on an excursion to get out of the house for the day, then I don't see why not, the guard can accompany whoever is taking them. I may need to stay behind with Patricia.'

David got to his feet and walked across to her, smiling. 'That's my girl, mon amie, you've returned.' He kissed the top of her head and hugged her. And that was all she needed in that moment, the strong arms of her loving man. If only she could have him with her all the time.

## *Chapter 18*

∞

'Patricia.' Laurel tried to rouse her mother from her afternoon nap. 'Patricia, there's someone here to say hello.'

She helped her sit up, the oxygen machine humming in the background.

'He's here already?' She looked towards the bedroom door, 'How do I look? Terrible, I suppose.' She patted down her wiry hair. 'I don't think I'm ready, Laurel.'

'It's ok, you're ok. Dad is Dad. He's delighted you wanted to see him again.'

'Really?' She looked up, doubt in her eyes.

'Yes, really.' She turned towards the door. 'I'll tell him to pop in now.'

Gerard was standing out in the hallway. To her, he gave the impression of a young, nervous man waiting to meet his crush on their first date, clutching the bouquet of flowers he'd purchased on the way from the airport. On arrival at their home, and after loving hellos with his grandchildren, he'd rushed upstairs to freshen up and change into his best suit. He looked so dapper. Ten years younger.

But he wasn't a young, love-struck man, and it wasn't their first date. She smiled at him. 'Go on, she's awake and waiting.'

He didn't hesitate and tapped on the door before entering. Laurel walked towards the living room, not wanting to look back or linger to overhear what would be said. Regret almost pained her brain. *Is it my fault or Declan's, or do we share the blame for Mam and Dad's marriage breakdown? Or was it their own fault? No denying he drank too much, and she was such an ambitious woman, both socially and professionally.* After the trial, he sold up what was left of the business and moved to California to live with Carl. That was hard to take, and she had to admit to being a bit miffed he didn't want to come to her in France. Even so, his decision was his own and right at the time. Carl made him promise there would be no drinking alcohol in his home, or anywhere else for that matter. When Gerard attended a few AA meetings, he admitted it dawned on him how reliant he was on booze. As months, then years passed, she saw the freshness and vibrancy return to him – the redness in his face calmed, and his eyes lost that awful yellow hue. She was delighted how

Carl helped him, and they reconnected through her brother's family and their love of 1950's American cars.

It didn't seem fair now that her parents' reunion would end all too soon. She shivered at the thought of her mother passing. The woman was such an immense part of their lives now. How would they ever return to the way things were before she came to join them? She shivered again as she entered the living room, pleased to see David sitting on the couch, relaxed as he read his script. As she watched her man, butterflies jumped in her tummy, which happened every time she found herself caught in a moment where he didn't know she was there.

Some contrast to their first meeting – how distant he'd acted, and how she'd disliked him, not fully understanding what he was going through. And then that second time, at their rock in the forest – his desperation, his mourning for losses he couldn't comprehend. How she'd hugged him, connecting in a way she wasn't aware of at that time. A few months later, he confessed to her that she'd saved him that morning, and she'd blushed listening to him explain what he had experienced that night. It was only then she realised he might not be with them now if she hadn't changed her jogging route and stumbled across him.

'Everyone lives on a cliff,' Jean-Pierre once said to her. 'There are those who hold each other tightly so as not to slip over the edge. Sadly, there are those who can't continue to hold on and fall, be it by choice or by destiny. Fate can play many tricks on our lives. When it pushes you to the edge of difficulty, it can catch you and teach you how to fly. Fate was good for you both that morning.'

As she watched David, her mobile rang and she took it from her back pocket. He looked up and smiled.

She swiped up to answer, not averting her eyes from his gaze. 'Hello?'

'Hi, Laurel.'

'Carl!' She raised her eyebrows at David, pointing to her phone like an excited child. 'Checking up on me, eh? Making sure Dad is safely here, I suppose.'

He laughed.

'Well, he is. We got here about an hour ago. All ok with you?'

'Yep, the kids are so excited about going to France for a holiday. How's Mam?' Although she called her Patricia, Carl never stopped calling her *Mam*.

'Tired all the time now.' She sighed. 'I think Dad being here will give her a boost, and she'll be good when you all arrive next week.'

When she sat beside David, he wrapped his arms around her. 'Ça va?'

She gave a positive nod in response as she listened to Carl chat away. For a while, with David's arms around her, she felt secure and, in that moment, luxuriating in his warmth and presence, forgot what was happening outside their embrace.

## *Chapter 19*

∞

David slid out from under the bedsheet, threw on shorts and T-shirt, then eased the door closed as he left Laurel sleeping. It was 4.30, with the sun beginning to rise – the perfect time to join Luc, one of their security team, for a morning run.

He found his new friend stretching outside in the back garden, and both greeted each other with a nod. They said little when out on their run, sharing a mutual respect for their individual fitness. At first, Luc admitted he was unsure how to converse with someone he'd admired through his own hobby of amateur dramatics. It didn't take long for David to fix that.

Within a couple of days of the security team's arrival, he'd checked out each guard's speciality, with Luc drawing the short straw being the least-athletic operative. The man admitted how the team assumed David just didn't want to compete with the fittest guards but, when he explained his reason, they all understood.

The speciality he was most interested in was psychology, and how to identify triggers and control tense situations, especially his own emotions. Luc asked him was it for a new movie project.

'No, I feel there will be a time when I may meet our antagonist and I want to be certain I don't…fuck it up.'

Luc nodded a couple of times, his lips pursed. 'Sir, I cannot support any notions you may have in taking on this gangster.'

'Please, it's David. And I fully understand your concerns – my request for training is not part of your job-spec – but this request is in case the situation does arise.' He shrugged. 'I need to be prepared.'

Luc remained silent for a minute as he chewed it over.

'While you think about it, there is a small area in the forest here I'd like to show you. I think it would be the perfect location for both the physical and mental training I need. It's a special place and you'll understand why I chose it when we get there.'

Luc agreed and followed him. 'You understand, David, I must report this back to Marc.'

David raised his brows in surprise. 'Are you all on first-name terms, even with the boss?'

'Yes, Marc would not have it any other way. He feels it creates a stronger alliance among us all, while we still respect the chain of command. It works, and helps those wanting to ease out of military or police structures.'

Once the men entered the clearing, David knew he was being analysed by his new friend.

'This small clearing is so hidden from anyone passing by, yet open to the person who enters. I feel it would be perfect for both types of training – that of the mind and for the physical side. Do you agree?'

'It was marked in our survey, and we are familiar with its advantages and its proximity to your home. We have a camera set up to ensure no-one can hide here.'

'Ahh, the professionals at work.' David laughed. 'I'm happy to know this now – this is a special place for myself and Laurel. We visit here when we want some privacy from the mad house beyond.'

Luc didn't laugh back, which David put down to his professionalism. He needed to rescue the situation. 'Look, the time may arise when I will meet up with Declan, and I don't want to lose sight of the end goal.' He rubbed his brow. 'I need to control myself, and any situation I might find myself in with that man. Do you understand what I'm trying to say?'

Luc nodded.

'I don't want him dead,' David continued. 'To be honest, I don't think I could do such a thing. But I don't want to mess anything up and put my family in further danger. If we do meet, I want to be in control.'

'You wish to learn from past mistakes?'

'Ah,'—he knew the security team were aware of his public outbursts in his former acting career—'yes, the old me. Best to move on.' He sighed. 'I no longer want him to return, under any circumstance.'

Luc nodded again, hands on hips. For a few minutes, both men remained silent as they watched the rising sun light up the space, appreciating the miracle of life awakening within the small forest.

'Let me speak to Marc, and if he is agreeable, we will begin tomorrow.'

David exhaled a sigh of relief. 'Brilliant.'

'Please be aware, David, this is not a simple exercise. There is a lot of self-control involved, even for the physical training. You want self-defence, I presume?'

David nodded.

'The psychological training will involve many challenges, including your readiness for any aggravated situation which may arise. Are you ready for such a task?'

'If it saves my Laurel, my family, then yes, I am ready.'

Luc nodded once more, then stretched his long body. 'Then we will begin with assessing your fitness.'

Once it was agreed with Marc, both men met every morning for their run and training. David learned there was so much more to simply calming his mind and body in any tense situation. Luc took no prisoners, and David struggled to control his temper at times; it took all his strength not to scream at some of the deceits Luc played. The man mixed both the mental and physical aspects many times, and, in the beginning, it fooled him. But he soon learned to anticipate and appreciate what his mentor was teaching him. If and when the occasion arose, and he met with Declan, he felt prepared for anything that gangster could put up to him. He just hoped he would never have need for it.

## *Chapter 20*

∞

Finished her final lunch preparations, Gabrielle hugged herself as she surveyed her baking creations covering her kitchen table. She so looked forward to her daughters coming for lunch, even if it was only once a month nowadays. Well, they were not her actual daughters but to think that way was no harm, she loved them so much.

Her family was growing and getting busier, and recently, it was decided that the weekly lunch visit to Marseille would change to a monthly occurrence, and be moved to the farmhouse so Laurel didn't have as far to go if she was needed back home. This day was just for the women, with the traditional Sunday dinner for all the family.

*Poor, poor Patricia. How much pain she experiences, yet showing such strength and courage to come here and face us all. I'm so happy Laurel decided to make amends and help her mother through this terrible time.*

She didn't expect anything less of Laurel or David, and she said so to Jean-Pierre when he told her of their plans. Her own worry now was that perhaps Laurel and the children were becoming too close, too loving towards Patricia. When the time came and she passed, would the family be aware of their needs as they grieved? Jean-Pierre reassured her but that niggly worry persisted. So much was happening – so much bad news with that brother of Laurel.

As she turned to make sure all was neat and tidy in her kitchen, something rankled her nostrils. She sniffed, searching for the source of the strange, pungent smell.

'Ohh la la! Has that cat brought another gift into the house?'

Oscar, who was actually a female, recently took to leaving dead field mice and even a rat at their back door. At first, they viewed it as a Mother-nature thing, their pet providing a gift – something cats were known for – but now with it happening every day, it was getting annoying, and even concerning. For ten years, Oscar never did such a thing and now it had been constant for the past two weeks. She was fed well so her reasons were beyond Gabrielle.

She lit a fragrance candle then went to open the back door. Everyone would be arriving soon, and family always came by the back yard. Thankfully, she didn't find a gift at the door this time, but looked around for Oscar.

'Ohh no! Oscar, what have you done!'

Their cat was lying under the window, her breathing laboured, with white foam coming from her mouth.

Gabrielle grimaced as Veronique's car pull up to the yard. At least none of the children would be coming today. She didn't want them to see Oscar this way. Veronique got out of her car and hurried over.

'What has happened?'

'I don't know,' Gabrielle replied. 'The smell from her is terrible.' She knelt and went to pick Oscar up but Veronique advised her to get some gloves and a blanket first.

She ran in and came back out as Laurel and Helene arrived. Veronique, tears welling in her eyes, turned to the two women. Oscar was not only a working farm cat, she was everyone's family pet, the boss of the working dogs, and mother to many kittens over the years.

'Did you give her some water?' Helene asked. 'Perhaps try to clean her down and rinse out her mouth.'

Gabrielle picked Oscar up and brought her into the kitchen, with the three women following. They all stood and watched as she ran water in the large sink, washing away the foam from Oscar's mouth and holding her small body under the running tap. But it was too late, their feline friend went limp, her laboured breathing coming to a permanent end. Gabrielle let out a silent cry, with Laurel hugging Veronique and Helene. The four women stood there, watching, crying, unsure what to do next, unable to move or turn away from the sad sight in Gabrielle's arms. While they were strong women, who could face any illness with their children, and any resulting mess, now they couldn't turn away, or even speak.

Oscar had passed and gone over the Rainbow Bridge right in front of them, and there was nothing they could do. Her line had always lived on this farm, but now it was gone forever.

'Perhaps we should bury her with her mother and grandmothers,' Gabrielle said, her voice almost a whisper.

'Should we check with the vet first?' Laurel asked, and the other women looked at her. 'To make sure it was nothing that will pass to the other farm animals.'

'I can call him now,' Veronique said, 'and bring Oscar down if he is free.' She touched Oscar's back. 'In the meantime, perhaps we should cover her with the blanket and place her in her bed.'

'And I will clean this area and outside, just in case,' Helene said. 'At least the smell is gone. It disappeared as soon as you started to wash her.'

Gabrielle lay Oscar back on the blanket and stroked her coat for a final time, then carried her to her bed.

'She was a good cat. Such a boss, and the other animals knew it. So like her maman and her grand-meres before her.'

Laurel put on the kettle as the others went about their tasks, then sat at the table. 'Did you always have female cats only, Gabrielle?'

She was kneeling beside the little bed, patting the blanket, hoping it gave Oscar the same comfort she was experiencing.

'Yes, Papa told me when I was a child that females were more reliable and provided a lineage. I think there could be a dozen or more female ancestors of Oscar buried in our forest.'

Veronique re-entered the kitchen. 'The vet is available. I'll leave now and be back in less than an hour.'

Gabrielle didn't miss the knowing look Veronique gave Laurel. She understood. Oscar's demise had been no accident, most probably poison. Their beautiful cat had been murdered.

## *Chapter 21*

∞

'Jesus, who's calling you at this ungodly hour!' Laurel rubbed her eyes as David got out of bed. She glanced at her bedside clock. It was 3 a.m.

He spoke in English so she knew it wasn't his family.

'And why are you commencing earlier than scheduled?' He turned to her, his hand over the phone. 'It's the L.A production team.'

When he finished the call, he sat on the bed and lay back with a groan. Laurel placed her arm across his chest in a silent show of solidarity. She felt exhausted with all that was happening, including preparations for Carl and his family, due to arrive in two days.

'They want me to start earlier than scheduled.'

'Yes, I caught that. When?'

'I need to leave here on Friday.'

'Shite, that's in two days! Ohh, David, you might miss meeting Carl.'

'I know, I'm sorry. But, if I can, I'll arrange to visit him after he returns to L.A. The only good thing is that I'll be home earlier than expected. It's just a month, with editing to start after, then the promo tour won't be until later this year.'

He kissed her head. 'I don't want to go back to acting. This only proves I don't want that life again.'

Laurel released a sigh of relief, hugging his body closer. 'We'll chat about it later. Sometimes, the grass isn't greener on the other side, eh?'

He let out a low growl, then kissed her head again before closing his eyes to fall back to sleep. No such luck for her, though. With her heart palpitating and an awful feeling of apprehension consuming her, she felt sure a panic attack was coming on. *Why did the production company call so late? Why are they moving forward with their schedule?*

She slid out of his embrace and walked to the bathroom, easing the door shut and turning on the small mirror light. Her reflection told her she was scared. Without warning, her eyes brimmed and tears trickled down her cheeks. Once the flow started, she couldn't stop it.

Being strong was such a huge task – taking care of Patricia, being there as support for her dad, for David, their family's safety, helping Emma come to terms with being Paul's daughter, and then all the prepping for Carl and his family – the whole lot exhausted her mentally and physically. She gasped for breath as her neck tightened, the panic gripping her like a vice. Her legs trembled and she held onto the sink to stop herself collapsing. *Was all this a huge mistake? Should I have allowed Patricia back into our lives? The children will be devastated when her time comes and they have to say goodbye.*

Then there was Declan, a growing, niggling threat at the back of her mind, starting to crawl under her skin like a cockroach, eating away her nervous system – never letting go.

And now this with David leaving a week earlier than expected. She stepped back and slid down the tiled wall to the floor, her hand over her mouth, afraid to let out a sound.

Somewhere through her emotional fog, she noticed the door opening and the love of her life walking in. He knelt beside her, wiping away her tears.

'I'm sorry,' he whispered. 'I'm not leaving you. I'm here for you.'

His soothing words cracked the shell of her turmoil and lifted her heart, providing that boost she needed. She looked into his dark-brown eyes, full of love and security, but she knew he would need to leave her. There was no way out of it. And she had to enable that. She took a shaky breath, resolving to be stronger for herself and for everyone.

He lifted her into his warm and strong embrace, then carried her back to their bed. She didn't say anything, her tears stopping as he kissed her, his passion overcoming all her doubts and fears. They made love, their exhaustion no longer mattering, and two became one as night turned to morning.

# *Chapter 22*

∞

Outside on the grass, the twins played as the sun shone down on the small group. Emma chuckled at her mother, being kept busy trying to ensure the youngsters had sufficient sun cream while they ran and laughed at her attempts to catch them.

After some time, David rose to help her and both parents laughed as they played chase. Chantelle and Pierre were in deep conversation, trying to ignore the chaos. Emma walked towards the forest, Facetiming Paul. Their bond was growing stronger now with the new awareness of their biological connection.

'So tell me,' she asked, 'what made you decide to hide this secret for so long?'

'Emma, we already explained, didn't we?'

'Yes, but I'm finding it hard to grasp. And I'm not being awkward or bitchy. Honest.'

An uncomfortable silence filled the space between them but she let it be to give him time to answer. She kept an eye on the path – the forest was shaded now and the incline could be tricky when multitasking.

‘I did ask your mam once, and she agreed it was time. But the difficulty was finding the time – the right moment – to tell you. To ensure we didn’t hurt you, not like that shithead did. I guess we should’ve worked harder to protect you, to prepare you. I’m so sorry, Emma.’

His apology, as far as she could tell, was genuine. ‘Do you think I’m being silly reacting this way?’

‘No, Emma, if it was me, I think I would react the same way, so it’s understandable. Well, in my eyes, it is. How is your mam?’

She turned back and walked towards the small group playing on the grass. ‘I think she’s still angry Declan got to tell me before she could. She said she’s annoyed she delayed telling me all these years.’

‘She really is sorry, too, you do know that, Emma?’ He nodded for emphasis. ‘She—No, we chatted about it plenty of times. It just never felt right. You were so happy with the status quo, so to speak. Are you mad at us?’

'No, I'm not annoyed with either of you, Paul.' It came out almost as a whisper. 'You both did what you felt was right at the time.'

While she spoke the truth, she was unsure if Paul would accept that, suffering constant guilt about the situation. She placed her hand in her jeans' pocket, touching that hateful letter. Each time it happened, a shiver shot down her spine.

'Are you ok?' Paul asked.

She couldn't hold back a sob. 'I keep reading the letter.'

Paul sighed. 'Burn it. Don't give him the satisfaction of thinking you still have it, or that it's causing you such pain. God, I want to hug you so much right now.'

Her tears flowed. 'It's ok. Mam and Pierre, everyone really, are great. They're all supporting me. Chatting away, trying to make things as normal as possible. Pierre is working with me for my end-of-year project. We're doing a bit of family history and checking out Patricia's side. Apparently, they had a farm in Carlow.'

'Is it helping?' he asked.

She laughed. 'A bit.' She looked at the house. 'And don't get me wrong, Paul, it's not the fact that you're my father, I'm actually so happy it's you and not someone I might never meet. It's the horrible words in his letter – the fact he knew and I didn't. It doesn't seem fair. It's unsettling, to be honest. He knew something about my life that I never even imagined.'

'Yes, believe me, he loves getting into people's heads. He's been doing it for quite a while with me and Marc.' He sighed. 'And now he feels it's you and your mam's turn. And it's such a nasty tactic. But that's Declan for you.'

'Do you think it'll ever stop?'

'What, Declan or the hurt?'

'Both.'

'I hope so. For Declan, I believe Marc will put an end to him soon and get him back into prison.'

Her grip tightened on the phone. 'He deserves more than prison.'

'Now, Emma, don't go there. I'm not only your father but as your family's solicitor, I can't hear you say things like that. Please, honey, don't let him twist your heart to evil thoughts.'

She smiled as she wiped tears from her cheeks. 'I'm sorry, it just feels like that sometimes.'

'Yes, I understand. Believe me, Marc is so troubled with what Declan is doing. He feels responsible.'

The strain in his face and sadness in his eyes brought guilt surging through her for questioning his and her mam's motives for not telling her the truth.

'I'm sorry, Paul, I shouldn't be burdening you with my little issue. No doubt you have your hands full as it is.'

'But that's why I'm here, Emma. That's why I've always been here for you. Always.'

A warm sensation filled her tummy. 'Thanks, you won't believe how much you're helping – how much I needed you to say that.'

The twins' laughter caught her attention. 'I think Mam needs me to help with the twins.'

'Bah, that woman can handle two toddlers. I want to chat about Trinity. I can give plenty of help with choosing the best societies to join and, of course, the best nightclubs in Dublin.' He winked, and she had to laugh.

'Somehow, I doubt if your nightclubs are still open these days.'

## *Chapter 23*

∞

The view from Patricia's room opened up before her as the sun rose. Her pain was getting worse, her breathing laboured, and she couldn't sleep. Laurel and David had been so kind, converting their home office space into her bedroom. From here, she could see for miles, her bed perfectly positioned to enjoy such a wonderful view and sunrise.

So much about the view appealed to her. Sometimes animals revealed themselves, or the odd person would walk or cycle by in the distance. Then there were the children, who would often play just outside and wave in at her. And the small woods to the side created a different musical movement every day. The inhabitants here, both human and animal, seemed to cast off their frowns and complaints. And it wasn't just the view – with the window opened just a notch, a fresh breeze, scented by the trees, at times blew away the pain for a while.

It wasn't a big window but the view it encased was magical – so peaceful. At night, the nurse would come in and close the curtains but as these late hours became more painful and sleep evaded her, she asked that the view not be shut away. Even in the darkness, it consoled her, helped with the pain, and made her thoughts and everything about her life so much clearer.

*What a fool I have been. You were a bitch, Patricia, a two-faced, deceitful witch. Constantly stabbing Gerard and others in the back when it came to the business, and your children. My poor children.* While she wasn't a sadist delighting in the pain she caused, she did consider her children a distraction from her business goals.

The kindness shown by Laurel and David, the forgiveness in Gerard's eyes, and now with Carl arriving today, it made her rethink her past life and what horrible things she'd done to achieve her objectives. Admittedly, at the time, it didn't feel like she was such an awful person but, now, looking back, knowing what she had become, it was nothing more than an absolute waste of precious time, especially compared to the family, relationships, and friends she could've had.

And she was scared. Afraid of the reality drawing closer and closer – her inevitable death. So much time wasted, so much love lost. She was so tired, and while she wanted to live, she also wished she could just slip into a deep sleep and fade away. When she'd first arrived, she felt invigorated and reawakened – the experience a breath of fresh air – but it didn't last as the cancer spread and her pain tightened its grip.

Her life had been such a mess before coming here, and it would end all too soon. She wiped a tear away. *No more pity, I can't let Gerard, Carl, or Laurel know how I feel.* 'You're doing this for them,' a voice inside her head whispered. Her breakdown with Laurel the other week was something they both needed. She'd wanted to clear her mind – to make peace. She needed her to know that she wasn't all bad as a mother, even if Laurel didn't remember many of those good occasions. It was time to clear the shadows away for her daughter to see there had been special times between them – the many Christmas mornings, the short holidays in Ireland and abroad. Hopefully she could do the same for Carl when he arrived.

*As for that other son of mine, if I had the strength, I would find him and make him see sense – get him to change his ways – such poison in his blood. What did I do to raise someone like him? Yes, my motherly instincts never kicked in but Laurel and Carl were good, there is no evil in them. Not like Declan.* When he was a child, he was stubborn, gave little time for others, and in his teens, he was accused of bullying and fighting in school. But with counselling, both she and Gerard thought his issues were resolved – they'd fixed him, so to speak. He'd fooled even the psychiatrist. When it came to working with him for his criminal dealings, she'd found him calm and cool – business-like – with no indication he was any type of low-down mobster, and no hint he could kill or order a killing. *You were blinded by all the money, Patricia, you fool.*

A surge of pain had her gasping for breath, and she closed her eyes as her body tensed. Perhaps it was time to start taking stronger meds. The morphine patch. Something to chat about with Laurel and the nurse later.

But she didn't want to be doped up when Carl arrived. It was fifteen years since she'd seen him. As soon as he got married, he'd emigrated to L.A. Couldn't get away fast enough. It was wonderful of him to come and see her now, albeit a sad way to rekindle their relationship. Maybe she could find the strength to hold back on stronger meds for another day or two. She also wanted to write some more, to add to the memories and letters for the grandchildren. Her view from her window had affected her in such a deep way, and she'd made it clear in her notes how she wanted a simple service, with her ashes spread in the woods below.

A gentle knock sounded on her door. She opened her eyes, knowing it would be Laurel – she was always up early to check on her before going out for her run, which she'd recently taken back up. Next would be Gerard. *My, he is an early riser nowadays.*

'Come in, Laurel, I'm awake.'

The door opened and her daughter greeted her with a wide smile. 'All ok, Patricia?'

'Yes, thanks. All is good.'

*Perhaps one day she'll call me Mam, just one more time.*

Once Laurel closed her door again, she sighed and looked out at the view. It was going to be a glorious day, with the sun rising into a beautiful blue sky. *Stuck indoors again.* But that was ok because she couldn't think of a better place to be.

## *Chapter 24*

∞

Laurel was panting and sticky when she returned from her run. Getting back in shape was proving more difficult than expected.

At first, one of the bodyguards ran with her but she felt uncomfortable and slow beside him. He was fit, unlike her, making her all too conscious of her heavy breathing against his rhythmic jogging. David had taken up running with another of the guards, and that was fine but it wasn't for her. She dropped a hint that she was ok to go alone, that she needed her own time, and if she thought anything was awry, she would call the guard on her mobile without delay. No-one was happy but it felt good to have some time to think alone and get her own rhythm back.

When she opened the front door, the scene that met her sent a wave of nausea surging into her throat. Two suitcases. It wasn't like she didn't know – it was a given this would happen, and she knew the night the production team called that delaying the inevitable wasn't possible.

David didn't need to get so worked up, arguing with Jacques over the phone. The man couldn't do anything about it; his hands were tied from a legal point of view. So, he was leaving, nearly a week earlier than expected. On a positive note, it meant he would be back sooner, giving them more time together before the promotional tour started. He could get things done out there, finish everything so they could return to normal life. Hopefully, Patricia would still be with them, although, as each day passed, she doubted her mother would have the strength to continue past the next couple of weeks. Was this the right time for David to leave?

Yes, it was, despite everything, or maybe because of it. This was one job she trusted he could do, put it in the past, finish it, and move on with their lives.

He came out from the kitchen, holding a cup of coffee for himself and some water for her. Her heart hurt to see his despondent look, and she put on her best smile to assure him that all would be ok.

'I'm sorry, mon amie.'

'Please, David, it's ok. Besides, they just want you over there earlier because they love you so much.'

He chuckled, the sound soft. 'But, of course, mon amie, one can't blame them.'

Their laughter filled the hallway, and the tension in the air dissipated, if only for a while. They hugged and kissed, and she didn't care if she tasted of sweat, or if his coffee dripped on the floor. She rested her head on his chest, breathing in his familiar scent, listening to his smooth heartbeat – a reassuring rhythm giving her solace.

'We will get through this,' he whispered.

A short time later, as they sat in the kitchen chatting about what they would do when this was all over, a car horn sounded outside. His taxi had arrived. Last night, they'd agreed she wouldn't bring him to the airport, as it meant she would need to go again three hours later to pick up Carl and his family.

'It's time, David, you need to go.' She sensed his reluctance to leave and tried to sound ok – strong – hoping her tone fooled him.

'All will be good,' he said, looking into her eyes. 'You know that, don't you? We will get through this.' He stroked her hair, and she, in turn, kissed his hand.

'Well, the timing could be better but, yep, we will. We got through worse, remember?'

She regretted saying that as soon as it was out because he looked tense as he rose from the chair and put on his jacket.

They hugged once more, then he looked into her eyes. 'I have confidence that you will be ok because I see strength and determination in your beautiful eyes.' He kissed her, his lips soft and warm. 'It is a strength that empowers me, and I thank you for that.' He leaned back. 'What would I do without you, mon amie? I think it is high time we got married.'

She blinked a quick sequence, studying his eyes. 'Is this your version of a proposal?' She laughed. 'And there's me thinking French men were the most romantic of all nationalities.'

Both fell silent for a moment, then the taxi horn sounded again. They looked at each other, knowing it was time. No more delaying.

***

As he got into the taxi, he struggled with his exasperation, unable to believe this was happening. He just wanted to have this ridiculous job sorted, get things over and done with, then come home to Laurel, to his family, as soon as possible. The taxi moved and he blew her a kiss before sitting back, his knuckles whitening as he clenched his fists.

*Why is this happening to us? Why does it have to be now? With everything going on, we don't deserve this.* He wiped beads of cold sweat off his forehead. *Why am I allowing myself to get so stressed? Calm down, David. Don't let Laurel see you like this.*

How he hated Declan. He had never hated anyone before, at least not like this. It had to be unhealthy to feel this way about anyone, and it showed in his and Laurel's mood swings and perpetual fatigue. It was all Declan's fault. The man was trying to ruin everyone's life – destroying everything they had built – threatening their sanity and upsetting their family and friends.

His rage left a sour taste in his mouth, and he took quiet, deep breaths to keep his anger at bay, not wanting it showing, even if it was only the driver who could see him. The taxi drove over a speed bump on their private roadway, jerking him out of himself. He had to keep control. With this trip, enormous changes were going to happen. He looked forward to the plane journey and the downtime it would provide. Better than dwelling on what would happen when he got to L.A. It was one of the things he liked when travelling from different shoot locations. The flight would take over fourteen hours, and he planned to take full advantage of it, to just think, maybe read a little, and sleep. With nothing to distract him, he would have time to mull over this situation, over recent events, and get things straight in his mind. He wasn't oblivious to all the crap around them but what was he to do?

As the taxi approached the gate, he shook away the sense of foreboding and looked back at Laurel, standing there alone, smiling and waving to him. He waved back. She looked strong. 'Mon Dieu, I hope you are, mon amie.'

## *Chapter 25*

∞

Veronique parked her car in their driveway, looking forward to some relaxation time after dropped off her children to Laurel's house. She'd laughed at the sight of all the gang in the garden: her own two, David's family, and Carl's three, chasing and playing, with no language barriers for them. It was going to be a busy day for everyone in that household.

This pregnancy had her exhausted. What were they thinking, having another child in their late-forties? All was ok with the baby, having passed with flying colours all the genetic screening and antenatal tests needed due to herself and Joel being *old* in the eyes of the medical world. She hadn't felt old when they'd started out but it was different now. Anyway, it didn't matter if this baby passed those tests or not, they were aware of the risk and would love their child regardless of anything he would bring with him.

She smiled as she thought of the baby's gender. *Finally, a boy.* Joel was delighted when they got the news.

He'd told her that another girl would be fantastic, too, but her heart swelled with joy when she saw the look on his face as the nurse told them.

With all his heart, he loved his two girls – his eyes shone every time they called him *Papa*, but she knew he longed for a boy. It was one of the reasons they'd decided to have this baby – to complete their wonderful family – and God knows how long it took them to have these children. Her heart broke each time she thought of the two miscarriages they'd experienced in the early days. By the time beautiful Sofie arrived, she had almost given up the thought of having their own family, and then, only a year later, she discovered she was pregnant again, with Adèle. Their joy was overwhelming.

They'd needed to keep this pregnancy to themselves for longer than anticipated. It was over twenty weeks before anyone except Gabrielle knew. She'd noticed practically straight away; rarely anything got past her wonderful mother-in-law.

As she got out of her car, she noticed the top window open. *Good man, Joel, keeping the bedrooms fresh.* She called out his name as she opened the door. No response. No surprise, he was a busy man, always out and about.

Heading towards the kitchen she decided some green tea would help her relax. Her thoughts travelled back to when she was first pregnant on Sofie and how her friendship and trust grew with Laurel.

***

'Don't tell me part of the job description now includes having to buy the clothes as well as delivering the new arrivals!'

Veronique shoved the pink and white baby dress back onto the rail, recognising the Irish accent attempting her beloved French language. Turning, she noticed Laurel was smiling, but it soon disappeared when the Irish woman realised Veronique's discomfort.

'Oh, I'm sorry. I didn't mean to startle you. Is it for a…friend?'

But Veronique didn't know how to answer. *Mon Dieu, an Irish woman is trying to talk to me in my own language and I don't know what to say.* Her cheeks burned, the shock of meeting someone she knew in this place bouncing around in her stomach. Normally she felt safe from prying eyes in the large city.

'Are you okay?' Laurel stepped closer. 'You look flushed.' She dropped her heap of shopping bags on the floor and took Veronique's arm.

'Yes, but of course. I'm sorry, too. You're the last person I expected to meet in here. Are you also shopping for someone?'

'No.' Laurel smiled, her shoulders relaxing down. 'I always stop here if I'm passing by. Just to window-shop, mind you. The clothes are so beautiful, but too expensive, if you ask me.' Brushing her hand along the line of soft material, she frowned. 'Ahh, I guess when you're a mother, the longing for the pretty pink and sky-blue stays with you forever, no matter how ridiculous the price.'

Veronique looked away, not wanting her sadness and anxiety showing on her face. She was dying to tell someone, but the scan was not until the end of the week. But then Gabrielle had told her how Laurel had refused to discuss anything about her meeting with David last week. Searching Laurel's fair face, an urge to confide her good news overwhelmed her.

'Do you want to go for coffee?' She looked into Laurel's blue eyes, hoping she would say yes, but still wondering if she could be trusted. *What am I doing? But then both Jean-Pierre and Gabrielle trust this woman, and look what she did for David.* 'I… I know a quiet little coffee shop just off Boulevard Eugene Pierre. It is not far and is halfway back to the hospital.'

Laurel responded with a smile, then nodded to the dress. ‘Are you going to buy it?’

Veronique giggled, relieved in herself. ‘No, not yet. I think I will wait and see what presents I get first.’

Laurel hugged her. ‘You’re right, don’t make it difficult for those bearing gifts.’

As the two women made themselves comfortable in the small veranda section of the cafe, Veronique checked her watch to see how much time she had left before she needed to return to work.

‘You’re on your lunch?’ Laurel enquired as she lit up a cigarette.

‘I have only ten minutes before I must leave.’ She sighed as she looked up. ‘I didn’t know you smoked.’

‘Oh, shite, you don’t mind, do you? I mean, with you being pregnant and all. I didn’t think. Sorry.’ Laurel leaned forward to stub it out in the ashtray. ‘I don’t even smoke in the house anymore. Emma gives out to me so I sneak out to the back garden.’

‘No, don’t do that. I’m used to it with Joel and Jean-Pierre, but I must admit, Joel’s cutting down now and, besides, we are outdoors.’

She smiled and looked down to her tummy, sure it was swelling with pride. How relieved she felt now that she'd finally told someone. It was only one person, but the sense of liberation she was experiencing from sharing her news was amazing. But then a panic arose within her. 'Laurel, please don't tell anyone. We have not informed the family yet.'

'You mean I'm the first to know?' She glanced around before leaning closer. 'You know,' she whispered, 'that night at the dinner, I had a feeling you might be hiding something like this.'

Veronique giggled again, touching her cheek as heat flushed into it. 'I caught you looking at me.'

'Really? I admit, I was quite nervous that night.' She shrugged and smiled, her teeth glistening in the light. 'Seriously, though, when are you going to broadcast the good news?'

'After the scan results at the end of the week.' A wave of sadness surged through her and she swallowed back the urge to cry. 'I am sorry, Laurel. I have not spoken about it so much yet. I have miscarried twice so we do not want to get anybody's hopes up. The pressure is bad enough being a mid-wife, welcoming new arrivals into our world when I cannot even do the simple task myself.'

Laurel held Veronique's hand, her gentle expression showing a deep sense of understanding and compassion that touched Veronique more than she expected. 'It's not an easy task, Veronique, and it doesn't get any easier once they arrive.'

Veronique was about to respond, but noticed something in Laurel's eyes – something dark that took the Irish woman far away without her actually moving an inch. She squeezed Laurel's hand and called her name, quietly, without shocking her.

'I'm sorry, Veronique,' Laurel said, her pale skin turning a deep red, 'my mind trailed back to when I had Emma and Jack.'

'Oh, have you also miscarried?'

'Oh, no, it's not that.' Laurel sighed and shook her head. 'I wanted children, but my husband didn't. Actually, I wanted a huge, loving family. Stupid, I know, in this day and age, and I thought with Peter coming from a large family, he wanted that too.' She ran the tips of her fingers through her hair. 'Before he died, I often wondered what we had in common. We married too fast, and didn't have any real time to think. We were only together for less than a year before we got married.'

'You didn't have to get married, did you? I mean, were you pregnant?' Veronique felt at ease asking her new friend such an intimate question. The vibes from her were good. 'I have heard Ireland is a bit religious like that.'

Laurel laughed and the sadness left her face. 'No, although some friends and family assumed that was the case when we announced our engagement after just four months.' She took a deep breath and released a long sigh. 'At the time, I really loved him. I did. I was fascinated by this high-flying, handsome and exciting young man, but now I…I know it was perhaps some entrancement too. I don't think I was ever in love with him. Do you know what I mean?'

Veronique nodded, knowing many friends who'd found themselves in such a situation. Thankfully there was divorce in France. 'I have seen many lives destroyed by such young ideas, but there are those that work out too, you know. Didn't I read somewhere that in Ireland divorce is illegal?'

'Oh, no, that changed a few years back,' Laurel replied, turning her cigarette pack in her hands. 'And I know a young or quick marriage can work sometimes. I like to think that if Peter and I had really tried, maybe we too could've worked it out, but…' Her voice trailed off, then she looked across to Veronique with a faltering grin. 'I'll never get the chance to find out now.' She shrugged and looked around the small café. 'C'est la vie.'

Veronique knew that was the end of the subject, and an awkward silence weighed heavy between them. Maybe she should lighten the moment, perhaps by letting Laurel into a family secret. She drummed her fingers on the table top, fighting a mad urge to giggle. 'David decided he needed to get married, you know. Thought he was doing the manly thing by standing by his pregnant girlfriend.'

Laurel's sharp look made Veronique think that maybe she had said the wrong thing, but then the Irish woman held her hand to her mouth to smother her giggles. 'Oops!'

'Oops, is right!' Veronique said. Both women side-glanced each other, then burst into laughter at the thought of David doing the manly thing.

They lingered over the remains of their coffee. 'Ahh, so what if I'm late,' Veronique said, rocking her cup on its saucer. 'Let's have another, shall we? And you can tell me exactly what is in all those shopping bags, because I know from the names they are not groceries and not day-to-day clothing, either.'

Laurel agreed, and it was obvious to Veronique that she thoroughly enjoyed showing off her new wardrobe and chatting with her new friend, as did Veronique.

***

Now heading to their sitting room, Veronique settled down on their couch, one hand resting on her stomach. *Only ten weeks to go, mon petit.* With a light rug over her, she opened her book and began to read. Just past the first chapter, she dozed off, until a loud bang shocked her out of it. Squinting against the sun shining in through the windows, she looked around, uneasy. Something wasn't right. While there were no signs of anyone else in the room, it felt like she wasn't alone. The air was different, with an odour she didn't recognise. She couldn't see anything obvious but the sense that someone had been in the room as she slept was strong. The air was wrong.

After a quick look around, she walked out to the hallway. The noise had come from upstairs – she was almost sure of it – like a door slamming. Then she remembered the open window in Sophie's bedroom.

'Tsk, you're paranoid,' she muttered as she made her way up to the culprit. Once she closed the window, she looked around her daughter's room, finding nothing out of place. She jumped at another loud bang, this time downstairs. Her heart fluttered as her anxiety heightened. The smell she'd sensed downstairs entered her nostrils and she put her hand into her pocket for her mobile.

'Merde.' It was in her handbag in the hallway.

Nothing to do but go down and get it. As she walked towards the stairs, yet another door slammed, so she quickened her pace. She was three-quarters down when something caught against her ankle. To stop herself falling forward, she grabbed at the stair rail but lost her balance and twisted to the side, the weight of her body too much. A million silly thoughts rushed through her brain as she fell. Then she landed, banging her head against the wall.

Her last thought was of her baby: 'Ohh, mon Dieu! Mon bébé!'

Then all went dark.

## *Chapter 26*

∞

Laurel and Jean-Pierre ran up the hospital corridor, towards Joel, who sat alone outside a room. When they got to him, she realised he was shaking.

'Joel?'

He looked up, his eyes bloodshot, his face red raw from tears. When he didn't stand to greet her in their familiar, friendly way, she assumed he didn't possess the strength to do so. As she sat beside him, she took his hand, feeling him tremble.

'I don't know when it happened.' He shook his head, staring down at his lap. 'Perhaps she was there all afternoon.'

'She left our house around one-thirty. What time did you get home?'

'I found her at three-thirty. No, maybe it was closer to four. Bah! I don't know.'

'It's not important, my son.' Jean-Pierre rested his hand on Joel's shoulder. 'She is here now, in safe hands. Let the professionals do their magic.'

He looked around, maybe to locate a nurse or doctor he could talk to. With Joel in shock, Laurel doubted he would be able to explain what was happening. As if on cue, a doctor in scrubs came out of the room opposite. She moved away from the door to allow others to rush an incubator to another area. It was covered by a blanket, and the nurses looked stressed as they almost sprinted past them.

The doctor let out a quiet sigh as she sat on a chair opposite them. Laurel noticed her bitten nails, and she looked pale, even with flushed cheeks – the combination of long hours and adrenaline rushes when working in a trauma unit.

Joel, looking lost and helpless, watched the incubator disappear down the corridor.

'Mon petit,' he called out after it.

'Monsieur Rousseau,' the doctor said, almost at a whisper.

He didn't respond, just stared down the corridor.

'How is Veronique, Doctor?' Laurel asked, feeling the need to acknowledge the medic's presence, as Joel was in no fit state to respond. 'Can you tell us what is happening, please?'

The doctor was hesitant to speak to her, looking to Joel for guidance. But he continued to stare down the now empty corridor.

'I'm Veronique's sister-in-law. We're all family here.' She gestured towards both Jean-Pierre and Joel to back up her little white lie. The important thing, as far as she was concerned, was to find out about Veronique and the baby.

'Veronique is sleeping at the moment. She needs rest after what she's been through. She has a broken arm, some bruised ribs, and a sprained ankle. Thankfully, we haven't found any head injuries but I'm pretty certain she will have concussion when she wakes.'

The woman was a work colleague of Veronique, and no doubt was aware she had taken a career break to raise her family. Laurel knew her from when she met with Veronique for coffee one morning.

'Monsieur Rousseau, your wife is going to be ok.'

Joel didn't respond. He tried to stand but collapsed back into his chair, covering his face with both hands.

Laurel put her arms around him as the doctor took out her phone, which was binging with alerts.

'And their baby, Doctor?' Jean-Pierre asked, his back straight as he looked down at her. 'What news do you have for us?'

She looked at him, then turned to Joel. 'Your baby, Monsieur, is in an incubator.' Her voice shook, and Laurel knew she was affected. 'At thirty weeks, he has a good chance of survival but the fall was… It was tough on his little body. The trauma to Veronique's abdomen – there was a partial placenta rupture… We are just grateful he is at thirty weeks. Any younger and…'

More nurses and porters came from the room, this time guiding Veronique's trolley. At least their walk wasn't rushed, their expressions not anxious.

'Please let us settle your wife into her room. Then we will allow two visitors at a time.'

When she got to her feet, Joel came to life and took her arm. 'But what of our baby? Can I see him?'

She covered his hand with hers, her head at a slight angle. 'Not yet, Joel. Let our staff do their work first.' She looked at Jean-Pierre and Laurel. 'The paediatric ICU is for parents to visit only. I'm sorry. He is strong but I can't guarantee things may not change. It is a wait-and-see issue with traumas like this.'

Laurel nodded, along with the other two. There was nothing to be done but wait, and support Joel while they did so.

'I'll go get some coffee, yeah?' She got up and gestured to Jean-Pierre to sit with his son.

'Yes, yes, please, Laurel. Put sugar in Joel's, he needs it for this shock.'

## *Chapter 27*

∞

Jean-Pierre and Joel came out of Veronique's room, and Laurel stopped pacing on seeing the drawn and serious look on their faces, especially Joel's.

'I need to see *mon petit*. Do you think they will let me now?' He looked to his father, who nodded towards the empty nurses' desk.

'How is she, Jean-Pierre?'

'She is awake but drowsy. I need to go look for that doctor or someone to advise us.'

Both men walked away, leaving her undecided. *Is it ok to go in?* Perhaps she wasn't the right person to go and hold her friend's hand. *What will I say to her? How can I comfort a mother who may lose her beloved baby because she slipped on a step? Should I say anything at all? It might be best to just be there – hold her hand and listen.*

When she entered the room, Veronique turned to look at her and both cried out and hugged.

'It was not an accident.'

Laurel pulled away from their embrace, her face going cold as goosebumps sprouted across her shoulders and arms. 'What are you saying?'

'There was a wire across the step but I didn't see it.'

'Have you told Joel? Anyone?'

She shook her head, then winced. 'Uhh, my head.'

Laurel offered her a glass of water. 'Who would do such a thing, Veronique?' She already knew the answer.

'Only those who wish evil on this family.'

'You think it was Declan?' She flinched as the awful reality hit her and grabbed her phone from her pocket.

'Him or one of his associates. Didn't Marc say he was no longer in France? I didn't tell Joel, I'm unsure how he will react.' She released a quiet sob. 'I've never kept anything from my husband.'

'The wire mustn't be there now, or Joel or the paramedics would've seen it. We all thought you slipped, as you had no shoes on.' She tapped into her numbers. 'I'm sorry, I need to call home in case he goes there.'

She wasn't surprised at this. How could she be? Shocked, yes, but surprised? No. Declan was warped – sick and evil. His potential impact on their lives if he wasn't stopped soon could stretch beyond their imagining. No, time for talk was over, with action their only option now. Her patience was gone, her anger palpable. Knowing Paul was holding Marc back, once she finished her call to her security team, he would be next on her list.

When she finished her call home, she hugged Veronique again, making sure not to put pressure on her injured side. 'I'm so, so sorry, my friend. I'm so, so sorry I've brought this on you all.' She glanced at the door. 'And I'm so, so sorry to ask you not to tell Joel or anyone about this. Not yet. Please?'

Veronique nodded, fresh tears streaming down her face. Laurel cried, too, but her tears were borne of anger.

'He could've killed you and your baby. That's it, no more hiding, afraid of what he'll do next.'

She hugged her sister-in-law once more before she got up to leave.

Veronique didn't let go of her hand. 'Laurel—'

'No, Veronique, don't say anything, please. I'm too angry to talk of this anymore. You get working on your recovery. Concentrate all your love on your baby boy. He needs you and Joel. I'll be ok. We'll all be ok, and sooner than you think.'

By the time she got to her car, she was calling Marc. She'd made up her mind – this chapter in their lives was going to end.

## *Chapter 28*

∞

'Are you sure about this, Laurel?' Marc's concern was clear in his tone.

'That bastard has made our lives hell, Marc. He tried to kill Veronique and her baby!' She took a sharp intake of breath to calm her voice. 'He's here in France, I know he is.'

The lengths Declan would go to destroy her life, and her family, shocked her to her core. If she wanted some sense of normality, some sense of security for everyone, then her plan needed to work. She rubbed at a muscle spasm in her neck but it didn't help. Some painkillers after this call would do the job.

'Look, we can't hide away anymore, enough is enough. Can you help?'

Her question was met with silence.

She looked at the phone. 'Marc, are you there?'

'Yes, yes, I'm here. Leave it with me.' Then he hung up.

She exhaled, sick in her gut. When he'd called her back on a secure line, she had to pull into a layby, unable to drive and tell him of her plan at the same time. In years gone by, she would've sucked on a cigarette or two but, now, thankfully, that was just a fleeting thought she dismissed without effort.

Her plan was extreme but not hard to justify considering Declan's behaviour. How could he do this? How could anyone be that cruel to try and kill a baby, who hadn't even taken his first breath in this world yet? Anger boiled up inside her again. *I did nothing to provoke his hatred of me but he still did what he did.*

As she drove home, she came to the conclusion, once again, that he was just pure evil. Nothing else could explain his actions. And he was only one person – one person she needed to shut down. Her main objective now was to get him out of her life once and for all.

Life wasn't meant to be like this – her brother hadn't been raised to hate her, but he did. Was Carl too far away in L.A to incur his wrath? When she'd first told him about Declan's attempts on her and David's lives, and now his silent threats, he'd been shocked and angry for her. He admitted he hadn't got on with Declan, especially in their teenage years, and the two rarely spoke when he'd moved to L.A, but he never felt threatened by him.

She recalled the confrontation in the Dublin office, and Declan's words: *'I found Peter, he was perfect for my needs...he knew from the beginning...he was mine...did all the leg work.'*

The madness in his eyes was palpable as he told her this. How scared Patricia looked witnessing his actions and confession. Perhaps that was the *lightbulb* moment for her, the realisation that her son was pure evil and not just in it for the money – enjoying the terror he created.

She tried to clear her mind as she focused on her driving. Some of the country roads from Marseille were hard enough to navigate, even after her years living here, and it was raining, not a light sprinkle but a hard downpour matching her mood. At least the drought had ended, after all the good weather. The kids would be disappointed but the farm and the forest would love it.

But her mind kept slipping back to Declan and her call to Marc. She thought again of what she'd just done, setting the wheels in motion. Her head was full of questions. *Did I do the right thing?*

It was such a mess. Right or wrong, it would all be sorted out soon enough. It was too late to change anything. In her mind, Declan needed to be out of their lives, for good – no more soft-touch prison time.

## *Chapter 29*

∞

A week later, Carl and Gerard were waiting in the kitchen as Laurel entered. Carl handed her a cup of tea, his look telling her all was not good. One of the palliative-care team sat hugging a coffee. A fantastic specialist with her job – her uniform was always pristine – and, importantly, she spoke English, which was a great help with everyone involved. But for the first time, Laurel noticed now how her deep brown eyes looked sad and tired.

She sat at the table and looked at Carl. 'What's happening?'

'The care team have upped Mam's pain meds. She's struggling, and I think it's time to…prepare. We need to chat, too, about what we're going to do when she passes.'

Laurel nodded once as she ran it through her head. 'She agreed to go on stronger meds once you arrived, and she seemed ok when I popped in this morning. Shite, that was only a couple of hours ago." She looked to her dad. "Is she still lucid? I mean, how long do we have? Will she understand what we're saying?'

Her father took her hand. 'Nurse Dubois said perhaps a few days, but…it could be today or maybe tomorrow. She was pretty forward and honest about it, and I appreciate that. Part of their job description, preparing the family… I suppose.' He sighed. 'We need to make her as comfortable as possible.'

*Today or tomorrow?* The heat from the cup burned into Laurel's palm. *The kids are on a day trip to the beach. They need to say goodbye too.* She felt lost. Too many things were coming at her at once. Patricia was dying. They'd just rekindled a relationship of sorts, and she wasn't ready for it. Now she thought about it, it was only twelve weeks since her mother had re-entered their lives. *And David's not here. I need him here too.*

She took a sip of her tea and winced. 'Christ, Carl, you make horrible tea!'

A nervous laugh erupted from them, including Nurse Dubois. It didn't last long, replaced by a heavy silence, which Laurel broke by walking over to the kettle to make a fresh brew.

This was moving too fast. She turned back to them. 'But she was sitting up having lunch with us all only yesterday. I know she didn't actually eat anything but she was lucid – she seemed ok.'

Her father let out a long sigh. 'She's in pain, Laurel. The poor woman can hardly breathe. And she's falling in and out of consciousness. It's time to make plans – time to know what she needs.' He glanced at Carl, the struggle clear on his face. 'Do you understand what I'm trying to say? We can't wait any longer.'

She bit her lower lip as she took stock of his words. 'Is she awake?'

'She's in and out,' Carl said.

The nurse cleared her throat. 'The morphine drip is allowing her to rest.'

Laurel nodded once. 'Thanks, you guys have been brilliant.' She looked at Carl. 'You're right, I know you're right. We need to chat with her about what type of service she wants. Where she wants to be buried.' She straightened. 'Or does she want to be cremated? Shite, I haven't asked her anything like this, have you?'

Both men looked at each other and nodded no.

'Will we go in now?' she asked. 'It's best we do this together.'

As they left the kitchen, Carl placed his arm around her. 'Do me a huge favour? Call her *Mam*, just this once. She needs it.'

She held a hand over her heart. His *favour* was a lot to ask. She hadn't called her mother anything but by her name since her early teens. Those years were the most horrendous, with constant bickering, screaming, and fighting. *Will calling her Mam now make any difference, to either of us? Is it not too late for that?*

When they entered the room, the nurse, sitting in the corner reading, closed the book and rose to leave.

'No, please stay,' Gerard said.

Laurel sat at Patricia's bedside, and Carl moved a spare chair over beside her. She didn't want to wake her as she seemed peaceful, even though her tired-looking body was just lying there, drained and almost skeletal under the light sheet. The ventilator whirred, and the slow beep-beep-beep of the heart monitor brought all focus to her chest, rising and falling in an irregular rhythm. Although she was still here, still with them, it looked like she'd slipped away to a land full of dreams. *Might be best to leave her sleeping. She needs her rest.*

'Patricia,' Gerard said, his voice low and soft. He took his wife's hand. 'Patricia, love, we're…here to have a chat.' His voice cracked as he spoke.

Her eyes didn't open. The three of them looked at each other. Carl was close to tears, and Laurel put her arm around him, wishing she was somewhere else – somewhere she could press rewind on her life with Patricia, to change their history. While their story wasn't unique in the world, it didn't make it easier to accept their lack of a relationship in the past or that it was too late to do anything about it because of her mother's cancer.

She knew her dad and brother were grieving, even though their grief was for someone who hadn't died yet. *When will it hit me? Will I grieve, too?*

Gerard leaned forward. 'Patricia.' Her eyes moved beneath before the lids eased open. 'Hello, love.' He smiled.

She tried to sit up, to move even her arms, but yielded to the reality that she had no strength left for such exertions. When she sighed, it came as a weak moan, as if she had surrendered rather than be annoyed at her limbs' inabilities.

'It's ok, Mam,' Carl said.

Gerard ran his thumb across the backs of her fingers. 'We want to…to ask you how you…want things.'

She took a moment to catch her breath. 'I haven't finished t-telling you…all I need you to know.' She could barely say the words, the three of them having to lean closer to hear. It was a minute or so before she could continue. 'I'm…running out of time.'

Then she stiffened, and her face creased in a pained grimace. She let out a weak cry and seemed to sink into the mattress.

Laurel took her free hand and held it to her own cheek. 'We understand, and we know.' Her mother's wizened hand was cold against her face. 'Don't let anything stop you from easing the pain you're feeling.'

Patricia looked at each one of them, then back to Gerard. 'I'm scared, Gerard.' A tear slipped out of the corner of her eye, as if released by her admission.

Carl nudged Laurel but she didn't turn to him, keeping all her focus on Patricia. She kissed her mother's hand. 'It's ok to let go, Mam. We're all here for you, and you've done great so far. We love you and we know you love us, too.' She kissed her hand again. 'We'll be alright, don't worry. D-don't be scared.'

Patricia looked at her, her tears flowing as she whispered, 'Thank you.'

'For what, Mam? There's no need for you to thank me. I'm the one who's thankful to you.' Her eyes brimmed over and she allowed her tears to fall. 'Thank you for showing me who you truly are.'

Her mother released her hand and held it out to Carl. 'I'm glad you made it, son.'

Carl lowered his head and sobbed, and Laurel rubbed his upper back.

'Gerard, I…' She struggled for her breath. 'My letters. It… It's all in my letters.'

'Don't talk, Mam,' Laurel said, almost pleading.

Patricia looked at her and touched her hand. 'It's such a beautiful view outside that window. The shadows are all gone.' She closed her eyes and released her final breath.

# *Chapter 30*

∞

A week had passed since Patricia's death and now Laurel was saying goodbye to Gerard, Carl, and his family. As she watched her brother pack suitcases into the hired car, she realised she had never felt so alone.

Paul and Marc flew in as soon as she'd phoned to let them know about her mother but could only stay until the morning after the funeral. No mention was made of her call to Marc and her plan to rid Declan from their lives once and for all. That thought stirred up all the unhappiness and frustration of the week, the swirl then turning to anger. She shook her head. *Stop it, stop it now!*

Due to production commitments, David couldn't get home on time but everyone else was present to give their help and support. It would be another two weeks before they could meet to embrace and support each other; a nightly Facetime call just wasn't enough to ease the enormous, emotional distance between them.

Veronique and Joel spent most of their time in the hospital with their little Simeon, who was a fighter and improving each day. Gabrielle, minding their two daughters, was a true blessing, enabling them to stay longer if necessary.

Jean-Pierre remained observant of everything, as ever, but hardly said two words to her throughout the week. It felt like he was keeping his distance, allowing her to support her young family through the grieving process. While she'd had many members of her family weep on her shoulder, since witnessing Patricia's final breath, she hadn't been able to cry. Yes, sadness and loss filled her but the tears never showed up, and she couldn't understand why. It was the same when she'd experienced Peter's death. Why was she so cold to these emotions?

The nurse gave her several envelopes just after Patricia's passing. She'd recognised her mother's handwriting, although it looked shaky and weak. Each one was addressed to individual family members. Her letter started with: *I know you're going to be the strong one for all this. Thank you for everything. I'm so proud of you and the wonderful world you created for your family.*

It contained a list with all Patricia's wishes for her service: songs to be played, readings, and where she would like her final resting place. Her ashes hadn't come back from the undertakers yet but they would be scattered in the woods below when the time came. Carl and Gerard were disappointed they wouldn't be around for that service but they needed to return to L.A – Carl's auto-repair shop couldn't stay closed any longer. His one employee needed to get back to work, with both having agreed to take their annual leave at the same time because of Carl's circumstances.

'Well, that's all packed.' Carl walked over and hugged her. 'It's going to be ok, you'll get through this.'

'I know, I just don't feel that I'll get there. Not with the way things are at the moment.' She touched her chest, just over her heart.

Carl rested his hands on her shoulders and made direct eye contact. 'Everyone grieves differently. When it hits you, boy will you know it.'

She rolled her eyes. 'Oh, thanks, you're full of good news today.'

Gerard joined them at the car. Harper, Carl's wife, was calling to their four children to hurry up or they'd miss their flight. Her strong New York accent grew sharper at being ignored by their eldest.

Laurel smiled. 'A man from Dublin and a woman from New York meet in L.A, fall in love and live happily ever after. You couldn't write a better romance.'

Carl laughed out loud. 'That *happily ever after* definitely had its ups and downs. And the romance? Well, ditto, but being here has helped rejuvenate that.'

'Well, that only means one thing, doesn't it?'

'I know, I know, come and visit more often.' He looked at Gerard. 'Perhaps it's something to consider, eh, Dad? With business picking up again, maybe I can take on more employees and there'll be no need to close up shop.'

Gerard nodded, smiling an enthusiastic yes.

Harper looked harried as she joined them with three of their four children. She nodded downhill towards the road leading to Laurel's home. 'Guess you've got a delivery, Laurel. Carl, honey, can you get that lazy teen of ours to come out and get in the car, please?'

Laurel couldn't figure who was delivering this early in the morning. It wasn't a courier known to her.

The van, old and large, struggled up the steep hill, barely fitting through the rutted, grassy lane. One of the security guards came out from the house to greet the driver, signalling to Laurel not to come any closer.

'Livraison pour Madame L. Rousseau?' The driver looked from the guard to the group.

Gerard chuckled. 'When did you two get married?'

'We haven't.'

She told the guard she hadn't ordered anything, which made him more suspicious. He signed for the small brown box, which contained the symbols of a well-known book store in Marseille.

'Perhaps it's a gift from someone who heard your mom passed,' Harper said.

Carl looked at her. 'Honey, take the kids inside for a minute, please.' She didn't question why.

Once the courier was gone, the guard placed the box on the grass and inspected it. He took his jack-knife out and made careful incisions to open it. Satisfied it wasn't a threat, he brought it up to Laurel, each of them releasing a sigh of relief that it wasn't anything more sinister than a book.

She realised the book was The Wizard of Oz, and when she attempted to take it out, the guard stopped her. He opened the lid and she saw a note stuck to it.

'That Bastard!' Gerard roared.

She couldn't believe the note's message: *Ding, Dong, the witch is dead, the wicked witch is dead! Rest in hell, Mummy Dearest. Lots of Love, Declan.*

## *Chapter 31*

∞

David arrived back to his condo in the plush L.A suburb of Marina Del Rey. The constant, repeated work had him exhausted. Voice editing in a small booth as he watched the film on a screen was not the ideal way to spend a hot day. It was air conditioned but still stuffy, sweaty, and a part of acting he hated.

This waterside area was beautiful, with many creatives selling their wares in a few nearby markets. When he sat out on the veranda, he relished the magnificent harbour views – the pace around him languid and peaceful. Had he decided to try a Hollywood career when he was younger, this would've been the place for him to live. But that would never happen. His life now, with Laurel, with their family, was all he needed to die a happy man.

He decided to order in. While there were many restaurants to choose from, last week he'd found a fantastic Mexican place called Tocaya in the Venice area. Their

Grilled Chicken Taco was beyond anything he'd tasted before. He wanted it now, with a nice glass of white Pinot Gris to wash it all down.

With his eyes closed, he released a long, slow breath. *So close now.* His impatience to be home with Laurel and his family was getting tougher to keep under control. What she'd told him about Veronique's accident, then Patricia's passing, and that book delivery, it killed him not being there for her, for everyone. His work schedule was shite – Laurel's favourite curse word. It helped him smile a bit thinking of her when she said it.

He turned a page in the novel he was currently reading – a thriller that would make a good movie. *Fingers crossed the ending is as good as the build-up.* Sometimes, he wished he had set up a production company so he could pick and choose his work, perhaps star in it, or simply be an executive producer. The choices would be his and his alone.

This book was written by an Indie author, with no agent or publishing company backing its promotion but it proved to be such a success and reviewers on many book sites couldn't wait for its sequel. He enjoyed independent successes like this. Was it pure luck or fantastic writing and strategic marketing? A bit of everything, he supposed. Without the big bucks to promote it, for a piece of work to shine through, it was all of the above and more. He'd found it in a local independent bookstore – smaller shops like that sometimes held hidden treasures.

A text pinged on his mobile. When he read it, he remained stock still in his chair. He'd been waiting for this, and wished it was just a normal text from a friend or work colleague. But, no, it was something far more dangerous: Declan.

The bastard had contacted him twice before, and he knew he would again and had waited for this particular text to arrive. He wasn't the only one to think this way. Marc and Paul knew Declan wouldn't harm Laurel – he wanted her to suffer, to watch her family and friends get hurt, to make her life a living hell. All those years in prison, planning – thriving on revenge – the man was a living monster who took so much satisfaction from watching his younger sister living a life of hurt and torment.

He decided to let him see that the message was opened, then he'd order dinner, enjoy the wait, and only respond when he was ready. The text should have upset him but he remained calm. *Five million, is that all you want?* He laughed to himself. They were comfortable with their finances but, even with all their assets combined, they were not that rich. He closed the message, clicked on the restaurant's number, and got up.

As he spoke to the person taking his order, he checked the wine bottles stacked against the cool stone wall. A 2006 Carr Vineyards & Winery Pinot Gris caught his eye. Not French but it was an excellent Californian white wine. He took it from the shelf and placed it in the fridge. Forty minutes until delivery – enough time for the wine to chill to his preferred temperature.

In that time, he could read a little, or sit back outside and watch people walking along the beach, some alone in their thoughts, some couples, and some with their dogs. Later that night, the sea would reconquer the sand and its waves would come close to his condo, the gentle sound soothing him to sleep. *Forty minutes – what to do in that time?* He placed his phone back on the table and returned to his novel. *Time to relax.*

Twenty minutes later, he decided on a quick shower. In the bathroom, he looked in the mirror, then opened one of the drawers under the wash basin. A mobile phone lay hidden beneath a small towel. He took it from its plastic holder and sent a text: *It's on.*

The reply was almost instant: *We're on our way. In New York now. Remember your training, don't antagonize him.*

## *Chapter 32*

∞

Laurel sat on the rock watching the sun rise. It was beautiful, her surroundings waking up with the emerging light, the earlier silence disappearing as the forest came alive for another day. She was here for one purpose: to spread her mother's ashes – though she felt hesitant as she held the urn to her chest.

At first, she'd found it strange that her mother chose this place – this forest – but then her final words came to mind: 'It's such a beautiful view outside that window. The shadows are gone.'

She wasn't sure what she'd meant regarding the shadows but understood about the view. Perhaps she had nowhere in Ireland to choose as her final resting place, though Gerard had mentioned a family plot in Glasnevin Cemetery, lying empty. Maybe Patricia had forgotten about it. Or maybe, after her time spent here, she wanted to be close to her *new* family. She smiled at that.

This area was a special place, almost sacred to her, and she didn't mind her mother choosing it. She patted the urn, remembering the fateful, rainy morning when she and David first bonded. With the turn in the weather, she'd decided to finish her jog early, taking a shortcut past a large rock in the centre of a small clearing in the forest. Other than Jean-Pierre, she rarely came across life of the human nature as she ran, so she pulled up with fright when she noticed somebody lying by the side of the rock. A man, his face covered by his arms. She didn't know whether to stay or run but was confident enough of the distance between them to make her escape if it proved necessary.

The man moved his head in a slow turn until he looked up to her. Her heart skipped a beat at their mutual recognition, but it was the desperation in his eyes that hit her hardest – a look she remembered seeing before, in Peter's eyes the night before he died.

David's dark eyes latched onto hers as she approached him. She knelt at his side and placed a shaky hand on his shoulder. 'Ça va?'

He tried to speak but all that came out was a groan, and in the end he just wrapped his arms around her waist, his head on her shoulder, and cried big sobs of grief and desolation. Laurel nearly fell over with his weight but soon settled into a supporting position. That he was releasing everything locked up inside him was so plain for her to see. Regrettably, she'd never let herself do that for Peter, and never gave him the chance, either.

Unsure whether to say something or not, she decided her best option was to remain silent and wait until he finished. They were there for only five minutes or so but it felt longer as she held him, afraid for him, her arms aching and the rain drenching both of them. After some time, his sobs ebbed to soft sighs, and then he went silent. Neither moved.

I'm sorry,' he said in English.

'Ohh, what for?' she asked, trying to sound casual.

He turned his head to look up at her but didn't release his grasp. 'For my rudeness last night. For now. I'm sorry. I don't mean to be so…'

'Now who's lost for words?' She smiled, probably because it was all she could do.

David didn't return the smile but closed his eyes and nodded.

She still held him, knowing that when he was ready he should be the one to release. But after a few minutes, he still hadn't, so she decided to give him the hint as her arms were about to fall off. 'Come on, mister, we're halfway between your parents' farm and my home. Where do you want to go?'

'Thanks.' He released her, looking in the direction of the farm. 'To my…to my…your house, please.'

She helped him up and linked his arm, saying nothing as he babbled on – the rain pouring down on them.

'Good Morning, Laurel.'

She jerked with fright and nearly fell off the rock at the sight of Jean-Pierre entering the clearing.

He chuckled as he approached her. 'Do you think you should be alone for this small but important event?' He shook his head. 'Emma called me last night.'

She smiled. Her daughter was as stubborn as her, insisting that she shouldn't be alone for this. In reality, she didn't feel the need for anyone's company. If Carl or her dad were here, then she would've appreciated their presence but not the grandchildren, who hardly knew her mother. They didn't have the memories, and would've attended for her and not for their grandmother. It wasn't fair on them or on Patricia's memory.

'How did you know I'd be here? I mean, in this place?'

'Your rock?' He smiled, a mischievous glint in his eyes. 'But, of course, my family have very few secrets kept from me.'

She looked away, hoping Veronique hadn't told him about her accident. Her guilt concerning how her problems affected everyone was bad enough, she didn't need Jean-Pierre or Joel knowing the shadow Declan cast on her was now creeping over everyone she loved. With that thought, she realised what Patricia meant about the shadows in her view. Her mother must have known something was in the works. *Why didn't she share her thoughts? Mmm, maybe that's what she was doing with that comment.*

'Thanks for coming, Jean-Pierre.' She turned towards the rising sun. 'This place is wonderful. You can see so much from this rock and yet it's completely hidden from those outside.'

'Is that why you chose here? So you can hide your mother – protect her from those outside?'

'I thought it was a good spot but now I'm unsure. Patricia asked for the forest and this is such an important place for me, and for David.'

'I think you are correct. If you do spread them here, she will have a peaceful, happy afterlife. You know she will be protected in this special place, no?'

Laurel liked the sound of that, and she liked how things were between them, here and now, with Jean-Pierre resting against the large rock. He reached into his knapsack and produced a bottle of red, followed by some bread and cheese.

She laughed. 'It's a bit early for the *Holy Trinity*, Jean-Pierre.'

'Ahh, but you see, it's not too early or too late to celebrate your mother's life and death.'

A soft breeze picked up, the leaves on the trees singing in the morning air.

'I still don't know what to say for her. I thought of a nice poem, then changed for some of my own words. Then I was just going to throw the ashes in the air but there was no breeze for her to fly away. Nothing feels right. Oh, Jean-Pierre, I don't think I'm ready.'

'But the breeze is with us now – it is beautiful and soft. And your maman said her goodbyes – she knew she was ready. But you? Believe me, you are ready. We all knew she was going to die, so holding that urn is not a surprise to you. It's not a problem to be solved, Laurel. There is a grace to be at the bedside of someone you love as they make their transition from this world to the next, and you were so blessed to be there with your maman.'

He spread a cloth beside her on the rock, then opened the wine and half-filled two small glasses. The bread and cheese were broken in two and placed beside them.

'What was the poem? Perhaps translate it to your own words to make it feel more alive for you.'

She thought of the poem by Christy Ann Martine, and the one line she felt was comforting for someone who regretted her past life: *There's no more pain, there's no more fear.*

Then she remembered another poem, its author anonymous, called *I'm there inside your heart.*

She slid off the rock and walked to the edge of the clearing, where it gave the best view of the forest. Jean-Pierre stayed where he was. She checked wind direction, then recited the poem as she opened the urn.

*'Right now I'm in a different place,*

*And though we seem apart*

*I'm closer than I ever was,*

*I'm there inside your heart.*

*I'm with you when you greet each day*

*And while the sun shines bright,*

*I'm there to share the sunsets too,*

*I'm with you every night.'*

She swallowed to ease back a growing pressure, then took a steadying breath.

*'I'm with you when the times are good,*

*To share a laugh or two,*

*And if a tear should start to fall*

*I'll still be there for you…'*

She stopped, unable to finish as she watched her mother's ashes fly away on the soft breeze. Something shifted in her then, deep down – a wedge of emotion she'd held back since Patricia's passing. It surged through her, taking her by storm, knocking the air out of her and sending her to her knees. When she landed, her tears came, the view blurring as her shoulders shuddered with the impact of her sobs. She cried like she hadn't cried in years, her head down, her mother in her mind, with flashes of childhood, her teens, and more recent times.

When she had no more to give, she released a long shaky sigh and wiped her face dry with her sleeve. She put the lid back on the urn and returned to Jean-Pierre, who handed her a glass of wine.

'Á ta santé.'

‘Á ta santé, Jean-Pierre. You always know the right place and the right time. Thank you.’

# *Chapter 33*

∞

Getting comfortable in the plush seat was an easy job for Laurel. She'd decided to book First Class, even though her jaw dropped at the price. With a fourteen-hour flight ahead of her, she wanted decent leg room and some comfort to sleep.

David would be so surprised. All the arrangements were made, with Gabrielle staying to help Emma and Pierre take care of the younger children. When they'd Facetimed last night, she was bursting to tell him but surprised herself with her self-control. The security team were informed she was heading to Paris to meet up with some friends, and she didn't think there was a need to tell anyone else. It would be a trip full of surprises, and maybe involving a visit with Carl and Gerard too.

Two weeks had passed since she'd said her final goodbye to Patricia; Jean-Pierre had helped her so much that morning. It refreshed her, gave her a new lease of life, and made any bad thoughts about Declan disappear, if only for a while. He'd gone silent. Maybe it was too much to hope he'd given up on his terror campaign. Perhaps, now he needed to go into hiding, he'd finally run out of money and favours owed to him. She hoped that was the case.

He was a serious threat but also such a coward. The quintessential bully, he knew what he was doing with his psychological war on them: his showboating in Cannes, that vile letter to Emma, his attack on poor Veronique and her beautiful baby, the silent phone calls to the house, and Gabrielle's Oscar. Thankfully, Veronique and Simeon were recovered now, with the baby safe in his parents' arms at home, and Emma had surprised her and Paul with her readiness to accept her new situation.

And then there was that book delivery. How low can a human go? Such a horrid man. Gerard and Carl were so angry and upset, not wanting to leave, determined to start searching for him and asking to contact Marc. But she and Harper were strong, and made them see sense. She truly hoped Marc and his team would find him soon and put him back in prison where he belonged. Paul reassured her that, because he broke his parole terms and left the country, the authorities would probably add more years to his sentence. She hoped this would be the case and she and her family could return to normal, forgetting he ever existed. But would Marc consider her request? It was a tough one, and she had sleepless nights because of it. *I can't believe I asked such a thing.* Maybe Marc's silence was his way of giving her time to calm down and rethink it. He was right, the longer she thought about it, the more she regretted asking.

'Some champagne and orange juice, Madame?'

The air steward smiled, and Laurel returning to reality and the luxurious journey ahead.

'Why not? It's not every day I get to fly First Class.'

Those few in the know about her trip to L.A were all delighted and promised not to tell David whenever they spoke to him. At first, she was a little on edge, wondering if she was doing the right thing but then she contacted Jacques to get the address, using the excuse she wanted to send him a present. When she googled Marina Del Rey, she knew their reunion would be so romantic in such a beautiful place. She bought some of his favourite red wine and chocolates in the airport, and her new sexy lingerie was packed away in her suitcase. Excitement buzzed through her at the thought of sitting outside the condo in the sun, waiting for him to come home from a long day in the studio. The timing was perfect – she would arrive only an hour before he finished. They would spend a wonderful week together, then fly home to their family.

As the flight left its stopover in Paris, she snuggled up and settled into reading her book. Soon, some food would be served and then she could sleep.

Once the plane landed in L.A and she collected her luggage, she sent a quick text to Emma: *Landed! Will call you later or tomorrow. Xx* Then she headed for the taxi rank. The dry heat was extreme and she felt both tired and excited, hoping the cab would have good air-conditioning.

As she waited in the long queue, she fidgeted and fretted – her timing needed to be right so she would be waiting for David at his front door.

Within a few minutes, she was sitting in the backseat of an L.A cab, cruising along Lincoln Boulevard to Bali Way. She chatted away to the driver, telling him of her planned surprise. He smiled at the appropriate places but she didn't care if he understood her Irish accent or not, it was good to be able to say it all out loud.

Venice Beach was within walking distance of the condo. She closed her eyes, thinking about the two of them walking to the Fisherman's Village and strolling down the boardwalk, looking out for sea lions and storks fishing and playing.

The cab slowed and came to a stop. *That was quick.* But then she remembered Marina del Rey was less than twenty minutes from LAX. She paid the driver, who helped her with her luggage up the steps to David's front door. The heat got to her again.

'Phew! I thought California had a wonderful Mediterranean climate.'

'M'am, we've been *enjoying* a heatwave for quite some time now. It's nearly a hundred, and hit one-oh-seven yesterday. You make sure you sit in that shade 'til that man of yours gets here.'

She smiled and gave him a second tip. He nodded, his hand up to his head as if tipping an imaginary cap.

As she watched him drive away, she sat on her large, over-packed suitcase. Although she was unable to see the ocean, the rumble of the nearby surf overcame the traffic noise, reminding her of a sonnet by Henry Wadsworth Longfellow – The Sound of the Sea – giving her inspiration for the next few days with her man. She closed her eyes, inhaled the scent of the ocean, and turned her head towards the sun. *This is going to be perfect.*

## *Chapter 34*

∞

After a long day in the studio, David was preparing a late dinner in the kitchen, frustrated by Declan's lack of contact. Last week, they'd communicated by text and, as advised, he'd asked him for a couple of days to get the money together. The creep had agreed to the time delay but now nothing – radio silence.

Marc had told him to wait for Declan to text, and under no circumstance was he to make contact, but it was exasperating. His stay in L.A was due to end in five days, and if they didn't get things sorted now, Laurel would know what was going on. At least with their distance, he could avoid revealing anything about this mission. *I'll feel more comfortable when everything is finished here.*

The longer Declan's silence continued, the more anxious he became. His irritation showed as he prepared his food, venting on his steak, bashing the mallet down too hard and turning it to mush.

'Merde!'

It was the only piece he had left. Last week, he'd decided to whittle down all his food stock so there would be little or nothing for the cleaners or the next resident to throw out. He groaned at the mess, now a poor excuse for a steak.

'Guess it's another Mexican.'

His phone vibrated and he took it out of his pocket. A video call from Emma. *Strange, I was going to call Laurel tonight. Two nights without answering my calls is long enough.*

'Ça va, Emma! Is your mother ignoring me and has you calling instead?'

She frowned, her silence odd.

'Emma?'

'Did you not like your surprise?'

'What surprise? What is your mother up to now?' His gut fizzed. 'Did she send me something?'

Emma looked nervous, her response confusing him.

'Where's Mam? I tried to call her twice yesterday and each time it went to voicemail. That's why I'm calling you now.'

'What are you on about, Sweetpea?' He noticed from the background that she was home. 'At this hour, she should be readying everyone for the school run.'

Emma had gone pale. 'David, Mam flew to L.A two days ago. She wanted to surprise you and be there for your last few days.'

He gripped the side of the counter, his legs quivering, as if he was standing at a great height. Emma looked like she was going to cry.

'I got a text to say she'd landed and would be in touch, but there's been nothing since. She's not answering her phone or reading my texts. I got worried, so decided to call you to see what the issue is.' She called out to Pierre, then turned back to him. 'I thought maybe she broke her phone or something like that.'

A chill ran up his spine, and he raced through to the bathroom and dragged out the cabinet drawer.

'Papa, Papa,' Pierre called from the phone screen. 'Papa, what's going on? Emma is saying Laurel isn't with you. Is it true?'

He didn't respond, speed-dialling the only number on the secret mobile. It answered right away.

'What are you doing, David? We said text only.'

'He has Laurel!'

'Where?'

'Here.'

'We'll be there in ten.' The line went dead.

He looked at Pierre. 'Son, I need you to speak with the security team, and contact the police too. But check with Marc's team first to see what is best. I will call you as soon as I have any news. Tell Emma not to worry, we will get her.'

'Papa, who has her? Declan?'

All he could do was nod in response. 'We knew he was here. When did Laurel decide to fly over?'

'Last week. She hoped to surprise you and then fly home with you. We all knew but promised to keep it secret.'

He realised it was a mistake not to tell her about Declan's latest antics and his suspected location. Now he knew why there'd been no word from him. He had what he wanted. Perhaps he wanted the money too. *Damn it!* They'd been so wrong, assuming his prime objective was to 'enjoy' tormenting Laurel over her family and friends suffering rather than kidnapping her. His gut turned and he had to swallow back a surge of bile. *What must she be going through? She is alive. I would know if she wasn't – I'm sure I would feel it.*

'Pierre, call Jean-Pierre, he needs to know what's happening. If Gabrielle hears you speaking to security, she will panic. He needs to be there with you all, and will contact your uncles to be on their guard. Keep everyone at home, I don't want them in school today or tomorrow. Not until this is all sorted and we know Laurel is safe.'

'Papa, will she be ok? Do you think we're safe here?'

He tried with all his strength to sound strong. 'Yes, son, and reassure Emma – all will be ok.'

# *Chapter 35*

∞

Back in the kitchen, David splashed his face with water, needing a clear head, his earlier hunger replaced by a sickening numbness in his stomach.

As he dried his face, someone knocked on the front door. He opened it to find Paul, Marc, and two other men – one looked like he belonged on Muscle Beach, Venice, with a tight T, jeans, and tanned, while the other was the opposite: tanned but wearing shades, in casual hoodie and tracks, and carrying a cloth laptop bag. Marc indicated for everyone to keep silent until they got the all-clear from his team.

All four entered, with Laptop Guy setting up at the table, his partner holding a small black device as he walked around scanning for hidden cameras or listening devices. He closed the door leading to the balcony, pulled the blinds shut, then continued checking the other rooms.

Marc stood beside Laptop Guy as he tapped away at his keyboard.

'What the hell happened?' Paul snapped, glaring at David.

He stayed calm, though he was close to losing it. 'Laurel, it seems, decided to surprise me and flew here two days ago. I don't know on what flight, what time she arrived, or even if she got any further than the airport.'

'Boss, she arrived on the Air France flight at three twenty-five on Tuesday afternoon. I'll see if I can access any taxi company data to see if she ordered one in advance.' Laptop Guy turned to David. 'Are there any security cameras here? I need to log into the system if there is. I'm Joshua, by the way.'

'Sorry, David,' Marc said, sounding calmer than Paul, though he looked exhausted. 'Paul isn't angry at you.' He darted a quick look at his partner. 'We were told she was visiting friends in Paris.' He sighed. 'It's just everything was going so well. We had Declan located in an area not far from here. We were so close, then, two days ago, everything went dead. Our sources couldn't help – they were as baffled as us. We checked everything and everyone. It wasn't a situation we expected.'

'And now we know why!' Paul's face reddened. 'Do you think they were paid to go silent?' He looked at the battered steak on the counter and then at David, who just shrugged in response.

'I don't think so,' Marc said. 'Why risk future payments? Besides, some are undercover cops. But I need to check in with France. They have to tighten security.' He looked at the laptop screen. 'Joshua, can you keep checking Declan's old IP address and any mobile numbers we have associated with him? Old and recent. See if any of them ping anywhere in this area. Check street cameras, traffic cams, shop security footage.'

Muscle Man walked back in, and Marc straightened.

'Bill, reconnect with your sources, there has to be something. He can't just disappear again. If needs be, offer more money for anyone with a definite line to locate him, even to your police contacts. That bastard is not getting away a second time.'

'On it, Boss.' Big Bill left to make his calls in another room.

'What do you need me to do?' David asked.

Marc looked at Paul, then to him. 'Text him. Tell him you have the money. Act like you don't know anything about Laurel.'

'I'll clear this mess, shall I?' Paul said. 'It looks like it's going to be a long night.' He opened the fridge and shook his head. 'Yep, I think pizza is on the cards.'

David picked up his phone and typed his message: *Have funds now, what next?* He showed it to Marc. 'Ça va?'

Marc nodded. 'Short and sweet.'

'Well, he's not going to get into a catch-up chat with the man, is he?' Paul cleared the mulched meat away. 'Anyone want burgers? Please tell me you have fresh baps somewhere?'

David didn't know how to respond, surprised by Paul's sudden change in tone. *No decent person would eat a burger out of that mess.* He turned to Marc. 'Well, do you want me to send it?'

'Go for it, and let's see what happens. Joshua, have you got David's phone linked as well?'

'Of course, Boss. I linked into the condo's security system too.' He flicked a look at David. 'She was here.'

All three men walked over to him, with David tensing as they watched the security footage. Laurel was paying and chatting to her cab driver. It seemed friendly, with both of them laughing. Then he waved goodbye and left.

Marc nodded to himself. 'Get in touch with that cab company and find out who he is.'

'Let's see the rest of the footage,' David said, his heart breaking at the turn of events. Laurel sat on her suitcase, smiling, her face turned up to the sun. She looked as beautiful as always. Then she took a book out of her bag to read, checking the road for him every few minutes. Joshua sped through the footage until she got to her feet on seeing another cab arrive. She walked down to it but hesitated when two men got out. David's scalp felt electrified as a struggle ensued, with the men bundling her into the cab as the driver ran up to get her luggage. Then the car sped away.

'Christ, can you get the licence plate?' Paul asked.

'Already on it, Boss.' Joshua's fingers danced over the keyboard.

David, his heart ready to burst, clicked send on his phone. The waiting game had begun.

## *Chapter 36*

∞

Laurel's head hurt from whatever they'd injected her with to keep her quiet. Unable to move, and with everything dark, she couldn't work out if she was in a room or box. *How long have I been here?* She'd lost all sense of time, going from nightmarish blackouts to this dark awakening, though she had a vague recollection of falling at one stage.

As she tried to stretch out again, pain shot up her leg and her whole body stiffened. She nudged left and right. Nothing. Restrained, with whatever they'd used cutting into her wrists. They'd made a thorough job of it, with her upper arms and chest bound as well.

*Shite, Houdini wouldn't get out of this.* 'Hello! Can someone help me? Please! I need to go to the bathroom. Please let me get up.'

Silence.

Her voice had travelled, so at least she wasn't in a box. She called out again, with no response.

*What the hell do they want?* She remembered it was three guys, who looked like gang members to her. *But, then, many people dress that way now, so who knows? Is Declan responsible?* There'd been no sign of him anytime she'd regained consciousness, just those three guys. He couldn't have known she was travelling to L.A – she didn't tell anyone outside the family. Even Marc's security team didn't know she was going anywhere until hours before she left, and they thought she was going to Paris.

Her head was pounding and she really needed to pee. She called out again, and this time something moved away in the distance. Was it a darkened room or was there a cover over her eyes? When she blinked, she couldn't feel anything. She gasped when rough hands grabbed her and dragged her across a floor, her sense of orientation shattered by the pain searing through her leg.

A door opened, and she wrinkled her nose against the stench.

'Try to escape and you're dead.'

He had an American accent. *New York?*

They untied her binds, then shoved her forward, though she had to hop with the pain in her leg. A door slammed behind her, making her flinch. She felt around her head. *It is a blindfold. Goggles.* She removed them and squinted against the bare light overhead, then looked around the small room. A few feet away, a single, filthy toilet pot beckoned.

*Ohh shite.* An appropriate phrase in the context.

When she took a step, pain shot through her leg again, right into her head. She clenched her eyes shut until it subsided, then looked at her ankle. *Is it broken? Just sprained?* She didn't know but it hurt like hell and the bruising was heavy. Using the wall to lean on, she hopped across to the filthy excuse of a toilet. The room stank, as if it had never been cleaned or aired.

While she did her business, she looked around. *No windows – wonderful.* But the sound of distant traffic filtered in, so there had to be some sort of ventilation shaft. She spotted a tiny air vent high in a corner. *Maybe a Chihuahua could fit in there but not this human.* She sighed as she thought of her grim situation. *What a mess you're in, Laurel. How the hell am I going to get out of this?*

Once finished, she banged on the door. 'I'm done!'

No response.

'Hello! I'm finished! What do you want?'

'Put the blindfold back on,' a man said. The same voice as before.

She followed the instruction. 'Done.'

The door opened. She was grabbed, then dragged across a floor again, trying to keep her injured leg up and losing one of her shoes in the process.

'Jesus! Give me a break, will you? I can walk.'

'Shut the fuck up, bitch!'

They shoved her down, and she banged off what might have been a cold wall. Then they tied her hands and legs again, pain shooting through her as they tightened the bind around her ankles.

She remembered Marc advising her that if this situation ever happened, and the kidnapper used zip ties, she should offer her hands with the insides of her wrists placed together, and she just about got time to do this. According to Marc, although her wrists would be bound tight by the ties, she could exert enough pressure to snap them. Now all she needed was the opportunity to get up so she could test it out. He'd given her and David many scenarios that might happen, and this was one of them. She hoped she didn't need to escape from a car trunk any time soon.

'Listen, if it's money, just let me know. I can arrange anything you want.' Desperation had her voice pitched so high, it didn't sound like hers. She needed to work out why they chose her. Like before, she got no reply.

After she'd regained her breath and the thump of her heart subsided in her ears, she heard distant voices, maybe over the other side of the room. More mumbled than distinct, she strained to work out what they were saying. Then a worn, rusty sound, maybe of a door opening, cut the voices off. During the following silence, she didn't dare breathe. Whoever entered, they'd had an immediate effect.

Unhurried steps approached her, growing clearer as they got closer. Something touched off her side and she flinched – maybe whoever it was had kneeled beside her. She tensed at the sound of a heavy sigh. When a hand touched her leg, she recoiled in fright.

'What d-do you…want?' She struggled with the words, her voice cracking as tremors ran through her. But then she remembered that cologne, that familiar smell of Tom Ford's tobacco vanilla, a favourite of her brother. The sweet but spicy woody odour could never be mistaken.

'Do you really not know, dearest sister? I'm so disappointed.'

'What the hell!' she cried out. 'Why are you doing this to me?' She jerked when something pricked her arm, then all went silent.

## *Chapter 37*

∞

David stepped out of the shower and towelled down. It was close to 5 a.m. He needed to get out of the house – out for some air and to think. Sitting around waiting for a response to the text was driving him crazy, and with some of the sharp talk between the team, fatigue and anger only added to the tense atmosphere in the small condo.

He couldn't believe this was happening again, that Laurel's brother was once more creating a living hell for them. At least he wasn't needed at the studio today. He doubted if he would be called on again, after sitting around most of yesterday. It was late when one of the production team came out and told him they were finished for the day and they'd call if they required him. The whole thing was crazy. He'd given all his experience and patience to that movie, repeating the lines again and again to appease the sound editors. Sometimes, he struggled to keep his temper when they'd let him know through his earphones that the take was wonderful but would he mind changing this tone or this word and go through a particular line again. He would be surprised if they called him again, with nothing more of significance to cover.

Throwing the towel to the floor in anger, he realised he could've been here for Laurel when she arrived instead of sitting around in an office waiting on the producers to decide if they wanted him or not. He needed to call home, to see how the others were. It would be around 2 p.m. there.

He got dressed and went to the kitchen to get some water. Paul was asleep on the couch in the living room, with Joshua in a corner, headphones on, his focus glued to his laptop. Marc stood at the coffeemaker. The remains of three large pizzas and fries littered the counter.

'Want some?'

'No, I need some water and to call home. It's afternoon there – they will all be in the house for the kids. I need to reassure them that we are doing everything here and that it will be ok.'

Marc's shoulders slumped. 'Be careful what you say. We can't be one-hundred-percent sure Declan hasn't got someone listening.'

David stared at him. The man didn't seem his usual confident self. He'd never seen him this way before.

Marc tapped his cup with his spoon. 'You know, if there is a God, then there's definitely a devil, and Declan is one of his disciples.'

'Hey, we will get her back. With your expertise, we will get him and leave him in some hellhole here in the States.' He tried to sound more confident than he felt, which wasn't too difficult with the adrenalin in his system creating an anger he'd never experienced before.

'Laurel asked me to do more than leave him in some prison,' Marc said. He shrugged. 'I was…looking into it when we got your message.'

David folded his arms and nodded. 'So if he was here, who set up Veronique?' He couldn't believe Laurel hadn't told him it wasn't an accident. Paul and Marc had filled him in on the true story yesterday evening over dinner.

'An associate who owed Declan a favour. We caught him leaving a dozen dead rats at your parents' back door.'

'That's sick. Now we know where the letters came from. And poor Oscar.' He pinched the bridge of his nose.

'Yep. Well, now we have him and his phone. Declan was told that myself and Paul are in France.' He rubbed his face. 'Can you imagine doing that to anyone? To a pregnant woman? It sickens me.' He took a sip of his coffee and winced.

David noticed the lack of steam but said nothing, feeling responsible for the man's coffee going cold.

Marc set his cup down on the counter. 'Having met Carl and Gerard and seen how decent they are, how the hell did Declan turn out the way he did? Yes, Patricia was money hungry but never violent, she never inflicted any physical hurt on anyone. I told her some of the horror stories I discovered about Declan, and it shook her up, made her see that it wasn't money or power he wanted. He enjoys the hurt he causes – the pain he inflicts on others – and loves to see people suffering. It's one of the reasons he got involved in the drugs' business.'

David put his phone on the counter and took water from the fridge. He struggled to balance his desire to contact his family in France and accommodate Marc's need to get this out of his system. To his surprise, the solution came to him and he just hugged Marc.

'Thank you, my friend. You don't know how much your help means to us.' He released him and stepped back, allowing him to continue.

'Laurel's request went against all my principles. But when I looked back at all that man has done – he killed Peter, destroyed my police career, Paul's life in politics, had you all living in terror, and to be so bad that his own parents hated him,'—he shrugged again—'I just folded. Perhaps Laurel was right – prison is too good for him.'

David remained silent, just watching as Marc made a fresh brew of coffee. He took the offered mug and nodded for him to continue.

'I know it was wrong, I should've said no when she first called me, but I think I was still in shock that he'd tried to kill Veronique and her unborn baby. I just told her to leave it with me.'

All David could do was nod his understanding. Joel and Veronique had asked Marc and Paul to be godfathers to Simeon. Both men were delighted and told everyone the news. The two couples were thinking of combining the christening with Paul and Marc's marriage, and the plans to have a wonderful weekend of celebrations were being set up. They'd made sure his promotional work for the movie wouldn't clash with any dates they chose.

He rested his hand on Marc's shoulder. 'Simeon and Veronique are ok. We'll find Laurel, then we will get that demon and all will be back to normal.'

Marc looked at him. 'The thing is, now more than ever, I still want him dead.'

## *Chapter 38*

∞

David walked along Venice Beach. Even at this time, there were joggers, some boot camps, yoga classes, and many dog owners out doing their early morning routine. Everyone seemed happy and relaxed. Not how he felt.

The call home had been strained. Emma looked like she hadn't slept for a week, her eyes red with tears, her words heartbreaking: 'I shouldn't have let her go alone. I should've told security or Marc or Paul the truth. Why didn't we think? Why didn't it dawn on us Declan would jump at this chance to get her?'

At one stage, she dropped the phone, only for Jean-Pierre to then come online.

'Son, tell me, have you any indication it was Declan? Do Marc and Paul know?'

David filled him in, and it didn't surprise him that his father was annoyed at not being informed about Declan's whereabouts.

'I'm sorry, Papa, but the advice was to keep all details within a small circle. Paul and Marc were waiting in New York, aware that Declan was in contact with me. Once he made his demands, they flew here, setting the plan in motion.'

'And now we messed it all up for you.' Jean-Pierre sounded dejected. 'When Laurel told me of her plans, I encouraged her, said it was a wonderful idea. I thought it would help her after Patricia's death.'

'Papa, no-one was to know.'

'But I should have! What was I thinking? I shouldn't have helped to ensure the children were taken care of. I should've told her to stay here and care for her family. To wait for you to return.'

David understood the guilt his father carried was connected to the break-up of his first marriage. Francoise told him that when he was away on a movie set or on promotion, Jean-Pierre would advise her to stay with them, that he would return, that his family would always come first. Whenever the tabloids were splashed with gossip about him, she wanted to leave and go to him but Jean-

Pierre would talk her out of it. His lack of maturity, ill advice from his *yes-men*, and his love of publicity destroyed the marriage. His father may have hoped the old David would change and save his marriage but it took longer than expected. Thankfully, that old David no longer existed.

He finished the call by reassuring his father that no-one was at fault. They would find Laurel, and her brother would finally be caught and sent to prison, where they would throw away the key. He had to say that because he needed to believe it himself.

Before he left the condo for this walk, he asked Paul to call Emma. She needed to hear from him. His calming voice and reassurance would be a great help.

As he walked alongside Big Bill, who'd insisted on accompanying him when leaving the house, he asked him if he knew Luc.

'Yes, sir. He's a good one, excellent in psychology, combat, and self-defence training. Why?'

'Please, call me David. I wondered is that your speciality too?'

'Nah, my thing is combat and weaponry. I'm also a sharpshooter, with US Army training. Not much time to specialise in self-defence – never had the patience to teach someone else. I'm a former Irish Ranger, and we often did training exchanges with the US military.'

'The Rangers is an elite force, yes?'

'Yes, it's their special-operations' force. I've lived here and worked specialist security for fifteen years now. The connections I made in the US military helped me establish my services here.'

'Is that how Marc found you?'

'We were in contact before this. He's hoping to expand here.' He flicked a look at a passing skater. 'I was a contact of a contact, so to speak.'

'Luc trained me in self-defence during his stay with us, and we worked together on how to keep calm in certain situations. How not to panic, I suppose. I feel I may not be ready – I feel the situation may arise where I will lose all control. It's happened before and, if the situation arises that I encounter Declan, then…I don't know if Luc's training will be enough.'

He looked at an area beside some tall palm trees. 'Marc gave the go-ahead for Luc to help me, and we went on early morning runs together, so it was easy to train in the forest where I live. Can you assist me too? It's been a month of sitting in a studio. I haven't forgotten what Luc showed me but I need the practice.'

'Not here, it would only attract attention. Let's go get some breakfast for everyone and we'll work out in the basement. The gym down there looks good – we can move some of the equipment aside.'

## *Chapter 39*

∞

'I got something, Boss!' Joshua yelled from the sitting room.

Marc, Bill, and David were in the basement, with Marc enjoying watching the two other men work through defence moves. Paul was already by Joshua's side when they entered the room. David's phone was connected to the tech-expert's laptop.

'Did Declan connect?' Marc asked, aware he sounded anxious. 'Did he mention Laurel?'

'Yes and no, you'll have to bear with me. It's a little too complicated for non-tech people.'

The man looked dishevelled – his long hair greasy and his normal attire of jog pants and hoodie looking *lived in.* No surprise to Marc, knowing he'd been up all night doing his thing. He was one of the best at his game. His fingers sped over the keyboard, then he turned the screen so everyone had a clear view.

'This is definitely the area he's hiding in. It's a commercial real estate section, a few empty units, but the ownership is registered to a suspect overseas' company.'

Marc remained silent, waiting for him to continue.

Joshua gave them an expectant look, then nodded to himself and shifted up in his chair. 'It's not a ten-minute drive from here, just off West Manchester Drive. It's so well hidden, no-one would think it was there.' His eyes widened. 'So goddamn clever.'

Marc understood his reaction. Declan was a tenacious tactician, and they would have to be at their best to capture him.

'How are you so sure?' Paul asked, sounding doubtful.

'He's good but he slipped up here. Maybe he got one of his cronies to send the text and they didn't take essential security precautions, like driving out of the area. Anyway, once the text came through, it was easy to trace the signal – the tower is only a block away. Once I found the units, I decided to trace ownership. West Manchester Drive is a residential area, with a lot of high-end apartment blocks. Unless it's a small store or bank, a commercial unit would be required to hide, to cover its existence behind soft-sanded walls and palm trees, so as not to encroach on the residential value of the area.'

'Ah,' Paul said. 'Right, good catch.'

Marc studied the screen map. 'Bill, contact your sources in that area, see if they can check it out without raising suspicion.'

As Bill walked away, Marc grabbed his arm. 'And I think we need reinforcements.'

The big man winked. 'I'm ahead of you.'

Paul looked at David, then to Marc. 'What do we do now? Should David reply?'

'What did Declan's message say?' Marc asked.

'Umm, yeah, here.' Joshua disconnected the phone and handed it to him. 'He wants to meet up. Said he wants some cash up front now, and will then provide details of the balance transfer when they meet.'

Marc gripped his bottom lip between his teeth. *Does he still not know we're here in L.A with David? He needs cash. Does that mean his finances for his team are running out? Why does he want to meet up with David? Why didn't he mention Laurel?* Too many questions filled his head from that brief message.

'Joshua, I'll leave the surveillance equipment to you. Make sure everyone has a wireless earpiece and mic – nobody gets lost on this – we all need to be in the loop if David meets up with Declan. Did he give a location?'

'No, Boss, nothing on that yet.'

'Ok, when we know, I want a complete assessment of the area.'

Bill returned. 'I've got some guys I trust set up and I'll meet them later. Local law enforcement now need to be involved but I've got colleagues in the department who know how this works. They won't try to take over.'

'Who's sourcing the surveillance van?' Marc's brain was in overdrive.

'Already on it.' Bill left the room again, phone to ear.

David finished typing a message into his phone. 'Is this ok?'

'Perfect,' Marc replied. *Ok, come on, Declan, it's up to you now.*

# *Chapter 40*

∞

Jean-Pierre stood in David's doorway and waved goodbye to Joel and Veronique. He would meet Joel later to check on his own house and the farm. Just as he closed the door, he received a text from Claude, in Japan receiving training on new cloud technology with his employer. He seemed concerned, wanting to fly home. Jean-Pierre replied, reassuring him that everything was going to be ok, and there was no need for him to return. Besides, what could he do? *Goodness, what can any of us do here in France?*

He returned to the kitchen, where Gabrielle was preparing dinner. The twins had already finished, and Emma was upstairs readying them for bed. Pierre and Jack were drinking coffee at the table. It looked like a normal evening, except it wasn't. The tension was palpable – the air sour.

'Shall I open the windows to let some fresh air in? The house is stuffy.'

Jack got to his feet. 'I'll go upstairs and open some there. Maman would be furious if we didn't open them at least for an hour a day.' He smiled as he left the room.

Gabrielle remained silent as she continued to prepare the food at the stove. She looked like she had aged ten years in such a short space of time.

'Grand-Père, should I call Papa for an update?' Pierre looked lost. 'It's still early afternoon in L.A.'

'No, he said to wait until they contact us.' He sniffed the air and wrinkled his nose. 'I'll go open some windows in the other rooms.'

He walked over to Gabrielle first, placed his hands on her shoulders and kissed her cheek. She didn't react, just kept cooking – a robot on automatic.

Despondent, he walked out of the kitchen, knowing she'd only reacted that way towards him once before. *This is all my fault. I should never have let Patricia into our lives.* Gabrielle became fond of the woman and they shared many memories of their children. Then there was the worry over Veronique's accident and little Simeon, Patricia dying so quickly, and his encouraging Laurel to leave for L.A. He never thought his wife would come to rely so much on Laurel. *I never thought Declan would be in L.A stalking David.*

He opened the door to David's office, what had been Patricia's bedroom. The bed and medical equipment were long gone – the room returned to how it had been before. It looked like nothing had happened here. He brushed his hand across some books, and took one out. The poet Charles Baudelaire: *Les Fleurs du mal* – The Flowers of evil. One of David's favourites. Reviewers referred to it as the poet's diary – a cry of terror and enjoyment. Laurel would have no time for such desolation. He placed it back on the shelf, not wanting to read such forsaken material at this time.

As he turned to leave, a shadow cut across the window and he jumped with fright, only to chuckle as the security guard passed the second window. *My goodness, he nearly frightened the life out of me.* They were on constant patrol – two outside, one inside. He left the room and returned to the kitchen.

Pierre was now helping Gabrielle with the dinner preparations. Emma came down from the bedrooms with the twins.

'Come on, tell everyone. *Bonne nuit à tous!*' She smiled, encouraging her little brother and sister with a nod.

'Bonne nuit à tous!' the twins chorused.

Their words brightened the room, and everyone smiled and responded, though Gabrielle just smiled at them. Pierre nudged her and pleaded for her to hug them, and she slipped from her robotic stance to take them in her arms. This routine of good-night kisses never changed for the twins – too young to know anything was wrong. The adults present didn't miss how those hugs thawed Gabrielle's tightness.

'I've roped Jack into reading them a story tonight.' Emma laughed. 'He was sorry he came up to open those windows.'

'A good talk with Paul earlier?' Jean-Pierre asked.

'Yes, I needed to speak with him.' She shrugged. 'It's good. We're good. We'll talk more when Mam is home, and I'll see him all the time next year while I'm in Trinity.'

'Good, it makes me so relieved to see you smile again.'

'Emma, tell Jack dinner will be forty minutes.' Gabrielle didn't turn from the stove. Pierre got tapped with her wooden spoon when he tried to take some meat from the pan.

'Have I time to check with Joel and the farm?'

She turned to him, her eyes sad. 'But, of course.'

It was a curt response, and everyone noticed it. But at least she'd replied.

As he walked down to the farm, he spotted Joel's torch in the distance coming from his own house, gathering the goats on his way so they could lock them in the pen for the night. He waved and his son flashed the torch in response.

It was a pleasant evening but he felt tired, and he found it odd that the air still smelled stale even though he was in a field behind the house, He stretched back his shoulders to ease a tightness in his chest, and realised that he was sweating. *I need to get a decent sleep tonight.* As he approached the gate, his vision blurred, and when he went to grasp the latch, he missed and stumbled forward, his body crashing to the ground.

'Papa!'

# *Chapter 41*

∞

Laurel lay in the same position as she'd first found herself, what seemed like days ago but was probably only hours. *Maybe it is days*. Her head was still woozy from whatever drug Declan injected into her, and she knew drool was seeping from her lips, even though her mouth felt dry.

The voices in the room were distant but it didn't take much effort to recognise the anger. She strained to work out what was being said. Something about cash…about going back on their word…and getting out. She shook her head to dissipate the fog, then imagined herself being closer. *Could it work?* She focused with all she had, and her heart leapt at the mention of police – just hearing it gave her hope. *Maybe Declan's time is up. Maybe he pulled too many favours, and now all I can do is wait and hope*. Another sound caught her attention – scuffling, followed by a man shouting. An American accent – not Declan.

She flinched when a door opened then slammed shut. More arguing ensued, then the door opened again.

The room was a hot hellhole to her, and the pain in her leg got worse each time she tried to move. She stiffened at the sound of someone walking towards her. *Oh, God, what now?*

The footsteps stopped beside her.

'Please, I need water.'

Whoever it was held her head as a bottle was placed at her lips.

'Now, we can't have you dying of thirst, can we?'

Declan. His voice was calm but breathless.

'What do you want, Declan? Why can't you just move on, forget I exist and do whatever evil you need to do without taking it out on me or my family?'

'Shut up, Bitch!'

Something clattered away from them and she realised he'd flung the bottle across the room.

'This is all your fault! My life was perfect until you interfered. You, Peter, and your little government friends had to go and mess things up, investigate me, trial me! Did you honestly think I'd sit back and cry?' He spat out each word and she visualised his face a burning red. 'I'm going to get my life back. Maybe not in Ireland but I will. I have powerful friends, and money.' He moved, and she sensed his heat. 'And you will be nowhere to be found.'

Although her mind was fuzzy, she knew if he was going to kill her, he would've done the deed when he first kidnapped her. No, there was something more, something he needed, and her life depended on it.

'Look, if it's money you need, I can get it. I can help you set up wherever you want.'

He grabbed her hair and jerked her up so his mouth was next to her ear, his hot breath creeping her out. As much as she wanted to, she couldn't hold back a cry of pain.

'Don't worry, little sister,' he whispered, 'I've got that all in hand.' He shoved her against the wall and walked away.

The pain in her head from the collision was all she needed. She curled up and cried. *This isn't happening. It's all a nightmare. I'm still on the plane, flying to L.A, to David.*

The pain got worse, spreading around her head, then all went silent.

***

When she woke, she lay still and listened, almost positive she could hear distant traffic. She clenched her eyes to focus, then opened them, flinching at the unexpected change. When Declan slammed her against the wall, it must have knocked her blindfold loose. She rubbed her head against the floor, working to shift it further. Though her hands were bound at her waist, she managed to scrunch up, getting her head down to finish the task. It was a struggle but it worked. Relieved, she rested her arms for a minute, then scrunched up again to get her hands to her mouth. She tried to force the ties but her strength was all but depleted, her sweat stinging her eyes as she listened for footsteps.

While the room was dark, it wasn't the pitch-black she'd become used to behind her blindfold, and she had to adjust her vision to it. As she looked around, she noticed fine lines of light higher up, what she assumed were blacked-out windows – too high to climb up to. Her only chance of escape was the door.

*You need to clear your mind.* She imagined herself back in France, her happy family surrounding her. The thought of them gave way to worry. *What if he's got someone to hurt them? Do they know he's kidnapped me? Christ, they must be so worried.*

The door opened and two figures entered the room.

‘Her blindfold is off!’

*The Americans. Declan must’ve persuaded them to return. Shite!*

## *Chapter 42*

∞

David and Paul entered the penthouse suite, right into a busy hub, with men preparing surveillance with stealth drones, checking maps on their phones, discussing tactics – several with guns, which made both of them nervous.

Joshua was sitting at the table, oblivious to all surrounding him as he focused on his laptop. David walked over to him.

'Any news?'

He smiled. 'Hi. So I'm trying to find out who Declan is working with. I sent a stealth drone over the commercial units and these are the shots of two guys. Do you recognise them?'

David studied their faces and nodded no.

'That's a shame, they are the same guys who abducted Laurel. Height, hair, build – everything matches. Three days and they haven't changed their clothes yet. There's no registered owner of the two vehicles. New York plates, so I'm running face recognition in some NY police systems.'

David gave an impressed nod. 'You have access?'

'Sometimes. If I can't get in, I phone a friend. This'll take a while. I think Marc wants to talk to you.'

He looked around for Paul's other half. The penthouse was small enough, with a kitchenette adjoining the living room. Marc was there, drinking more coffee. His face looked drained but his eyes were wide, probably helped by the caffeine. *His bloodstream must be flowing with coffee at this stage.*

'You're looking for me?'

'Yeah, your brother's been calling you.'

'Oh?' They'd held onto his phone before meeting the team.

'He needs to stop and keep the line clear. There's still no word from Declan on the meet time and location.'

'I'll text him now. Has Joshua got it?'

'No, it's here. He's finished with it for the time being. I think he has a wireless link to it.'

David checked the phone and counted eleven missed calls from Joel, with another three from Pierre. *Something is wrong. A text won't suffice, I need to call.* Something in his gut told him all was not good in France.

'Why didn't you answer?' he asked Marc.

'If I answered, they may have thought the worst, especially as you weren't with me to take the call.'

He speed-dialled his brother's number, and it was picked up right away.

'Joel, est-ce que tout va bien?'

'David, what is going on? Why didn't you answer? It's Papa, he is in hospital – a heart attack. Why didn't you answer your phone?'

'What!' David roared. 'Is he alive?'

Marc tried to take the phone from him but he jerked away and listened to Joel's report, barely able to hold himself together. The news wasn't good. His father had been rushed to hospital with a suspected heart attack. He was stable, but being so far away and not able to attend just added to this nightmare. The news from France, Laurel kidnapped, it was all too much – he couldn't take it anymore. Everything he was holding back rushed out: his anger; his feelings of helplessness – it all exploded to the surface like a volcano. It took Marc, Bill, and Paul to hold him down and pull him to the couch.

'I'm going to kill that bastard!'

Another man in the room walked over, hunkered down in front of him, and showed him his ID. 'No, sir, we hope we might have that honour.'

David could only look at the sincerity in the operative's eyes. It gave him no choice but to calm down. These guys were deadly serious about their work, and they didn't need him getting in the way with emotional outbursts.

Marc sat beside him. Paul and Bill loosened their grip.

'Everything is arranged. We will get him, David. Dead or alive, we will get him.'

Joshua, still ignoring the chaos around him, called out his now familiar line: 'I found them, Boss!'

Marc, Bill, and the other agent walked over.

'They're two members of a drugs cartel called Cypresse in New York. Low-ranking from what I can work out.'

Marc turned to the agent. 'You were right, Declan is more international than I first thought.'

'Yes, sir. These cartels are as big as some multi-national companies. They pay their taxes, and sometimes more, to keep under the radar of the IRS and other countries' tax regulators. But their underground side is huge, worldwide, and networked with many other criminal cartels. They keep in each other's pockets so the logistics of their illegal operations run smoothly.'

'Who are they? Will they co-operate or run?'

As they discussed what to do next, David's phone pinged. It was Declan.

'Guys, we have contact. Time and place set.'

'Let's get moving then,' Bill said to everyone in the room. He turned to David. 'Sir, I need to set you up.' He called over a colleague. 'We need a ballistic vest under his shirt, an earpiece, etcetera. Everything needs to be covered, we want no injuries on this op.' He turned to the group. 'Thank you, gentlemen. We have a time and place, all systems go.'

Everyone set about their individual tasks, some on their phones, some putting on bulletproof vests, some checking their weapons. David and Paul looked around, then at each other, both in disbelief at the scene surrounding them.

# *Chapter 43*

∞

Declan nearly growled as he waited for the Frenchman's reply. Unlike previous messages, the response was almost immediate, with the three dots flashing to show it being typed.

'C'mon, you asshole, there's no need to write a book.'

It came through, and he nearly let out a yelp of delight. The fool had the money and was ready to meet. 'Finally!'

He rubbed his arm. For the first time since he was a young teenager, he felt nervous. Too many favours had been called in. It took a lot of promises and the remainder of his cash as a down payment to persuade those two idiots to stay with him and watch over that bitch. He'd lost his temper with the goons Cypresse had sent him – a rare occurrence. And all he could use them for was to babysit her. They didn't know the area and had no contacts here. So amateurish. It was clear Cypresse had no respect for him since his time inside. *That will soon change – let there be no doubt about that.*

They were fools. Inexperienced, and the wrong choice for what he needed. Once he'd mentioned kidnapping the target, they wanted to back out. No problem with murder, though – much easier than kidnapping. At least you could dispose of the body, with no witness to worry about, and no long-term issues arising in years to come. Although he'd threatened her earlier, he didn't want the bitch dead. No, he wanted her to suffer the consequence of her actions towards him – to agonize throughout her petty life, knowing he'd made sure that every piece of happiness she tried to gain was wiped away by him.

Her lover boy was going to die today. He would make sure of that. But he needed that cash. Once he had it, he could pay off the two idiots, get rid of them, then disappear to Columbia. He could set up his network again, reconnect with some other cartels, and settle some scores against those who'd betrayed him. Not forgetting those who'd dropped all connection with him while he was behind bars. The first he'd hit would be the head of Cypresse. *What the hell was Yiannis thinking sending me two clowns?* Next would be Politician Paul and his little sidekick Marc. Thankfully, Patricia was out of the picture – one loose end he didn't need to tie up. Still, it disappointed him that he wouldn't enjoy the thrill of killing her. *To murder my own mother, how orgasmic that would have been.*

In Columbia, he would reconnect with a few retired cops, and some old partners and politicians. He could become another Escobar, without the ending his hero endured.

On his approach to the shopping mall he'd told David to meet him at, he checked all the car parks, the side lanes leading to the back of the shop units, and the rooftops. Nothing could go wrong and he wanted to make sure the frog hadn't called the cops in. Nothing looked out of the ordinary, with the usual security guards walking around, all armed, as expected. The main square of the retail park was packed with people either window-shopping or just sitting around. *Nice and public. No-one will try anything here.*

He sat at one of the many open cafés, continuing to people-watch, holding the menu as if to see what food was available. It took a moment before he realised this part of the food mall was self-service. *No harm, there's not too many around – the table should still be free if I just order a coffee.* He passed two security guards as he headed for the counter, their guns looking so easy to grab. Bringing his own was too risky, with the high possibility of the mall having x-ray machines at the entrances. The amount of gun incidents in the US was too great a risk for many commercial places to be lax about protecting their clients. *Besides, there are other ways to skin a cat.*

Back at the table, he looked at his phone. Still an hour before the meet – plenty of time to ensure this wasn't a set-up, and that the soon-to-be-dead David was alone in his actions.

His contacts in France had gone quiet, instructed to only message him if something came up. The last he'd heard was that Paul and Marc were there just before Laurel left for L.A. *Strange her man didn't ask for her. Does no-one care for her safety? From all accounts, it was a surprise arrangement, but why hasn't he contacted France? This is the third day since she was taken. Does he still not know? Did Romeo not call his Juliet at least every night?* He smirked at the thought of his dear bitch of a sister having marriage difficulties.

He got up to get more coffee, taking his time, checking around to make sure no-one was concealed in the roof areas, or in any of the sections leading to other parts of the mall. Various staff moved about, with some shifts changing. A young tattooed woman called out to her group of friends at the far side of the courtyard. They shouted and gestured for her to join them. A group of teen girls, their phones glued to their hands, gossiped as they passed him. One teen's shoulder clashed with his but she didn't apologise, just giggled with her friends. Children skipped alongside their parents. Some were obvious tourists, some locals. A normal working day in the life of a US shopping mall.

*Yep, it all looks good. Won't be long now.*

## *Chapter 44*

∞

As the agent set up his equipment on the rooftop of an apartment complex, he checked the area on the other side of the road. The shopping mall was the perfect location, the open food court neat and clear to view and locate the target through his scope. He checked the photo on his phone again. A recent image, which always helped. He checked in with coms, confirming he was in position.

The response was clear: do not fire unless necessary and not before confirmation that the victim was found. He took off his hat and wiped his brow, the heat from the rooftop's metal flooring extreme.

Now in his fifties, his work with the department was coming to an end. He didn't know anything else, and would be bored with retirement. The only option was to take on jobs like this. The calls kept coming in, and he couldn't resist them. With his role as a sniper, he played the scalpel rather than the surgeon – he didn't need to know the details.

Bill was trying to pull him into his high-security firm, and it didn't seem like a bad idea. It would be a change from the regulations and conformity of the FBI. But he could adjust. His expertise was as a sniper but he also had training and experience as a high-speed tactical and close-protection driver.

He scoped the area again. Still no sign of the suspect. He called to coms to confirm this was the correct mall.

'Suspect spotted at the WideAwake coffee unit, now returning to his seating.'

The agent checked the food court area again. *Ahh, he's grown a beard now. He's early, too, and looking nervous.* The suspect had his phone in his hand, pretending to read something but really scanning the area, paying great attention to the security detail and looking up if anyone shouted or moved to another table. Checking the rooftops too. The agent eased back as the target turned in his direction. His rifle was set up and ready for positioning. He checked his watch. Another thirty-five minutes until the appointed time.

'Be advised, suspect is scanning the area, checking side entrances and rooftops. Inform me when I can take position.'

He sat back, took out some food and water, and relaxed. It was going to be a hot half hour.

## *Chapter 45*

∞

Gabrielle held Jean-Pierre's hand as he slept. Still no news from L.A to keep her worries at bay, and now her silly husband went and had a heart attack.

*What to do with all this worry?*

Joel was asleep in the chair beside her, exhausted, having come straight here after checking on Veronique and little Simeon. *So many worries. When will this family return to happy days? Will we ever return to a normal life?* She was confident they would. *We always overcome any obstacles in our way. This is nothing more than a little hiccup.*

Claude had called earlier. He was trying to get a flight from Japan. Helene, his partner of ten years now, was going to Laurel and David's house, to work from there. He would keep in contact.

Such support from her boys, showing much-needed maturity. She felt such love and pride for everyone around her. *And now to fix my husband.*

When he woke earlier, he was drowsy and kept apologising, though she couldn't understand why. It wasn't his fault she was like this. Nothing was his fault – he was the champion of calm and security for her, and for the family.

'Mon Dieu, Jean-Pierre, there is no need for sorry. Why would you say sorry when it is not anyone's fault?'

With her words, he fell back asleep. The doctors, while keeping him under observation, were happy he was out of danger. *So good to know, the first good step to our return to a happier, normal life. Now to get David and Laurel home safely to our nest. To our wonderful, safe nest.*

After Joel had managed to get in touch with David, he'd called again, this time sounding calmer and more confident than before. Thankfully, with video calls, she could see their faces – her family were unable to hide their feelings when she could see them. He looked tired but his wonderful smile returned when she told him that Jean-Pierre was stable and the doctors were happy with his progress. She updated him on the progress of Simeon, too.

Marc and Paul then joined the call. They all looked tired but she took some delight that her news was lifting their spirits.

All she'd felt in the past day was numbness but Jean-Pierre's heart attack had kicked her out of that state right away. She was silly to let such worries get to her when she had many strong people around her. The last time she felt that way was when Francoise died – it was such a shock to everyone. For her, the best way to control her grief was to concentrate on her work in their home. So much cooking was done, scrubbing floors, counters, and windows that had been cleaned only the week previous. Each time Jean-Pierre asked her to stop, to rest, she ignored him and continued on, afraid that if she spoke to him, she would break down. Perhaps it had been a mistake to cover her feelings through work but it was the only way she knew to cope. She hoped Jean-Pierre and the others did not feel her distance.

As she looked out the hospital window, she struggled to understand why Declan or anyone would want to hurt or kill any member of her family. Nothing convinced her any person could live in this world and be so evil.

She turned back to her husband, now awake and watching her.

'Ohh, my sweet, sweet husband! How are you feeling now?'

'Good, good. Is there any news from David? Did they find Laurel?'

'Not yet, but he and Marc assured me they were close. They said we were not to worry anymore.'

He groaned and shook his head, the action slow. 'This is all my fault.'

'No, no, mon cher, please don't fret. Don't do this to yourself. This isn't your fault, it is no-one's fault! How were we to know?' She sobbed. 'And now, I am so sorry, too. I didn't mean to be so numb to you, so distant. I thought my housework, my cooking, would clear my bad feelings.'

They held each other's hands and talked.

Joel woke up, looked around, then smiled at his parents. He checked his phone and his eyes lit up. 'Maman, Papa, we have good news. Claude has a flight home, he will be here by tomorrow afternoon.'

'See, Jean-Pierre? All our family will be home soon, I feel it.'

## *Chapter 46*

∞

David wished a few windows were open. He was too hot and uncomfortable, with the bullet-proof vest too tight, and anything but light.

'You ok?' Bill asked.

He checked his image in the long mirror. His outfit, a light shirt, jeans, and leather jacket, wasn't ideal in nearly one-hundred degrees but it hid the outline of his vest.

Bill handed him a tiny earpiece. 'Now, remember, listen to what we're telling you to say. It's important you follow our instructions. Any false move, or you decide to take the situation into your own hands, can cause us issues – even lead to someone dying.'

David looked at the big man. 'There's only one person who might die today.'

Bill frowned, looked at Marc for a moment, then turned back to him. 'Look, David, I'm not doubting your acting abilities but this is life or death. If I speak, you listen. If I say turn right, you turn right. Any order I give into that earpiece, you need to obey without hesitation. You got that?'

'David, please,' Marc said, his tone calm, 'this isn't the time to play hero. You need to get your head straight for this. If we don't capture Declan this time, he'll go underground. God knows when we'll get this opportunity again. If ever!'

'I know, I'm ready. Just ensure you tell me when you have Laurel.'

'The drone didn't bring back any confirmation she's there, but I promise we'll let you know as soon as we hear word. Paul is with the second team – purely as an observer, but he'll be there for Laurel.'

'Right, let's go then.' His stomach churned, and he shook himself down, shrugging the feeling off and releasing a long breath.

As they left the bedroom, only Joshua remained in the penthouse, glued to three laptops set up at the large dining table.

'Boss, still no confirmation Laurel is in that unit.' He looked over the top of his glasses. 'But Declan's two associates are popping in and out for a cigarette or food.

From their constant pacing while smoking, they're pretty agitated about something.'

'Good, let's hope they're not trigger happy and will surrender to our team without question.'

'Can they not go in now?' David asked. 'At least I'll know if Laurel is safe when I get to Declan.'

'Don't let that concern you,' Bill said. 'Rest assured we'll be in full control.'

'Just keep him busy talking,' Marc said, sounding a bit more anxious than a few minutes ago. 'Our team will be everywhere, and he needs to be focused on you. He'll try to rile you, to test you, so do your best to keep control of the situation.'

David stopped at the elevator and laid his hand on Marc's shoulder. 'He won't get to me. I've seen what he can do. Anything he says won't be a shock to the system.'

The elevator brought them down to the underground carpark. No-one spoke but, when they entered the carpark, they were met with a flurry of activity, with about a dozen men running from van to van, checking equipment, updating Joshua in coms. No-one paid attention to them until Bill called them to attention.

David turned to Marc. 'How the hell are we going to pay for all this?'

'This is networking with potential partners, it'll all work out in the end. Money doesn't come into play with these guys. They want people safe.'

David let out a long sigh, saying a silent prayer that everything would go to plan.

Another agent pulled up in a rented car. 'This is yours, sir.' He handed over the key.

David got in and looked at Bill. 'I promise, I'll listen, and I will do whatever I'm told.'

The big man nodded. 'Good.'

## *Chapter 47*

∞

Paul tried to swallow back the sick feeling coming from the pit of his stomach. It was a situation he never imagined he would be involved in. *What was I thinking? What if Laurel isn't there? What if she's dead?* The men in the van with him appeared so casual yet were fully focused and confident as they waited – another day in the office for them. He had refused a short arm. Wearing a bulletproof vest was overwhelming enough.

He'd waved to David as the first team left the carpark but he didn't respond, looking so serious, so focused. *I wish I could feel the same way.* His instructions were to stay in the van, wait for confirmation that the area was secure, and then enter the unit to identify Laurel, if she was there.

As they drove through the streets towards West Manchester Drive, he thought he was going to puke. An agent looked at him, one brow raised.

'Car sickness. I'm usually ok but in this heat.'

The man said nothing but gave him a bag.

'Thanks.' He looked up to the heavens. *Please let this go ok.*

Once the van slowed, he knew it was time – there was no going back. Then it stopped. He let out a shaky breath, louder than intended. No-one noticed, all silent – waiting – ready.

The vehicle had the markings of an electric supply van, local to the area. Their driver got out and banged on the gates. No-one answered and he banged again.

After what felt like an age, someone answered, but with the partition between the group in the back and the driver, Paul couldn't work out what was being said.

The gates opened. They were in.

When the driver got back into the van and started it up again, he rolled down his window and thanked whoever had opened the gates, then eased forward. He stopped again and spoke to the same person, confirming directions. The van veered off to the right.

The team around Paul were prepared, their submachine guns and handguns at the ready. All had the full gear on, including helmets. He didn't have one – he didn't think he'd need one. As if reading his mind, the same agent who'd handed him the sick bag, handed him a helmet.

'Stay here until you're called.'

He jerked when the back door shot open and they all rushed out, one agent carrying a battering ram. One loud bang followed, then shouting, but no gunfire, which he was grateful for. A long silence ensued, broken only by his heartbeat in his ears. He didn't know what to do, so he sat there, sweating, his stomach in knots.

An agent appeared at the back of the van. 'Sir, the two suspects are now in custody. There's no sign of any other assailants and no further defences to breach.

'And…Laurel?' He nearly choked on his words.

'Please come with me.'

He climbed out of the van, a lot slower and more awkward than the team a few minutes earlier. His mouth was dry as sand as he followed the agent into the building. The van driver was placing a man in handcuffs, while other team members questioned the second prisoner. One operative checked their phones, probably to ensure they hadn't sent out any messages to warn Declan.

It was a larger area than he'd expected. Some of the team members were searching and clearing rooms off it.

Then someone called out and everyone stopped, all looking to Paul.

'Sir, please come this way. I think you're needed.'

He followed the operative into a darkened unit, fearful of what they'd find.

'Don't touch me! Who the hell are you?'

A woman, in a room down the far end.

His legs shook as he let out a huge sigh of relief. The voice, while croaky, could only belong to his beautiful friend Laurel. He ran down to where an agent stood just inside the door.

'Christ, Laurel, am I glad to see you're here, and alive!'

'Paul?'

He knelt beside her, a lump forming in his throat as he looked at the mess of a woman before him. One of her ankle's had severe bruising, and she was all bound up with rope and ties, which one of the operatives was cutting free with a mean-looking knife.

She cried into his shoulder, and held him tight when her binds were released. 'My leg and head hurts.'

'It's ok, all is ok now.' He failed to hold back a sob and had to bite down to pull himself together. 'Can someone radio in, please? Everyone needs to know she's safe. We have Laurel.'

# *Chapter 48*

∞

The crowd in the food mall was getting smaller as the temperature broke the hundred mark, with many shoppers opting to sit in the comfort of air-conditioned cafés and restaurants.

Declan had his phone in his hand, pretending to read something on it. He scanned the area – the meet time was close. As far as he could tell, there was nothing out of the ordinary, no unexpected threats, just a mixed crowd enjoying the weather and their shopping. Then he spotted the Frenchman. He smirked as he watched him approaching, checking around for him. *Should I wave and pretend to be his long-lost friend?*

Just as he was about to stand, David turned his way, and both men stared into each other's eyes. Declan nodded once. *No, this isn't going to be a friendly meeting.*

***

David turned away to get some coffee from WideAwake, taking his time, just as Bill advised. He would make this meeting as casual as possible to the unaware public and workers.

With coffee in hand, he sat opposite his adversary, the one person in Laurel's family he had never met but wanted to kill so many times. On too many nights, he'd held his soulmate as she cried after a nightmare, and too many times, he woke with a start, remembering the attempt on both of their lives.

'We finally meet.' He kept his voice dead calm.

'Yes, nice weather for it.'

'Fuck the niceties and the weather. Here's the money you want.' He placed the bag on the table.

'Don't go off-script, David,' Marc said, his voice a tinny whisper in his ear.

Declan eyed the bag, then looked around, checking the rooftops once more.

'Don't worry, I'm alone.'

Declan spun around when a lone customer scrapped her chair as she rose to leave an adjoining table. Once she walked in the opposite direction, he frowned, as if annoyed at letting himself get so paranoid.

He smirked. 'Are you not going to ask about my dearest sister? You know I have her. Surely you know she's not in France?'

David blinked, then flicked a look, as if hiding something, hoping Declan would spot it. He did. *I have you now, you bastard.*

He leaned forward. 'I know you have her, and you won't get a penny more until I know she is safe.'

'No, my dear brother-in-law—'

'Don't call me that!' he snapped. 'Laurel and I never married. So, thankfully, I have no connection to you.'

'Ohh, so sorry, sir. My mistake. But, as I was saying, until I know that the rest of my funds are in my account, you won't be receiving any reassurances from me about that bitch.'

'Then our work here is done.' He got up to leave.

Declan grabbed his arm. 'What the fuck do you mean? Sit down!' His raised voice had a couple of people looking their way.

'David!' Bill's powerful voice was unmistakable in his ear. 'David, don't fuck this up.'

He remained calm and took his seat again, staring at Declan, waiting for the man to say something. The swine's mouth twitched – a possible tell.

'I must say,' Declan said, 'I'm very impressed at your cool nature. We could've worked well together had things been different. Maybe in the future, if the bitch lets you, who knows?'

'Ohh, so you are letting her go?'

'I didn't say that.'

'Then what more do you want?' He knew the man was struggling, despite his bravado. Evidence that this excuse of a human sitting in front of him was just a man – a ruthless monster, no doubt, but a man all the same. Luc came to mind. They'd discussed many situations, and one just like this was played out a couple of times in the forest.

Declan took hold of the bag's handles, sweat beading his forehead.

'Incoming message,' Bill said. 'Keep your head when you see it.'

His phone pinged and he opened the message, doing his utmost not to react, even though his heart was fit to explode. He looked up at Declan, unable to hold back a wide smile.

'What the fuck have you got to smile about?'

He showed him the photo of Laurel and Paul together. 'I'm led to believe you will recognise the two handcuffed men in the background.'

Declan looked around, sweat running down his face, then shot up and broke into a sprint, bag in hand. Two security guards attempted to stop him but he outmanoeuvred them and pushed through a group of shoppers, scattering them in panic.

David looked after him. 'Coward!'

Declan stopped at the sight of two men dressed as electricians moving towards him, then turned to face David, his eyes narrowing. A security guard grabbed at him but he pivoted out of the way and lunged, trapping the man's arm around in an arc and palming him under his nose, sending blood spurting. As he fell, Declan pulled the gun from his holster, snapped the breech back, and ran towards David.

'Coward? You think I'm a coward! Let's see who—'

A shot rang out. Declan stopped dead and looked down to his chest to see blood seeping from a single wound. He fell to his knees, his mouth working words that didn't come out. As he lifted the handgun, his arm shaking, another shot rang out and he jerked forward and landed flat on his face.

An agent, handgun pointed, walked up to Declan's body, kicked his weapon away, and felt his neck for a pulse.

'Subject is dead,' he said into his mic. 'I repeat, subject is dead.'

## *Chapter 49*

∞

'I'm ok, stop fussing Paul, but I need to see David. What the hell is going on?' Laurel had allowed the medic to strap her ankle and clean the wound on her head. But, now, with Paul keeping shtum about David's whereabouts, she thought something was up. What was he to do? They were in the same position.

The van entered the underground car park. Several agents had stayed behind, waiting for technicians to arrive to search the area further. Even if Declan escaped from their sting, his partners would not be happy to discover one of their hidden drug dens had been raided, and the Cypresse gang would be worried that two of their lowlifes were in custody for kidnapping, and possibly much more, on the West Coast.

'Laurel, just wait until I have word from the other unit. Stop being so bloody awkward!'

'Hey, I'm no damsel in distress. I need to know what's going on. I can handle it.'

'Wait!' he snapped. He was just as worried as her, with Marc also involved.

She went silent, and he regretted shouting at her. She'd been through enough. 'I'm sorry. It's just everyone's been so worried for you. We need to find out what the situation is with the other team before I can fill you in.'

They took the elevator up and he helped her enter the penthouse suite. Joshua, wearing earphones, looked up from his screens, his hand out to signal them to keep away.

Paul guided Laurel over to the couch. She cried out in pain as he lifted her leg onto a pillow.

'Can handle it, huh?' He smiled.

'Sorry.'

'They got him!' Joshua shouted out, his excitement making Paul and Laurel jump.

Paul rushed over to him. 'What's happened? Is everyone ok?'

Joshua gave him the thumbs-up, and he turned to see Laurel attempting to get up, only to collapse back, no doubt realising she needed to stay put.

'They have him, Laurel. It's over, it's ok.'

Fifteen minutes later, she had her hair brushed and face washed. Paul gave her a hoodie to change into. It was huge on her but she told him she didn't care. The elevator door closed and they watched as its arrow showed it moving down to the carpark.

'Jesus, can it move any slower!' Her face showed her frustration.

'Don't worry, David will be here any minute.'

'And Marc.' She smiled at him.

The elevator door opened and Bill walked in, followed by David and Marc. Both men ran to their partners, Paul taking Marc into his arms and hugging him tight, delighted at the look on Laurel's face.

'Ohh, David!' she cried. 'I really thought I'd never see you again.' They kissed, David's arm around her.

'Mon amie, that is it, we are never parting again. We travel as a family from now on.'

'Is he really gone, like...*dead* gone?'

'Dead as a doornail,' Marc said, with Paul running his fingers through his hair.

'Ohh, God, I hope he didn't suffer.'

David kissed her head and caressed her cheek.

'M'am,' Bill said, 'make no mistake, my agent ensures his targets don't suffer. Don't fret over evil men like him.' He turned to Marc. 'Sir, it's time for you all to disappear now. My colleagues are ensuring this mess is cleaned up, with no detail left behind. That includes you three.'

'Already?' Laurel asked. 'But what about our luggage? Our personal stuff?'

'Already waiting on the plane.'

Paul liked the sound of that. He particularly liked having his man back, safe and sound.

David stood up and shook Bill's hand, then walked over to Joshua, already packing away his IT gear. 'Thank you for everything, for finding Laurel. *Thanks* simply doesn't express what I need to say.'

'I guess that's our cue to go then,' Marc said. 'Bill, you'll be in touch for future prospective business?'

'Leave it with me. Take some timeout, sir. I think you all need it.'

Paul took Marc's elbow and guided him towards the lift, eager to get back to normality.

# *Chapter 50*

∞

**Six Months Later**

The church bell rang out as everyone gathered outside the Town Hall, all full of anticipation and excitement as they looked to the main door, waiting for the happy couple to come out. Then the doors opened.

A loud cheer erupted around the small main square of the village as Marc and Paul walked out to their waiting guests. Emma threw rose petals and light sweets into the air to squeals of delight as the children rushed for them. Once the photos were taken, the crowd headed over to the small church, where Simeon Paul Marc Rousseau was christened.

Later that day, the celebrations moved to Laurel and David's home for a picnic, with a vast selection of Irish and French foods on the menu. Jean-Pierre, now fully recovered, and Gabrielle took charge of the fine French cuisine and wine selection. Gerard, Carl, and his family made sure to be present for the special celebration, and Paul and Marc's family and friends were amazed by the friendliness and welcome of the Rousseau family. Nearly every hotel and B&B was booked from there to Marseille.

The newlyweds' first dance to *Stand By Me* didn't last too long alone, with everyone soon joining in. Then Paul danced with Emma, to everyone's applause. With dancing and singing running late into the night, many children, and some babysitters, were retired to their rooms so the parents could enjoy the festivities without concern.

Laurel couldn't hide her joy and kept hugging Paul and Marc, one after the other, then together. She kept doing it all night, until they told her she was drunk and to behave. This sent her into a huff, and she looked for David.

'Ok, so, I'll find someone who appreciates my hugs.'

'Honestly, please do!' They laughed as she walked away.

'Now, where is my man?' She looked around, then spotted a light turning on in one of the rooms.

'Aha! So here you are, Mister!'

David was sitting in the large soft chair. He laughed at her. 'Oui, mon amie, here I am, and you're drunk.'

'Pfftt! I'm not! Paul and Marc think the same. The cheek of ye all!'

She sat on his lap and cuddled into his arms. 'So, what are you doing here? It's very bad manners to abandon your guests, you know.'

He smiled. 'Just admiring the view from our window. Look, mon cher, what a wonderful view, everyone so happy, so alive.'

The picnic lights streamed around the dancefloor, twinkling in the light breeze. Tall encased candles flickered on tables and provided an ambient atmosphere away from the dance area.

Laurel kissed him. 'Yep, lots of happy light. Mam was right, the shadows are gone. It's a wonderful view.'

THE END

Made in United States
North Haven, CT
06 July 2023

38598462R00182

The Official

# Wolves

Annual 2014

Written by Paul Berry
Designed by Iain Donnachie

A Grange Publication





Photographs © AMA Sport Photo Agency, Sam Bagnall, Dave Bagnall, SM2 Studio and the Wolves Archive.

ISBN: 978-1-908925-54-1

BILLY
WRIGHT
CBE

# CONTENTS

# JACKETT A GOOD FIT

## "Is it always this sunny in Wolverhampton?"

**So asked Kenny Jackett as he breezed into the Compton training ground on the day he was officially introduced to the media as Wolves Head Coach back in June.**

After two seasons of desperate disappointment and back-to-back relegations which had taken Wolves from Premier League to League One, there hadn't been much sunshine knocking about for those of a gold and black persuasion.

But in over two hours of media interviews, defying the sweltering conditions as he moved around the different pitches of the training ground, Jackett's measured delivery and clear, unflinching ambition started immediately to shift some of the gloom.

Out of Darkness Cometh Light? Everyone certainly hoped so heading into the 2013/14 season with the new man at the helm.

There were 75 serious applications for the Head Coach position as Wolves sought a new era of stability following the departures of Ståle Solbakken and Dean Saunders.

Among them were some household names boasting plenty of quality and experience, with Head of Football Development and Recruitment Kevin Thelwell tasked with the job of sifting through the contenders and carrying out initial interviews.

Chief Executive Jez Moxey then joined the process for a more formal interview of 12 candidates, which were whittled down to a final shortlist to be put under the microscope by both Moxey and Chairman Steve Morgan.

Throughout the process, there was one candidate who continually impressed.

"We're a club with a fantastic tradition and history, and everyone anticipates us being successful, so it's about managing that expectation," said Thelwell.

"So it was about finding someone of that level of expertise and experience.

"It was also about someone who has an excellent coaching record, which Kenny has with the UEFA Pro Licence, and his background as a coach is highly regarded in the game.

"Then there was the fit, and anyone who has been a success at Millwall, which is not an easy club to manage, certainly has the qualities to be able to manage Wolves.

"All of those qualities culminated in Kenny being the standout candidate as well as his huge knowledge and understanding of where we are, what we are, and what we need going forwards."

As a player, Welsh international Jackett was the archetypal one club man, making 428 appearances for home town club Watford which included a runners-up finish in the top division and FA Cup Final

appearance in 1984.

Staying on in a coaching capacity at Vicarage Road he eventually assisted Graham Taylor in helping the Hornets achieve back-to-back promotions into the Premier League, before moving on to cut his managerial teeth at Swansea and then Millwall.

Both clubs were left in a far better condition than when he arrived, helping avert Swansea's decline and provide the spark for recent resurgence with promotion from League Two, and then doing likewise with Millwall a division higher, establishing the Lions in the Championship with an FA Cup semi-final appearance at Wembley in April to boot.

Wolves offered a new and fascinating challenge for Jackett in the summer of 2013 – the chance to try and rebuild a club following successive relegations and to do so from a foundation of young and vibrant talent.

"I was extremely proud to become the Head Coach of Wolves, and the potential of the club attracted me," said Jackett upon taking the job.

"I want – and I'm going to need – people who are committed to the cause and want to be here and see this as the type of fantastic opportunity and the fantastic club that I do.

"There has to be a team here with players that are proud to pull the shirt on.

"Wolves have obviously been struggling in recent times but I feel confident I can turn that around with plenty of hard work.

"I can see a tremendous football club that has the potential to go a long way."

Jackett's arrival was the start of a new structure at Molineux which sees him working closely with Thelwell. He also reignited the managerial team, which enjoyed so much success at Millwall, by bringing in Joe Gallen as his assistant.

With both Jackett and Gallen well known for the quality of their work developing younger players, and a burgeoning group at Wolves who have come through the Academy and tutelage of Steve Weaver, the signs were certainly promising for a new era.

"With the Category One status in place with the Academy, we have to back our own players," says Jackett.

"Young players can surprise you.

"They won't all necessarily do that, but if there was ever a time to be a Wolves player between 18 and 23, you won't get a better chance than now.

"You won't necessarily do it with a whole team of young players – there must be some reality to my selection.

"But I have seen a high number of them play and they look like they're ready for their chance."

And another item high on the agenda for Jackett this season? Rebuilding the relationship between the players and the fans.

"There has definitely been a distance between the players and the fans, and so adjustments need to be made because that is such an important link.

"It's key at any club and if you get it right, one can bounce off the other and it can drive you on to successful times.

"When it becomes a negative, the pressure builds up and it becomes very difficult to become successful so that link is an important one.

"It is always player-led – players have to take the responsibility to put on a good performance and get good results.

"We have to make sure now we have no hangover from what has happened and come out fighting with a young, fresh and vibrant Wolves side."

If Jackett can achieve that during the 2013/14 campaign, then the sun will once again be shining over Molineux.

# SAM THE WOLVES MAN!

**There was a certain symmetry to the arrival of new Wolves captain Sam Ricketts ahead of the 2013/14 season.**

Because it was ten years earlier that – while playing just up the M54 in non-league with Telford United – Ricketts was first handed a chance in the professional game with a move to Swansea City.

And the manager that signed him? Kenny Jackett.

Small wonder then that once 31-year-old Ricketts had come to an agreement on his contract with Bolton, he was Jackett's first choice not only to become his first signing, but also skipper as well.

"I did feel I needed a captain and my own captain," said Jackett.

"In terms of this stage of Sam's career, he's ready for that responsibility and he's been around for long enough to take that on board.

"It will be quite a youthful squad, so his experience will help us."

As for the man himself, taking on the armband was clearly a sought-after privilege.

"It's a big responsibility but it's something I'm relishing," said Ricketts.

"At this stage of my career, I've got the experience to go with it to help what is generally a young team here and start to get the club back where it belongs.

"I'd have been proud just to be at Wolves anyway but with it being such a big club as well – you look at the captains of the club from the past and who's played here before and it's a massive club and a great honour for me.

"I'm not a shouter and a bawler – I think those days in football are

long gone.

"As a captain I will just try to lead by example – I've always tried to do the right things."

That previous link-up with Jackett was also important.

"The gaffer signed me from non-league and taught me a lot – he started my career to be honest," says Ricketts.

"Within six or seven months of him signing me, I made my Wales debut and as a manager he instils the organisational side of the game into his players, which I think is hugely important.

"You must have ability to go with it, but there's no point having that if you don't know what I'm doing or my teammate next to me is doing.

"He teaches people the game, and that reflects on the team performance.

"You pick things up from every manager, but he was the first one at the time when I was a utility player who sat me down and got me playing full back.

"He taught that position and that's where my career took off."

Ricketts was, of course, well known to Wolves fans not only from their own footballing knowledge, but also – painfully – the clash between the two Wanderers at the Reebok Stadium on the final day of 2011.

Because it was then that Ricketts, in his first game back after a rare long-term injury, despatched a superb shot from distance beyond Welsh international team-mate Wayne Hennessey!

"It's always nice to put one past Wayne!" was the captain's verdict.

"He's an international teammate of course and being my first game back from injury it was nice to put one past him."

Ricketts' ability at all levels of the game – from non-league to Premier League – certainly made him an excellent acquisition for a new challenge with a young Wolves team, spells at Swansea, Hull and Bolton marking him out as a consistent and versatile performer.

Not to mention being, in Jackett's words: "the most two-footed player I have ever seen."

And that, as Ricketts, explains, is all down to his Grandad!

"I was born naturally right-footed and every time I went to see my grandad when I was a kid, he used to coach me – and does right to this day, he tells me what I've done, good and bad.

"I'd flick the ball up with my right foot, and he would say 'now do it with your left foot'.

"And from a young age, every time I saw him, he would only let me use my left foot.

"Unfortunately he can't go to the games anymore, but I have them copied and sent down to him.

"He will watch me and say 'in the warm-up, you kicked eight balls with your right foot and only two with your left – you need to do five on each foot'.

"That's what he's been like all the way through.

"Luckily, my debut for Wales was at left-back and I gave him my shirt and if it hadn't have been for him, I would have never played left back."

And Ricketts is now ready to channel all his experience, and Grandfatherly advice, into trying to help Wolves enjoy a successful season.

"Wolves are a big club – this club doesn't expect to be in League One, this was one of the biggest sides in the Championship and it's been in the Premier League recently as well.

"The challenge for all of us this season is to start to get this club back where it belongs."

## AUGUST/ SEPTEMBER

The now familiar surroundings of Carton House Hotel in Ireland greeted Wolves for their pre-season trip, but there was a change at the top with Norwegian Ståle Solbakken kicking off the 2012/13 campaign as the club's first overseas manager.

It was 5-1 Shades of Bray in the first friendly as Wolves ran out comfortable winners in the Emerald Isle, but the game's three outstanding performers – messrs Kightly, Jarvis and Fletcher – had all departed by the closure of the transfer window with the lure of the Premier League too strong.

New faces arrived in their place, including a potentially exciting attacking threat from the likes of Bakary Sako, Björn Sigurdarson, Razak Boukari and Slawomir Peszko.

The Capital One Cup provided a different to normal start to the regular season, Wolves coming through on penalties against Aldershot, but after then seeing off Northampton, a 6-0 defeat to European Champions Chelsea ended any interest in the competition by late September.

In Championship terms the first two months of the campaign saw Wolves bounce back from winning only one of their first four games to chalk up four victories in succession.

That man Sako was proving a particular star in the early season, scoring in his first two outings against Northampton and Cardiff, and following up with further assists and goals, including a free kick winner against Sheffield Wednesday on the last weekend of September.

Prior to downing the Owls, wins against Leicester, Ipswich and Peterborough had certainly raised the spirits of a Wolves fanbase understandably affected by the disappointment of relegation.

There was one notable departure in September, as Terry Connor – after 13 years of loyal service – left Molineux, later joining up with former Wolves boss Mick McCarthy at Ipswich Town.

# OCTOBER/NOVEMBER

The first fixture of October proved a disappointing one as Wolves lost their unbeaten home record in a tightly contested midweek game with Crystal Palace.

Wolves actually went in front through Sylvan Ebanks-Blake, and Kevin Doyle then hit the post before a quickfire brace from Manchester United-bound Wilfried Zaha saw the Eagles fly off with the points.

But the Molineux Men bounced back just five days later with a thoroughly professional all-round display at Blackburn, Bakary Sako's excellent second half strike helping to regain third place in the table and prompting an intense post-match celebration from Ståle Solbakken in front of the delighted travelling following.

Unfortunately, however, victory at Ewood Park was not to prove the catalyst for Wolves to reaffirm their early season promise, but was instead as good as it got as the team's fortunes slumped dramatically following the international break.

Nine league games came and went without success, in which Wolves' only points came from draws with Bolton, Charlton and Brighton, the latter marking Roger Johnson's redemption with a late headed equaliser.

Wolves could justifiably argue against certain decisions which didn't go their way during the dismal run, one example coming from Christophe Berra's early dismissal at Watford, which was later rescinded.

And injuries were also mounting in specific areas, notably on the wings where summer signings Razak Boukari and Slawomir Peszko both picked up serious injuries while Stephen Hunt suffered a setback.

The result of this was to see Jermaine Pennant arrive on loan from Stoke, German coach Patrick Weiser also joining assistant boss Johan Lange in Solbakken's backroom team in October.

Off the pitch there was a night packed with nostalgia as the new Wolves Museum officially opened its doors, a string of legends from Ron Flowers through to Steve Bull making the most of a special preview.

Meanwhile there was plenty of perspective at the home game with Brighton, Wolves' annual Armed Forces day, including children of serving personnel surrounding the centre circle before kick off as the matchball was delivered by fan - Sapper Clive Smith - who lost both of his legs serving in Afghanistan.

# DECEMBER/ JANUARY

The first four fixtures of December brought about a Wolves revival with three wins and the only defeat coming in controversial circumstances at Middlesbrough.

The 4-1 victory at Bristol City, featuring a superb solo goal from Kevin Doyle, was particularly impressive while a Friday night pre-Christmas success at Blackpool owed much to the continuing excellence of keeper Carl Ikeme.

In between times came a hard-fought Midlands derby victory against Birmingham, and the late defeat at 'Boro sparked initially by a hugely debateable penalty.

But the outcome of the improvement in results was to send Wolves into the Christmas programme with Peterborough and Ipswich boasting some solid foundations for more.

However, this was where it once again went wrong, Posh prevailing 3-0 on Boxing Day and then Mick McCarthy's Tractor Boys producing an equally comfortable 2-0 victory three days later.

Another convincing reverse at Crystal Palace on the first day of 2013 was followed by an even more damaging defeat to non-league Luton in the FA Cup third round, shortly after which it was revealed that Wolves had relieved Ståle Solbakken of his duties after just over six months at the helm.

Solbakken's replacement arrived swiftly in the form of Dean Saunders, who had guided Doncaster to the mid-season automatic promotion spots in League One, and was officially unveiled as manager 48 hours later.

Saunders' first game in charge was a lively 1-1 Friday night draw with Blackburn, followed by another share of the spoils – this time without troubling the scorers – at Sheffield Wednesday.

But then successive defeats by the odd goal in three against Blackpool and Leicester sent Wolves into February closer to the bottom end of the table than the top.

# FEBRUARY/ MARCH

There was a stirring late finish to Wolves' first fixture of February as Academy graduate Danny Batth continued his impressive initial senior impact with an injury time equaliser in front of the South Bank against Leeds.

And when this was followed up by a solid display featuring new loan arrival Kaspars Gorkss in a goalless draw at Derby, there was the suggestion Wolves were starting to find their feet under the new manager.

Another loanee, young Liverpool full back Jack Robinson, then arrived ahead of the crucial trip to Barnsley, but on a stormy night at Oakwell Wolves suffered a 2-1 defeat that saw them overhauled by the Tykes and, for the first time, dropping into the bottom three.

There followed back-to-back Molineux dates with the division's two pacesetters at the time, and after a narrow 2-1 defeat to Cardiff it was Bakary Sako's injury time leveller against Watford that provided the prelude to a far more encouraging Wolves run.

A midweek match at Millwall saw Saunders register his first win thanks to a goal in each half from two players recalled to the side, Dave Edwards and Sylvan Ebanks-Blake, the latter via a superb overhead kick.

A 3-1 defeat to Nottingham Forest at the City Ground was far closer than the scoreline suggests, but it left Wolves facing two monumental home games with Bristol City and Middlesbrough.

It needed a second half comeback to see off City, quickfire second half breakthroughs from Ebanks-Blake and Kevin Doyle overhauling David Davis's own goal on an afternoon when Wolves lost Carl Ikeme, Edwards and Sako to injury.

But Doyle, now captain, helped Wolves overcome those key absentees with another winner in a five goal thriller against 'Boro which also featured an excellent solo effort from Björn Sigurdarson.

# APRIL/MAY

Wolves picked up in April from where they had left off in March, a blistering first half display at St Andrew's seeing them build up a 3-0 lead against Birmingham.

Blues hit back with two second half goals to prompt a slightly nervy finale, but Wolves, now buoyed by a resurgent Stephen Hunt, saw out injury time to make it four wins from five and suggest more upwardly mobile times to come.

However, the man who struck two of the three goals – top scorer Sylvan Ebanks-Blake – limped off in the second half with an injury which later turned out to be a broken leg, thus ruling him out at the time he was playing his best football of the season.

David Davis had produced all three assists as Wolves completed a derby double, but when he limped off – also with a season-ending injury – in the early stages of the following fixture at Bolton the list of key personnel on the injury list was starting to look ominous.

The prognosis was further bleakened both by the 2-0 defeat at Bolton and then a 3-1 reverse at home to fellow survival battlers Huddersfield, leaving Wolves in a perilous position ahead of a Tuesday night visit of second- placed Hull.

But a solid all-round display, coupled with a well-worked Kevin Doyle goal, breathed fresh life into Wolves' efforts to maintain their Championship status, as Molineux basked in the delight of such a crucial 1-0 win.

The team were then within a minute or so of picking up a point at Charlton the following weekend – which would have kept them out of the relegation zone – but after Doyle again cancelled out the Addicks opener a 90th minute strike from Jonathan Obika hammered a dent in Wolves' hopes.

It left three points from the final home game of the season as a 'must', but in truth this never looked likely against a Burnley side who took full opportunity to see off any lingering doubts about their own safety

with a 2-1 success in which Wolves' goal came late from loan signing Nouha Dicko.

It needed various permutations to go Wolves' way on the final day but as it turned out even victory at play-off heading Brighton wouldn't have been enough.

The 2-0 defeat was perhaps overshadowed by the excellent support from the 2,000 travelling fans who overcame their own disappointment to earn rave reviews from the Seagulls' faithful for their backing of their team.

So it was that a double dip relegation was signed and sealed, and with Wolves condemned to League One, the club parted company with Dean Saunders, embarking on an intensive recruitment process culminating in the appointment a month later of new Head Coach Kenny Jackett.

# FINDERS KEEPERS

**There have been some pretty special goalkeepers who have turned out for Wolves down the years.**

**And we've managed to hide 15 of them within the wordsearch below! See if you can find the 15 – including not only the four senior goalkeepers at Wolves during the 2012/13 season, but also some legendary names from the past as well. Answers on page 61.**

- PAUL BRADSHAW
- DORUS DE VRIES
- MALCOLM FINLAYSON
- TIM FLOWERS
- MARCUS HAHNEMANN
- WAYNE HENNESSEY
- CARL IKEME
- PAUL JONES
- AARON McCAREY
- MATT MURRAY
- MICHAEL OAKES
- PHIL PARKES
- GARY PIERCE
- MIKE STOWELL
- BERT WILLIAMS

M A L C O L M F I N L A Y S O N
A I T I M F L C A R L I B D T A
R E K M I T I M F L O W E R S A
C I B E R T W I L L I A M S W R
U D S E S W A Y N E H Y I P W O
S O K E R T Y L M T H N C E A N
H J J O N T O E H P H E H C H M
A A R O N O K W L H P H A R S C
H E N E T I J F E I R E E E D C
N K K T L W M L O L A N L I A A
E I A R O I A B U P L N O P R R
M M A T T M U R R A Y E A Y B E
A C S T L J A C K R P S K R L Y
N O R I E L I A M K Z E E A U V
N E H C K H E N N E S Y S G A R
B P S E I R V E D S U R O D P X

# ONES TO WATCH

**With Wolves aiming for a fresher and perhaps younger approach to life in League One for the 2013/14 campaign, two players hoping for a chance to be involved in the new era were Lee Evans and Liam McAlinden. Evans, who arrived from Newport in January 2013, is a central midfield player from whom much is expected. McAlinden, meanwhile, has been at the club for over a decade, progressing through the Academy and landing a first team debut as substitute against Burnley in the last home game of 2012/13. Ones to watch? Let's hope so!**

## LIAM McALINDEN

Liam McAlinden can still vividly remember his days as a youngster supporting Wolves at Molineux.

"I used to come to games most weeks as a kid," says the striker.

"I always enjoyed watching Kenny Miller play, and really liked Henri Camara, although maybe that's not the best thing for me to say!

"But it's been great for me to come through the ranks at the Academy at the club where I have always been a fan.

"Then in recent times to be able to train and work with the first team has also really helped me improve.

"When you're training alongside strikers like Kevin Doyle, Sylvan Ebanks-Blake and Björn Sigurdarson, you can always pick things up and that is what I have always tried to do."

McAlinden has been with Wolves' Academy since he was eight, and has followed the likes of David Davis, Anthony Forde and Danny Batth in progressing through to the senior scene. With Wolves continuing the Category One Academy status, which puts them up alongside some illustrious company in English football, it is hoped many more will follow that same lead over the next few years.

McAlinden, a tall and agile frontman who was one of the leading scorers in the Under-21 league last season, was in and around the first team squad for the last eight fixtures of the 2012/13 season, then coming off the bench for his debut in the final home game against Burnley.

Having almost scored himself with a curling shot just wide of the target, McAlinden then set up Nouha Dicko's consolation against the Clarets, but the striker admits that the delight at his debut was tempered by a lingering disappointment about Wolves ultimately being relegated.

"It was great for me to be involved, but also difficult because it was really disappointing with the team being relegated," he said.

"But for me to be around the first team set up and get on for my debut was something I will personally remember given I have been at the club since I was eight and am a big fan.

"I learned a lot from being around the first team set up for the last eight games and it helped me settle in alongside them.

"And having had a lot of games for the 21s at a good standard, I was looking forward to coming back this season and, like the other young players, trying to impress.

"We are all keen to show what we can do and if we carry on working hard and improving then it is all about taking the opportunity when it comes along.

"It has been a very difficult time for Wolves over the last couple of years but I think now it is about looking forward.

"League One will be difficult but we will all be thinking positively and it would be something special for any of us to be involved in a push for promotion.

"We've got a new Head Coach in and it's a fresh start and up to us to make the most of it and do what we can to help the team."

# LEE EVANS

When Lee Evans joined Wolves from Newport County in January 2013, the two clubs were separated by three divisions. Now, thanks to Wolves being relegated and Newport winning promotion via the Conference play-offs, the gap in leagues has been reduced to just one.

But Evans certainly has no regrets. Indeed his delight at seeing his teammates help end Newport's 25-year absence from the Football League – Wolves won the old Fourth Division as the Welsh side exited in the opposite direction – is matched only by a determination to break through into the senior picture at Molineux, despite still being a teenager.

"I had all the banter from my Newport mates saying we'd end up playing them in the Johnstone's Paints Trophy," says Evans with a smile.

"I was really glad to see them get promoted and back into the league again and I hope they can go on and do well.

"But my focus now is on helping Wolves have a good season and do as well as we can - I'm settled here and have absolutely no regrets.

"Wolves are a massive club and when they come calling then you don't turn the opportunity down.

"Relegation was a massive disappointment for everyone at the club but once that has happened it becomes all about looking forward and, for me, trying to be involved around the first team."

Evans remains indebted to Newport – particularly manager Justin Edinburgh and Academy director Glyn Jones – for the grounding he received at Rodney Parade.

Having broken into the first team during the 2011/12 season, he was picked – as a 17-year-old – for the FA Trophy Final against York at Wembley.

Wolves' senior scouting team of Stuart Webber and Chris Badlan had kept tabs on the midfielder for a considerable time, and after the Club made their move Evans spent the second half of last season producing some starring roles under Steve Weaver for the Under-21s.

He also chipped in with four goals, the only real setback coming when an injury forced him out of a potential Wales-Under-21 debut against Moldova.

"It was good that the Under-21s were involved in the Elite League from the time I arrived to the end of the season," Evans explains. "It gave me some decent experience playing against some of the best Under-21 players in the country and was good to be involved in.

"It would have been nice had Wolves been safe in the Championship to maybe get a few games at the end of the season to see what I could do but it wasn't to be and, sadly, we were relegated.

"Now I have to concentrate on this season and trying to make a breakthrough for Wolves.

"It was a case of coming back for pre-season, working as hard as I can, and trying to impress.

"There is a new Head Coach in Kenny Jackett who has proved he will give young players a chance if they are good enough and that is all you can ask for.

"If we'd been in the Championship and I'd not been involved than maybe I could have gone out on loan to a League One club.

"But now we're in League One I'd like to feel I could play there, although it's up to me to prove that in training or if I get the chance."

And Evans certainly got off to a good start in pursuit of that aim, winning a place in the midfield for the opening few games and scoring his first senior Wolves goal in the 4-0 win against Gillingham.

## THROUGH THE FANS' EYES

The agony and the ecstasy. The joy and the despair. Wolves fans suffered their share of both during the 2012/13 campaign. And photographers from SM2 Studio captured the Molineux Mood every step of the way. Here are a selection of their shots from the season as supporters young and old go through the Wolves experience...

sportingbet

KEEP
CALM
HAVE A
PIE
W.W.F.C

**SINCE making his Premier League debut against Blackburn in March 2012, David Davis has emerged as a player with plenty of quality and the potential to become a midfield mainstay at Wolves for many years to come.**

**He has played alongside and against some top players even in his short career so far, and now we ask David to dish the dirt on both himself and his Molineux teammates past and present, exclusively for the Wolves Annual!**

**Who has been the best trainer at Wolves? And the worst? Who's got the best banter? What has caused him embarrassment? Read on to find out!**

## BEST TRAINER?

Karl Henry. He's always been very consistent in training and keeps his standards high. He never stops.

## WORST TRAINER?

Hunty. Yes Stephen Hunt. He's 100 miles an hour all the time and so can be very erratic!

## BEST PLAYER YOU HAVE EVER PLAYED WITH?

Steven Fletcher. Technically he is a very good all-round player and his finishing was superb.

## BEST PLAYER YOU HAVE PLAYED AGAINST?

Paul Scholes when we played Manchester United in one of my first games. Because he's 'the man' isn't he? Just a complete midfield player.

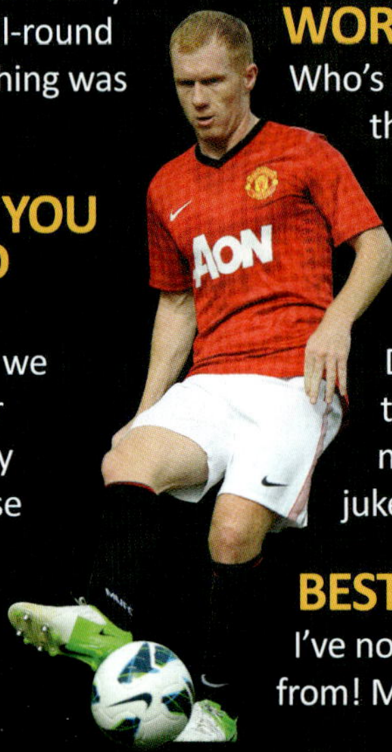

## BEST BANTER IN THE DRESSING ROOM?

Sylvan Ebanks-Blake. He is always on people and never gives them a rest. If he's coming for you there's no escape. He's had Phil Hayward our physio on toast.

## WORST BANTER?

Who's got horrible banter.... there have been a few. I'll pick a couple. Stephen Hunt. Because I could never understand a word he said. And Danny Batth. You have to put a 50p in him to make him talk – he's like a jukebox.

## BEST GOAL SCORED?

I've not got many to choose from! Maybe the own goal against Bristol City? Picked my spot for that one! Okay then I'll take one in training. A volley. My best for Wolves in a match is yet to come!

## BEST PERFORMANCE?

Probably against Birmingham towards the end of last season when I set up our three goals. I then got injured in the next game against Bolton which was really disappointing given the stage we were at.

## WORST PERFORMANCE?

I would have said that Bristol City game when I scored the own goal but we then turned that around and won. I'd go for Derby towards the start of last season when I don't think I played very well.

## MOST EMBARRASSING MOMENT?

Having to sing in front of the lads as you do here on your first away trip. I sang 'Old McDonald Had A Farm'. I got away with it. No idea how. It was in the away game at Swansea in the 2008/09 season.

## FOOTBALLING HERO?

Thierry Henry. When I was growing up he was such a player and a finisher and I supported Arsenal. I wanted to be a striker – but I couldn't finish.

## BEST THING ABOUT BEING A FOOTBALLER?

Playing for Wolves against some of the top players like Paul Scholes.

## DAVID DAVIS ON FIFA?

I play it but don't play as Wolves or as myself. That would be too much! Anyway I don't think my character is very realistic. I'm faster and stronger than what they've done – they're mugging me off. And I'm definitely better looking!!!

# TEAM-MATES with David Davis

# TONY'S TALES FROM THE TERRACES

**There are many wonderfully loyal Wolves supporters who travel great distances to see their team home and away. And one in particular – Tony Cowley - has now spent over 40 years of his life crossing both land and sea to follow his gold and black heroes. Because he lives at the Point of Ayre in the Isle of Man! The Wolves Annual met Tony on one of his visits to Molineux to enjoy a few of the stories of his travels....**

### First of all then Tony... why Wolves?!

**TC:** There were a few different reasons really. As a kid the colour of the shirts always appealed to me and I followed a team in the Isle of Man who played in gold and black. And in the 1930s and 40s my Dad played for a team called Wanderers. My favourite players at the time were also the likes of Bert Williams, Billy Wright and Peter Broadbent. There were a lot of Liverpool, Everton, Manchester City and Man United fans in the Isle of Man but not many Wolves!

### And so you started going to games?

**TC:** Yes. I trained to become a teacher in the mid-1960s so it was easier to go then, but I was never going to be a teacher! I went back to the Isle of Man to work as a stocktaker for a brewery and eventually managed to do a deal where I went self-employed which freed me up more to organise my travel arrangements. I used to come and stay at the York Hotel before home matches – you could say I had a Season Ticket as I would do the stocktake for the hotel and Indian restaurant next door as well! It was while I was there that I met my wife Karen, who was working at the hotel.

### What does Karen make of your footballing travels?

**TC:** Erm. She's okay with it! Karen is from Tipton and her Dad is a big Wolves fan too. We have four children and the first two were named after Wolves players! It was August 1987 and our first arrival was imminent but I still managed to get across for a Saturday away game at Hereford. Fortunately I got back home to the maternity unit in the Isle of Man in plenty of time for the birth on Sunday, and was then back to Molineux for a game with Scunthorpe on the Monday. I was sat in The Fox pub (now The Wanderer) and I said to the people I was with that we were going to call our baby after the first Wolves goalscorer. I was secretly hoping it wasn't Floyd and, sure enough, Bully duly obliged so when I got back home again it was agreed to name our son Stephen! Our second son is called Robbie, after Robbie Dennison scored that great free kick when we drew 2-2 with Sheffield United to clinch the Third Division title. I didn't manage to get the third one as well – he is called Daniel (see picture above)! – although I remember going to watch Wolves in PSV Eindhoven when we were all in a restaurant and a guy asked us to sign a team photo as if we were the players. And I signed as Peter 'Daniel'! We also have a daughter Kristen who, like her Mother, isn't really into football!

### Time for some stories then – give us some of your favourite games!

**TC:** Obviously the League Cup Final wins at Wembley in '74 and '80. The Sherpa Van final and the play-off final win, too. The amazing comeback to beat Leicester 4-3 after being 3-0 down in the Premier League, not to mention beating that lot from Old Trafford – twice! For the win back in January 2004, we nearly didn't make it as the plane was circling in heavy fog around North Wales and just couldn't land. We had to go back to the Isle of Man and were walking through the airport thinking where we could

watch the match on telly and someone spotted us to say there were spare seats on a flight to Birmingham. We dashed across the airport, and after the flight and a rushed taxi journey just got inside Molineux in time for kick off. It was of course a lunchtime kick off, and by the evening we had stopped at a pub in Hale enroute for Liverpool and the return flight. The pub was full of Liverpool fans watching their game with Tottenham live on Sky and when we arrived wearing Wolves colours there were hugs and cheers all round!

## ○ Many other travel difficulties over the years?

**TC:** One or two! I remember the Sherpa Van Trophy semi final at Torquay the year after we won it. We were at Weston Super Mare when it was called off due to a waterlogged pitch. We kept on going and the game was eventually played the following night, before which we saw the team train at Paignton. Incidentally, Torquay is probably the longest journey I have ever made in one go after I had to pick people up in Wolverhampton, then London, and then go down to Plainmoor for a Saturday night game. By the time I'd done the journey in reverse it was over 1,000 miles! Another time my hire car broke down en route for Bristol City and by the time it was fixed it was too late to get there. Instead I stopped at Wolverhampton and watched the reserves against Stoke when those games were played on a Saturday afternoon. There was also one occasion when I travelled on a mail plane, tied to the floor, and another when we'd been delayed and the pilot, who knew of my Wolves links, called me up to the cockpit and rushed me through to his car after landing before giving me a lift to the station!

## ○ It's not always been that difficult though?

**TC:** No. One of my most memorable experiences was travelling with the team to a UEFA Cup tie in Porto in 1974. The firm running the Wolves Supporters' Club trip had gone bust, and so six of us travelled with the team from Birmingham Airport which was a great experience. We all felt very important on the team bus. Although sadly we ended up getting thrashed in the game!

## ○ Any favourite players who stand out?

**TC:** Peter Knowles, the Doog, Waggy, Mike Bailey. After I featured on Match of the Day 2 a few years ago, Peter sent a signed framed copy of a League Cup programme against Spurs featuring him and brother Cyril to Wolves historian Graham Hughes to pass on to me. From there I managed to meet Peter in Wolverhampton, which was great.

## ○ And now, in League One, you're enjoying it as much as ever?

**TC:** Oh yes! I was pleased with the appointment of Kenny Jackett and couldn't wait for this season. I've seen us go from the First Division to the Fourth before – I've seen Wolves at over 100 grounds and I'm not going to pack it in now! It's not been a great couple of years but we've still got some good players and hopefully better times are ahead! ○

**A TYPICAL TONY TRIP**
(vs Huddersfield 13/04/13)
**5am.** Get up
**5.45am:** Leave house for 30-mile trip to Ronaldsway Airport
**7am:** Flight to Liverpool John Lennon Airport
**7.30am:** Arrive in Liverpool and bus to South Parkway Railway Station
**8.15am:** Train from Liverpool to Wolverhampton, arriving at 9.30am
**3pm:** Match
**5.20pm:** Train to Liverpool cancelled so catch train to Stafford and then Runcorn where met by taxi to ensure I don't miss flight
**7.50pm:** Flight from Liverpool to Isle of Man
**8.30pm:** Arrive back at Isle of Man Airport
**9.15pm:** Home!

# NIGHT AT THE MUSEUM

The Wolves Museum has proved a very popular attraction for fans since opening its doors in November 2012.

And Head Coach Kenny Jackett made it one of his early priorities to take a look around with his family not long after his appointment.

A number of Season Ticket Holders won a competition to meet Kenny, talk through some of their Wolves memories, and sit down to watch the cinema-style show in the Museum auditorium.

# WOLVES MUSEUM: FROM THE ARCHIVE

**As well as the various quizzes, interactives, a relative minefield of information and a spellbinding cinema-style show, the Wolves Museum also houses many impressive exhibits from the club's proud history.**

**These will be rotated over time, with the Wolves Archive now containing many vastly contrasting items telling the story of Wolves through the years.**

**Here on this page there are just five examples from different generations of the club's history of the sort of artefacts contained within the Archive!**

## 1888: HARRY ALLEN'S ENGLAND CAP

This is an international cap awarded to Wolves and England's Harry Allen at the Home Championship match against Scotland, staged at Hampden Park on March 17, 1888. Allen, who made his second England appearance in the 5-0 win, was a centre half whose stay at Wolves from 1886-1894 included the 1893 FA Cup triumph.

## 1939: RADIO TIMES

This edition of the Radio Times magazine from April 21, 1939, showcased the build-up to the 1939 FA Cup Final between Wolves and Portsmouth, displaying the two captains Stan Cullis and Jimmy Guthrie.

## 1960: BARCELONA PENNANT

This pennant was exchanged at the European Cup Round Two first leg tie between Barcelona and Wolves at the Camp Nou on February 10, 1960. The final score was 4-0 to Barcelona.

**Remember the Wolves Museum is a fun-packed experience for all the family. For opening hours and prices visit *wolvesmuseum.co.uk***

## 1971: TRADE CARDS

Trade cards were all the rage at this time and here are three examples – Derek Dougan, Jim McCalliog and Derek Parkin – of the Wolves set produced by A&BC Chewing Gum Ltd.

## 1993/94: HOME KIT

One from the vast array of Wolves kits down the years, this was used during the 1993/94 campaign, and featured the return of the town's crest as the club's badge. This shirt was worn, donated and signed by Wolves' record goalscorer Steve Bull, who had won 13 England caps several years earlier.

# WELCOME KEVIN McDONALD

**Wolves were delighted to add Kevin McDonald to the squad shortly after the start of the 2013/14 season, the midfielder arriving from Sky Bet League One rivals Sheffield United.**

**The Scotland-Under-21 international was keen to join Kenny Jackett's new era at Molineux, and contribute towards the Club's aims of a successful season.**

THE SIGNING: 'Big Mac' checks in!

THE TRAINING: Warming up for his debut.

THE PLAYING: Eyes on the ball.

THE WINNING: Applauding the fans.

# WHAT'S IT LIKE TO SCORE A GOAL?

**There can be no better feeling than scoring a goal, even more so if it's a late goal. Matt Doherty has emerged as a key talent for Wolves, and it was the defender who popped up at Bristol City early in the season to secure a crucial three points at Ashton Gate. Here's how...**

Doherty has met Sako's cross and his effort is heading for the line

Ave it! The goalkeeper is distraught, Doherty is delighted.

Time to do the aeroplane....

...and let all the passion out!

How about some crowd surfing?

And a bit more for good measure!

# PICTURE PERFECT

**Wolves were once again making their presence known in the community during the 2012/13 season, whether via the work of Wolves Community Trust, donations from Wolves Aid, or inviting people to enjoy a day out at Molineux.**

**Here are a selection of some 'off the pitch' photos from the season.**

Popular Wolves favourite Graham Hughes enjoyed a special party and presentation from captain Karl Henry to mark his official retirement.

Baroness Rachael Heyhoe-Flint led a half time presentation for some of the Midlands' Olympic and Paralympic heroes, including bronze medallist gymnast Kristian Thomas, from Wednesfield.

St Peter's Collegiate Church Choir entertained the Molineux crowd during half time of the pre-Christmas fixture with Birmingham.

Björn Sigurdarson and Sylvan Ebanks-Blake visited Compton Hospice as part of the players' Christmas visits.

Wolves legends Ron Flowers and Steve Bull laid a commemorative wreath pitchside after the club's annual Memorial Service at St Peter's Church led by Rector, the Rev David Wright.

25 years on from the Sherpa Van Trophy win at Wembley, several of the squad returned for a day out at Molineux, along with Mark Kendall's widow Gaynor.

Wolves Women were boosted by some sponsorship from the London Wolves Supporters Club, Jody Craddock also involved here at the photocall.

Kevin Thelwell addresses a press conference as it was confirmed Wolves Academy had achieved the highest standard Category One status.

Young fan Harry Evans, who has battled cancer, led the Wolves team out as mascot for the Friday night fixture against Watford.

Steve Morgan and Jez Moxey were among club officials who faced supporters at a special Fans' Parliament held at Molineux.

Chairman Steve Morgan chats to Wolves legend Ron Flowers at the opening of the Wolves Museum.

Wolves once again joined forces with Tettenhall Rotary Club to support the Power Pleas wheelchair charity, Bakary Sako pictured here with some of the beneficiaries.

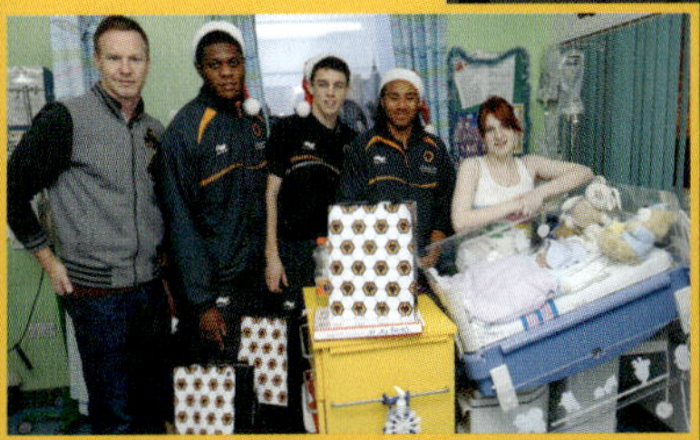

Wolves Academy players joined Jody Craddock in visiting several wards to spread some festive cheer at Birmingham Children's Hospital.

George Elokobi presents a cheque from Wolves Aid to the West Midlands Disability Swimming team.

Wolves Community Trust's Soccer Schools continue to prove extremely popular for all those in attendance.

Matt Murray, Carl Ikeme and Tongo Doumbia met the pupils at Westcroft School and Sports College.

**Jody Craddock confirmed his retirement in the summer of 2013, after a playing career spanning two decades, 581 senior appearances and 24 goals.**

**And, with ten years' playing service at Molineux, the hugely popular defender was awarded a testimonial with a series of events to take place during the 2013/14 campaign.**

**Here Jody looks back at a few memories from a career in which he will always be remembered fondly for his conduct both on and off the pitch.**

# CAPTAIN CRADDOCK

## First up Jody, can you remember your debut?

**JC:** Yes I can. For Cambridge against Stockport. (CORRECT! A 0-0 draw on 11/12/93). I was 18 and playing against Kevin Francis – who was 6ft 7in – and Andy Preece, who was around 6ft 4 as well. So quite a baptism! I think I did alright, held my own and won my headers. And we didn't lose!

## Best goal you scored?

**JC:** For Wolves against Bradford in the League Cup. Definitely. It fell really nicely and I just hit it! To be fair I have always had a volley in the locker and it was nice to actually produce one in a match. I hit it really sweetly and just knew it was heading for the top corner.

## Best individual performance?

**JC:** It's difficult to try and remember and certainly pick anything out. I never really thought about individual games too much – for me I always liked to be consistent. I was never going to really stand out but measured myself on managing to keep a decent standard.

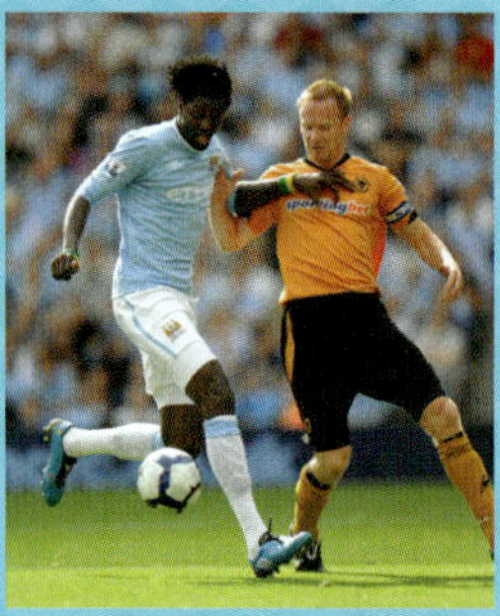

## Worst performance?

**JC:** I don't think I was ever that bad that I was substituted. Although I remember scoring one or two own goals, which is never any good! I remember an own goal for Wolves. I made a block at the near post and as I got up it hit my knee and went in. That hurt! And you don't forget

Keep an eye on Jody's testimonial year by checking the website at *jc6.co.uk* or by following the Twitter account at: *twitter.com/JC6Testimonial*

those! When you get beat by big numbers as a defender it's also not great.

## Any games particularly good memories?

**JC:** The derby games were ones I always enjoyed. Wolves against West Brom had a great atmosphere, Sunderland against Newcastle. Celebrations in those games always felt that bit bigger. And the promotion with Wolves as well, beating QPR to clinch it and then lifting the trophy with Karl Henry after the final home game with Doncaster.

## A bad memory?

**JC:** Relegation. Any one of them. It's never just one game or one thing but a collaboration of so much that means you get relegated at the end of the season. It's a horrible feeling and leaves you feeling dreadful all summer.

## How many times did you smash your head up?

**JC:** Loads! Probably about ten I reckon. Those bandages became a regular occurrence. I remember one game when I took a whack scoring against Southend. I came off on the stretcher and wasn't completely with it. I remember coming around again in the tunnel and saw our kitman Trev. He told me I'd scored and we were winning 1-0 but I didn't believe him.

## Best thing about being a footballer?

**JC:** Do you know what? It never felt like a proper job. It was like I came out of school, went into playing football and was lucky enough to make a living out of it. It never felt like a proper job, just something I loved doing and got paid to do.

## And the worst?

**JC:** Training at Christmas, particularly Christmas Day and travelling over Christmas. In the early days it was being on my own at that time and then when you've got kids as well. Training in the summer holidays when they are off school! Just missing out on a few family things like that.

## Best player you played with?

**JC:** There's a few to be honest. Probably at Wolves it would be Joleon Lescott who was a great centre half and has gone on to play for England. At Sunderland Kevin Phillips and Niall Quinn up front formed a fantastic partnership.

## Biggest character you've played with?

**JC:** Graham Stack. Without a doubt. Nothing I can repeat here, but he was ridiculous! Just what you'd expect from a goalkeeper.

## Many dressing room pranks in your day?

**JC:** Always. There's always stuff going on in a football dressing room. All the usual stuff – clothes getting pinched and hung up somewhere else, socks getting cut in half – all dressing rooms are the same.

## And what now?

**JC:** I'm hoping to enjoy a great testimonial year meeting fans and putting on some good events. And for my career it's my painting, which everyone probably knows about! I've been doing it throughout my football but now I've finished playing it's something I will be involved in even more.

# JUST THE JOB FOR JACQUI...

**Jacqui Oatley, born and bred in Wolverhampton, has risen through the media ranks to become one of the leading broadcasters for BBC Sport, chiefly reporting and presenting on football. And, she is also one of us – a lifelong Wolves fan – to boot! The Wolves Annual caught up with Jacqui to find out more about her life and times!**

## First things first Jacqui, how did you get into journalism and broadcasting?

Bit of a long story really! I did a degree in German, travelled around the world for a year, and then thought: 'What do I do next'? I moved to London and fell into a job in intellectual property because of my language skills but it wasn't something I really wanted to do. At the time I was watching Wolves home and away every Saturday with London Wolves and playing football every Sunday for a team in the Greater London league and that gave me my football fix. Then I injured my knee badly playing football which left me on crutches for ten months and was told I could not play sport ever again, apart from swimming and cycling.

## That must have been a terrible moment?

Yes I was devastated. And when it was clear I couldn't play anymore then I wanted to be involved in football in some other capacity. I started doing lots of research, evening courses and so on, and worked on Hospital Radio for six months and decided this was definitely what I wanted to do. I gave up my job, gave up my flat, and went around doing

work experience at places such as BBC WM while sleeping on friends' floors! I knew then for certain it was what I wanted to do so I completed a postgraduate degree in Broadcast Journalism in Sheffield, from where I started with BBC Leeds working on non-league football. I absolutely loved it, and things moved on from there.

### Can you remember the first game you ever broadcast on?

I can. And it was the most nerve-wracking moment of my life! I couldn't actually believe I was being sent to cover a football match. It was while still on my postgrad course and I was sent to cover Bradford Park Avenue against Ashton United in the Unibond Premier League for Radio Leeds. I will never forget the stress of it as the traffic on the M62 was a nightmare and I was panicking about getting there on time. I did get there, and it was one of those grounds with an athletics track around the pitch and an enclosed press box from where you couldn't really see very much! I went into the press box alongside some senior gentlemen who had been working in the industry for many, many years and they were probably thinking 'who is this blonde girl coming in talking about football'? Everyone fell silent when I did my radio reports and it was all a bit daunting but I am sure it stood me in good stead for what was to follow.

### The vast majority of your work is now done for the BBC with the likes of Five Live and Late Kick Off. That must be a source of some pride?

Absolutely. I still can't believe I get paid for watching football matches. Of course you are not just sitting there with your arms folded, you are working. But it is still an absolute pleasure whatever the standard of the game you are at. I started with non-league and loved doing that and, while I mainly cover Premier League and Championship games for Five Live, I also do a few in League One and League Two. I cover a lot of women's football as well and I love covering any match or any tournament wherever it may be. Having worked in another job which wasn't fulfilling I am hugely appreciative of the opportunities I now enjoy.

### Do you cover a variety of sports?

Football is the main sport I cover as it's my obsession but I have done a lot of others including tennis, rugby league, snooker and even Royal Ascot! It's good to get a variety and I have done news reporting as well, for BBC WM. That was good fun, before the days of Sat Nav, driving around Birmingham City Centre in one of those huge radio cars trying to get to a story in time to get it on air. I've also been fortunate enough to cover different tournaments, such as the World Cup in Germany in 2006 where I did a TV show and I was also a BBC TV reporter at Euro 2008. I commentated on the 2010 World Cup in South Africa for Five Live which was amazing. I had a commentary per day over seven days in different cities around South Africa which was incredible. And then at Euro 2012 I did TV punditry for Norwegian TV. I have covered Women's World Cups for TV and radio such as the one in China in 2007 and I presented the BBC's coverage of the European Championships this summer in Sweden.

## Any horror stories you can tell us about equipment failure or something similar?

I've generally been fairly lucky but there is one incident I particularly remember. I was interviewing Arsene Wenger just before the final game Arsenal played at Highbury. There was just me and a chap from another radio station. It was just a lovely interview with Arsene speaking so eloquently and reminiscing about the Marble Halls of Highbury. It was a real pleasure to be listening to him. Then I got to the end – and the recording equipment had failed! The guy from the other station tried to help by sending us his recording but unfortunately there was a hissing noise on it and it couldn't be used either. Arsene was fantastic because he came back despite having done so many other interviews and did another couple of minutes with me but sadly he was fairly tired by then and it was nothing like the relaxed, nostalgic one he had done first time. It was never going to be! That was such a let-down and I will never forget it.

## Of course you were the first ever female to commentate on a game for Match of the Day back in 2007, which caused a fair amount of attention. How do you reflect on that experience now?

I'm still glad it's over! I'm pretty sure I won't have to go through anything like it again. It was an absolute honour to commentate on Match of the Day but the way it happened turned it all into a very difficult scenario. It came out in a newspaper on the Tuesday before the game on the Saturday, and just gave the story time to grow legs. By the Wednesday *The Daily Mail* had done a big spread on it and on the Thursday it was on the front page of several papers, including *The Telegraph,* and *The Guardian* carried a picture with the headline: "Is football ready for Jacqui Oatley?" My phone never stopped ringing. I felt trapped and isolated and because of all the attention I didn't manage to do my preparation until late the night before the game and felt so tired and drained on the day. My head was all over the place and it ended up being something I just had to get through rather than enjoy. It was still an honour though and I have been fortunate to do games for MOTD and the Football League Show on several occasions since.

## Do you think there are more women now getting a fair crack in football and sports broadcasting?

I am involved in the Women in Football organisation which is a group allowing women working in football to network and share experiences. Quite often women are the only one at their workplace, be it an office, company or medical room if they are a physio. When I first started in Yorkshire I felt I was a bit of a weirdo because there were hardly ever women in press boxes. That has changed now and there are more female journalists and female press officers although I still think, from some of the stories I have heard, that there are some issues that need to be addressed.

## And you do get to work alongside some household names as summarisers?

I still find it strange but of course a privilege to be working with some of the top names in football. I'll be looking through my mobile to find a friend's number and these football names will pop up! One of the best things about this job is getting to hear what really goes on behind the scenes. It's great to work with people who have so much experience and knowledge of the game.

## Any stand out moments?

There is a bitter sweet one when I did full commentary of Wolves against West Brom in the FA Cup a few years ago on Five Live. To be working at Molineux doing a full commentary of Wolves against Albion was another 'pinch yourself' moment. Of course, we lost that game – Kevin Phillips again! There was also another Wolves memory – the 6-0 defeat at home to Southampton in 2007. I think that was the most incredible game of football I have attended in my life. The fans were singing 'Super Mick McCarthy' as Southampton made it 4-0.

## Any other memorable commentaries away from Wolves?

All those World Cup matches in South Africa were pretty special, particularly as my mum Sonja comes from the country. One in particular was Cameroon against Holland played in an absolutely fantastic new stadium in Cape Town, overlooking Table Mountain. I was working with Graham Taylor and did have to pinch myself during the National Anthems looking around this stadium and wondering how on earth did a girl from Wolverhampton manage to end up commentating at a World Cup Finals with a former Wolves manager – and England of course?! It was spine-tingling.

## As mentioned, you are a lifelong Wolves fan...

Yes. I used to go home and away most seasons even midweek trips as far afield as Grimsby.

My Dad would give me stick for spending all my pocket money on watching Wolves. And when I was in the Sixth Form at Wolverhampton Grammar I used to go to Molineux regularly at lunchtimes, just to see if anything was happening. We'd go into the old club shop which was the dingy and damp portakabin behind the North Bank. There was one time when somebody invited me inside to meet Steve Bull.

## Is it difficult to remain impartial when you get to cover Wolves?

Not at all. When I used to stand in the South Bank I don't think I could ever imagine being neutral at a Wolves game. But now I actually find it extremely easy. When you have a microphone in your hand your entire focus is on conveying what is happening in the game and what you can see and who is or isn't playing well. If Wolves are attacking you are not thinking 'come on score' but more who is crossing to who and who is going to get the final touch because you are going to have to explain everything that has happened in close detail. I do find it easy to criticise Wolves if they are not doing well or praise them when they are. When the game is in progress it is very much a 'job'. It is only when you switch off and drive home in the car that you look back from a fan's perspective.

## It sounds like you are still living the dream?

Yes and I'm really lucky. A lot of my friends who are mums haven't been able to go to back to their jobs but because I am freelance I am able to manage my diary. I love spending time with my little girl, Phoebe, but also I am still able to go to work in such an enjoyable job. Sometimes people fall into careers but I worked extremely hard to get into this one and spent my life savings on going back to university and worked for free which gives me even more satisfaction. I could have carried on in my well-paid job but it didn't inspire me like the one I do now. Being able to report, commentate and also present as well is a real privilege and something I really appreciate.

Wayne 'Liam Neeson' Hennessey in Star Wars

Liam 'Adam Sandler' McAlinden in The Wedding Singer

Sam 'Bradley Cooper' Ricketts in The Hangover

Kevin 'Ed Norton' Foley in The Bourne Legacy

# PLAYERS AS FILM STARS

**If you have a quick look at the Wolves team coach en route to away games you will often see most of the squad sat and engrossed in a DVD or two.**

**Yes footballers and films tend to go hand in hand when it comes to a leisure pastime!**

**So we put one question to the Wolves class of 2013/14 – who is your favourite film star, or indeed, who should play you in a film about your life?**

**Here are the pictures!**

**With thanks to our 'Director' Abbie Groom for the pictorial handiwork!**

Aaron 'Liam Neeson' McCarey in Batman

George 'Vin Diesel' Elokobi in The Fast And The Furious

David 'Eddie Murphy' Davis in Beverley Hills Cop

Carl 'Denzel Washington' Ikeme in Training Day

Jake 'Jason Statham' Cassidy in Death Race

Anthony 'Alan Garner' Forde in The Hangover

Dave 'Ryan Gosling' Edwards in Only God Forgives

Danny 'Bane' Batth in Batman

Matt 'Matthew McConaughey' Doherty in Surfer Dude

Björn 'Mark Wahlberg' Sigurdarson in The Perfect Storm

# THE BJORN IDENTITY!

**Wolves Annual caught up with Björn to discuss the differences between his home country and where he now plays his football, including why he used to drive around all day back in Iceland and what he thinks of a good English steak!**

**Björn Sigurdarson showed plenty of promise during the 2012/13 season, his first as a Wolves player since joining the club from Lillestrom.**

**The affable striker hails from Iceland, where he started playing his football with Íþróttabandalag Akraness.**

### England and Iceland then – what are the main footballing differences?

When I went from Iceland to Norway I was 17 and that was a big step in terms of better football but not nearly as big as the one from Norway to England. It is also very different over here. Football is popular in Iceland and there are a lot of good teams but there are not as many good players as there are in England. Training is also very different and it is a lot more physical here and you have to be mentally tougher as well. When you were young you went to training and everyone was friends and it is more like that in Iceland. Here you have to be strong because it is a very competitive environment and you have a lot of people yelling at you making sure you do things right!

## Fans?

There are not as big crowds in Iceland as there are in England. When I was playing in Iceland 2,000 was a big crowd but here of course at Wolves there have been many more fans. The supporters don't sing as much in Iceland – there are some fan clubs who try to cheer everyone on but not as many get involved as they do over here.

## Teammates?

I played in Iceland for my home town team, so I knew everyone there from when I was maybe six years old. So everybody was friends as well as team-mates. Here I have met new people and it has been different, but in a good way. There have been some very different personalities at Wolves while I have been here. I know a lot of the players called me strange in the matchday programme last season, but I would say the same about a few of them too!!! This is my chance to say that back to them!

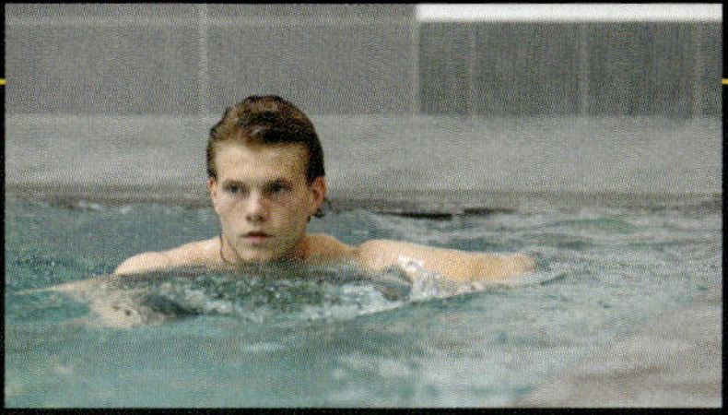

## The weather?

It is not as warm in Iceland but it is a bit different. A good day is maybe 10 degrees which feels like 20 here because in Iceland we get a lot of wind and rain. To be honest, the more I think about it, there are probably a lot of similarities between the two countries.

## The traffic?

There is a lot of traffic in Iceland, but way more here. There are so many people on the roads all the time!

## The food?

I think the food is better in Iceland. But I would say that! It is different that's for sure. Fillet steak here is quite similar and I eat that a lot! But, for example, the lamb in Iceland tastes a lot different the way it is cooked. Over here it is like you are smelling the sheep! It's just the traditional foods that I miss from back home, but there are other options over here.

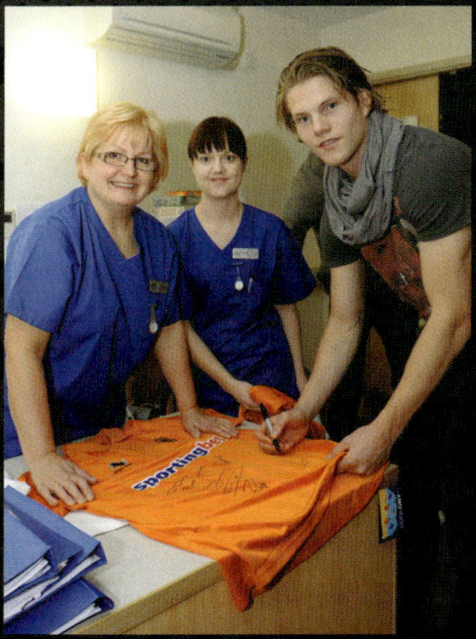

## The people?

People come up to me in the street here and will say 'hi' or 'you're doing great'. When people did that in Iceland it was people that I knew, either your friends or their parents. Everyone here has been really friendly. I probably wasn't expecting them to be this good. People suggested I should be careful because they might have a go at me if things weren't going well but they never have and have been great.

## Their personalities?

We do have a lot of people in Iceland who rush around like they do in England! But I think maybe people can be a bit more aggressive in England. There are probably more laid back people in Iceland who just sit back and enjoy life.

## Social life?

I play pool here and like going to films but there are a lot of cinemas in Iceland as well. Back home, when you are 17 and get your driving licence and when you do that everyone just drives around town all day. You end up meeting everyone like 50 times a day and just wave to each other! You just drive around! And then you grow up! Here I just stay home or go out for something to eat with my girlfriend.

# MURRAY'S MEAN MACHINES

**It is often said that strikers get all the glory, and that goalkeepers are plain crazy, so here at Wolves Annual we are trying to redress the balance!**

**When trying to look back over five great goalkeeping performances from the last couple of decades, who else could we ask but a former Wolves keeper himself – Mr Matt Murray.**

**Murray, now a well-respected pundit on Sky Sports and Free Radio, has taken a look back through his memory bank and picked five of the best from his fellow former Wolves glovemen.**

## CARL IKEME
### 21/12/12
### BLACKPOOL 1-2 WOLVES

To see Kemes come in the team was great for me.

We needed a win big time going down to Blackpool last December.

He made some brilliant saves which included all different types of saves.

With some he had to stand big to make one-on-one saves and with others had to show his agility and block a shot which had come through a sea of bodies.

There were three saves in the space of a minute just after half time which was a big spell when Blackpool were pressing.

I think a lot of Kemes and it was great to see him do well last season.

Some saves are brilliant but also important for the time and his all-round display on a very difficult surface – including his catching and distribution – was spot on.

## WAYNE HENNESSEY
### 27/12/11
### ARSENAL 1-1 WOLVES

I have seen Wayne put in some excellent displays for Wolves, including Bolton away when we lost 1-0 in injury time.

At the Emirates it was like the Alamo at times and Arsenal had scored early on through Gervinho.

They had chance after chance.

Again he pulled off a range of saves including one when he got across his goal really quickly and made the save with his feet.

You can't always make the perfect save – what you have to do is whatever you can to keep the ball out of the net.

He showed great desire and bravery to keep Arsenal at bay and we went down to ten men as well but hung on for a 1-1 draw.

If you could get close to the perfect goalkeeping performance then I think that would be it.

## MICHAEL OAKES
### 17/01/04
### WOLVES 1-0 MANCHESTER UNITED

A team like Manchester United have got players with a bit of magic and as a goalkeeper you always have to expect the unexpected.

You have to be ready for them to suddenly let a shot go and the Nike balls that you had in the Premier League then were also fairly lively.

Oaksie made some really good reaction stops in that game and as a result, thanks to

Kenny Miller's goal, we won 1-0.

United were sweeping aside everyone in their path at that stage so it was a great result, and Oakesie also stayed strong and his handling was great particularly in taking crosses.

He also followed it up with an excellent performance in the following game when we got a 1-1 draw with Liverpool.

So many people will remember us beating United on that day and you have to pay tribute to Oakesie for keeping the clean sheet.

He is such a modest guy that he wouldn't have taken any credit though!

## HANS SEGERS: 07/03/98 LEEDS 0-1 WOLVES

Hans had been at the club and had been injured, so I had been on the bench for the first team.

I was close to making my debut against Stoke, but then Hans was fit and had a little run in the side.

We'd done well in the FA Cup and went to face Leeds in what was a really tough quarter final at Elland Road.

Don Goodman got a goal in the 82nd minute and from there it was all about hanging on.

Leeds were flying high at the time with Hasselbaink on top form and again you need your keeper to be right on their game in a fixture like this.

Hans hadn't been in our team that long but had made some smart saves before Leeds won a penalty in the 88th minute.

There were a few mind games going on but Hans made a great penalty save, which was so vital.

If they had equalised, then they might have even gone on to win the game or certainly fancy their chances in a replay back at Molineux.

For Hans to guess right, and then get a strong hand on it to keep it out, was awesome.

I was pulled out of the England Under-16 squad at that time in case I was needed to be on the bench, but Stowelley had recovered sufficiently to do that, so I watched the game instead.

## MIKE STOWELL 03/01/94 WOLVES 1-0 BOLTON

I know this is one of Stowelley's favourite Wolves performances. There had been a massive downpour before kick-off leaving pools of water on the pitch and those conditions can make it difficult for a keeper.

But Stowelley made some great saves including one in particular late on from Jason McAteer to ensure Wolves kept a clean sheet and won the game thanks to a goal from Robbie Dennison.

Goals win you games, but saves can be equally important and that one, particularly so close to full time, is something which always gives a goalkeeper great pleasure.

Stowelley has always been a big help to me as well – when I was a schoolboy and YT at Wolves he was the first choice keeper but always had time for everybody.

He's a brilliant pro and someone I still speak to a lot now.

He was also very consistent in his performances, rarely letting in soft goals, and it's because of that he managed to break the appearance record for Wolves goalkeepers.

I think he should go down as one of the best Wolves have had.

## ... And what about MATT MURRAY

Well he is, of course, far too modest, so it's up to the Wolves Annual to select three of his best Wolves performances...

### 26/05/03 SHEFFIELD UNITED 0-3 WOLVES

Where else to start but the Millennium Stadium and the game which clinched Wolves' return to the big time? Three first half goals made the scoreline look comfortable, but only thanks to a man-of-the-match display from Murray with a string of saves, including one from the penalty spot from Michael Brown shortly after the interval.

### 30/01/07 NORWICH 0-1 WOLVES

Wolves were reduced to nine men by full time, but clung on to win despite being "absolutely battered" according to boss Mick McCarthy. And that was thanks to Michael Kightly's goal and umpteen Murray saves, particularly in a first half when Wolves were completely outplayed. "One of the best in the country," was McCarthy's verdict on Murray's performance.

### 11/03/07 WOLVES 1-0 WEST BROMWICH ALBION

Jay Bothroyd's late goal won this tension-packed Black Country Derby but again much of the credit had to go to the man between the sticks. Another raft of saves from the imperious Murray included three outstanding stops in a one-on-one duel with Diomansy Kamara.

# PRE-SEASON FUNNIES

**Pre-season was a fairly intense affair at Compton and in Scotland – but there is always time for the Wolves Annual to have a bit of fun!**

**Check out our captions on the pictures below!**

Who's nicked my water?

No Stears I promise – this is how you do it.

You know I'd much prefer a proper pillow.

Hands up who wants this to stop.

Preparations for the synchronised walking competition are going well.

Are you ticklish...

Remember the wheelbarrow race?

Come on then, who put Superglue on the bottom of my boots.

Yep, someone did that to me as well....

# FAMOUS FACES

**Can you identify the seven Wolves players included in these photos, all of whom have turned out for the club at some stage over the last four decades?**

**Might be one for the Mums and Dads this!**

**Once you have all seven names, the 14 initials also provide an anagram of a Northern Ireland winger who graced Molineux and had a special liking for finding the net at Wembley in the late 1980s.**

**Good luck!**

**Answers on page 61.**

# KEEPERS' CORNER

# PLAYER PROFILES

**Here are a selection of the players charged with taking Wolves into a new era, including some vital statistics and their footballing hero when they were growing up.**

**WAYNE HENNESSEY**
**BORN:** 24/01/87
**POSITION:** GOALKEEPER
**HERO:** NEVILLE SOUTHALL

**CARL IKEME**
**BORN:** 08/06/86
**POSITION:** GOALKEEPER
**HERO:** PAUL MCGRATH

**AARON McCAREY**
**BORN:** 14/01/92
**POSITION:** GOALKEEPER
**HERO:** SHAY GIVEN

**MATT DOHERTY**
**BORN:** 16/01/92
**POSITION:** DEFENDER
**HERO:** DENNIS BERGKAMP

**RICHARD STEARMAN**
**BORN:** 19/08/87
**POSITION:** DEFENDER
**HERO:** STEVE WALSH

# PLAYER PROFILES

## KEVIN FOLEY

**BORN:** 01/11/84
**POSITION:** DEFENDER/ MIDFIELDER
**HERO:** ERIC CANTONA

## GEORGE ELOKOBI

**BORN:** 31/01/86
**POSITION:** DEFENDER
**HERO:** ROGER MILLA

## SAM RICKETTS

**BORN:** 11/10/81
**POSITION:** DEFENDER
**HERO:** JOHN BARNES

## JAMIE RECKORD

**BORN:** 09/03/92
**POSITION:** DEFENDER
**HERO:** ROBERTO CARLOS

## ETHAN EBANKS-LANDELL

**BORN:** 12/12/92
**POSITION:** DEFENDER
**HERO:** RIO FERDINAND

# PLAYER PROFILES

## DANNY BATTH
**BORN:** 21/09/90
**POSITION:** DEFENDER
**HERO:** RIO FERDINAND

## DAVE EDWARDS
**BORN:** 03/02/86
**POSITION:** MIDFIELDER
**HERO:** GARY SPEED

## DAVID DAVIS
**BORN:** 20/02/91
**POSITION:** MIDFIELDER
**HERO:** PATRICK VIEIRA

## JACK PRICE
**BORN:** 19/12/92
**POSITION:** MIDFIELDER
**HERO:** ROBERT PIRES

## LEE EVANS
**BORN:** 24/07/94
**POSITION:** MIDFIELDER
**HERO:** STEVEN GERRARD

# PLAYER PROFILES

**KEVIN McDONALD**
**BORN:** 04/11/88
**POSITION:** MIDFIELDER
**HERO:** ZINEDINE ZIDANE

**ANTHONY FORDE**
**BORN:** 16/11/93
**POSITION:** WINGER
**HERO:** CRISTIANO RONALDO

**ZELI ISMAIL**
**BORN:** 12/12/93
**POSITION:** WINGER
**HERO:** ZINEDINE ZIDANE

**BAKARY SAKO**
**BORN:** 26/04/88
**POSITION:** WINGER
**HERO:** CRISTIANO RONALDO

**SCOTT GOLBOURNE**
**BORN:** 29/02/88
**POSITION:**
DEFENDER/MIDFIELDER
**HERO:** RONALDO (BRAZIL)

# PLAYER PROFILES

**BJORN SIGURDARSON**
**BORN:** 26/12/91
**POSITION:** STRIKER
**HERO:** JOEY GUDJONSSON

**JAKE CASSIDY**
**BORN:** 09/02/93
**POSITION:** STRIKER
**HERO:** STEVEN GERRARD

**LEIGH GRIFFITHS**
**BORN:** 20/08/90
**POSITION:** STRIKER
**HERO:** MICHAEL OWEN

**LIAM MCALINDEN**
**BORN:** 26/09/93
**POSITION:** STRIKER
**HERO:** THIERRY HENRY

**KEVIN DOYLE**
**BORN:** 18/09/83
**POSITION:** STRIKER
**HERO:** ANYONE FROM THE IRELAND 1990 WORLD CUP SQUAD

# WOLVES' NUMBER NINE

**Wolves headed into the 2013/14 season with hopes of a new hero in the form of their new number nine.**

Kenny Jackett made the return of Leigh Griffiths after a successful loan spell at Hibernian one of the priorities of his early days at Molineux, and in return 'Griff' started banging the goals in during pre-season. Here are nine photos of the man in action as he took on the coveted number nine shirt.

# GOLDEN MEMORIES – WOLVES' FIRST TITLE

**It is 60 years this season since a fairly important moment in Wolves' history – a first ever top flight title!**

**And what is more, the Championship success of Stan Cullis's class of 1953/54 was achieved after a titanic battle with local rivals West Bromwich Albion.**

**So let's mark the 'Diamond' anniversary of that epic triumph with some happy Golden memories.**

- Wolves posted their best ever unbeaten away run of 11 games during this season, the sequence from September to January covering 11 matches, of which six were victories.

- Out of Darkness Cometh Light, Wolves' first ever title also arrived during the season when floodlights were installed at Molineux for the first time. The first ever floodlit game took place on September 30, 1953, with goals from Jimmy Mullen, Peter Broadbent and Roy Swinbourne securing a 3-1 win against a touring South African side.

- Six of the Wolves squad involved in the season had also featured as Wolves won the 1949 FA Cup Final. Bert Williams, Jimmy Mullen, Johnny Hancocks, Roy Pritchard, Billy Wright and Bill Shorthouse all played in the 3-1 victory over Leicester at Wembley.

- Roy Swinbourne scored the very first goal of the 1953/54 season – after one minute 50 seconds of the first game away at Burnley. But Wolves actually lost the opening day fixture 4-1.

- Wolves inflicted the heaviest league defeat in Chelsea's history on September 26, 1953, winning 8-1 at Molineux. Scorers were Johnny Hancocks (3), Roy Swinbourne (2), Peter Broadbent, Jimmy Mullen and Dennis Wilshaw.

Wolves won the title by four points from local rivals West Bromwich Albion, helped by doing the double over the Baggies. Wolves won both games 1-0, Jimmy Mullen on target at Molineux in November and Roy Swinbourne at The Hawthorns in April.

Leading scorer for Wolves in the season was Dennis Wilshaw, with 27 goals in all competitions. Roy Swinbourne and Johnny Hancocks both notched 24.

The Football League trophy was not present at Molineux ahead of the final game of the season against Tottenham, which Wolves won 2-0. It would have needed a major turnaround of results and goals for Wolves to have lost the title to Albion, but officials had learned the lesson of 1947 when turning up at Molineux to see Wolves fail to beat Liverpool which would have secured them the Championship.

The title was marked with a banquet for 500 people at the

Civic Hall on May 10, 1954. West Bromwich Albion chairman Major Wilson Keys and director Horace Thursfield were also present and were congratulated on their FA Cup triumph against Preston North End.

Billy Wright: "First duty on one of the proudest days of my life is to pay tribute to the lads for the way they have played throughout the season, from start to finish, despite the fact we lost two of the first three games. Success, I think, has come because everybody in the team has pulled their weight all the time."

WOLVERHAMPTON WANDERERS: FIRST DIVISION CHAMPIONS

Back row (left to right) : J. Short, W. Slater, R. Flowers, B. Williams, R. Swinbourne, R. Pritchard. Front row (left to right) : J. Hancocks, P. Broadbent, W. Wright, D. Wilshaw, J. Mullen. Inset : W. Shorthouse

Stan Cullis: "Let me put the credit where it rightly belongs – on the players, who have won this championship because they have given of their best from start to finish. I feel I must pay a tribute to the captain Billy Wright. I have made many demands on him this season but he has answered them all without question."

# YOUNG WOLVES AND DRIBBLERS

Wolves run plenty of initiatives for junior supporters, including the hugely popular Young Wolves club, and the more recently formed 'Dribblers', which proved a major success in its inaugural season.

Well both are back again for the 2013/14 season, with Young Wolves open to fans aged 3 to 16 and Dribblers for supporters under three.

See the page opposite for more details.

But in the meantime feel free to relive a pictorial look back at some of the highlights from last year.

From Christmas parties to Open Training Sessions, mascot opportunities to snowman competitions, there was certainly never a dull moment!

# Wolves Dribblers

Become a member or renew your existing membership for **only £10**, and receive one of two exclusive gifts....

### Members will receive:

- Welcome certificate
- Various competitions
- Exclusive Mother and Toddler event
- Smartcard and rewards

### New members

will also receive this exclusive poncho towel

### Renewing members

will also receive this exclusive backpack

# Young Wolves

### Membership just £15 for the season!

- Exclusive **Young Wolves** football shirt joining gift
- Cash Rewards earned on Ticket and Merchandise purchases
- 100 Loyalty Points
- Free match tickets to:
  - Wolves v Sheffield United,Saturday September 28th
  - Wolves v Crewe Alexandra Boxing Day fixture
  - Wolves v Peterborough United, Saturday April 5th
- **PLUS LOADS MORE!**

Membership can be purchased online at **wolvesmembership.co.uk** or by calling the Ticket Line on **0871 222 1877**

# ROOM-MATES WITH VIEWS!

**We've already heard from midfielder David Davis in the Team-Mates feature. Now he stars in Room-Mates too, alongside fellow Academy graduate Danny Batth. Players generally tend to find the same team mate to room with on away trips or during pre-season tours – and David and Danny are among that number. The Wolves Annual gatecrashed their room to find out more!**

### ⬡ How long have you pair known each other?

**DD:** Too long.
**DB:** When did you sign?
**DD:** When I was 15.
**DB:** Since we were 15!

### ⬡ And you always room together when you're in the squad?

BOTH: Yes.

### ⬡ Let's cut to the chase, what is your room-mate's worst habit?

**DB:** He blows his nose without a tissue.
**DD:** He snores. So loud that sometimes I cannot sleep.

### ⬡ Ok then, moving on swiftly. Good habits?

**DB:** He makes me a good cup of tea.

**DD:** Can't you talk about my banter? I'm always making him laugh. He's got some decent music to be fair.

## How are those tastes in music?

**DB:** Very similar.

**DD:** Yep house music. Deep house. You have to spell it Haus.

## Do you play FIFA?

**DB:** Sometimes yes.

**DD:** But it all depends on whether we can plug the console into the TV on away trips!

## And who wins?

**DD:** Come on, out with it...

**DB:** He wins if his team is away.

**DD:** It's me. All the time!

**DB:** It's because he plays five at the back.

## Anything else to keep you entertained?

**DD:** Football Manager usually, when we can't play FIFA.

**DB:** Or just watch a bit of telly. Or a film. Selfish films. It's difficult to find one we agree on.

## Who gets up first in the morning?

**DD:** Usually me.

**DB:** But he's very quiet so he doesn't wake me up!

Cheers guys!

# PICTURE SPECIAL
# GEORGE'S MARVELLOUS MEDICINE!

After a 2012/13 season damaged via no fault of his own through injury, George Elokobi's positive and determined attitude both to his rehabilitation and life in general certainly provided a major tonic after a spell of disappointment.

The message heading into the new campaign was clear and simple – Big George is back! Here are a few shots of the Cameroon-born defender preparing for the new season:

# QUOTES QUIZ – WHO'S THE BOSS?

**Wolves have reaped the benefit of being led by some impressive managers since being founded in 1877, many of whom have achieved success with league titles, promotions and cup victories.**

**And of course, managers are always called upon to give interviews and talk about games, passing on their thoughts to supporters via the media. Here below are ten comments made by Wolves managers down the years – can you link them to the correct boss from the list provided? It's fair to say some will be easier than others!**

**Answers on Page 61.**

1 If I'm honest with myself, if it was any other club than Wolves I wouldn't have taken it on. The reason I did? I was a Wolves supporter who followed the club closely as a kid and had a favourite player in Billy Wright.

2 You only have the one life – and I gave mine to Wolves.

3 I told the back four: 'I'm glad you lot weren't defending me in my court case. The judge would have put his black cap on'.

4 Wolves are in such a state it's frightening. I won't be party to killing off one of the greatest football clubs in the world.

5 The initials on my tracksuit may say 'MM', but I'm not Merlin the Magician.

6 Stan (Cullis) is the best defender we have by a mile, but he gets a nosebleed everytime he crosses the half way line.

7 Wolves was a big club that needed to get into the Premiership and it was immediately obvious to me that they needed a proper training ground. So I used to spend my evenings driving around the area looking for suitable sites we might be able to develop.

8 I'd watched Wolves from the age of ten and used to be almost the first in the ground at Molineux, jumping off the bus and taking my place in the North Bank, with my box of sandwiches.

9 When I came into Wolves it wasn't just about rebuilding a club, but about rebuilding my life. I've been building, not just to get into the Premiership, but to stay there.

10 Andy Gray does not miss many chances like that. I do not normally single out individuals for praise but George Berry deserves some today – I thought he was superb.

| | |
|---|---|
| GRAHAM TAYLOR | DAVE JONES |
| MICK McCARTHY | TOMMY DOCHERTY |
| GRAHAM TURNER | MAJOR FRANK BUCKLEY |
| JOHN BARNWELL | GRAHAM HAWKINS |
| STAN CULLIS | BILL McGARRY |

# NEW SPONSORS NEW KIT!

**The 2013/14 season saw a double change at Wolves with new main club sponsors and new kit manufacturers secured at the Club.**

Whathouse.co.uk, the specialist new homes portal, became the new main sponsor, seeing their company name move from the back of last season's replica kit to the front.

In a move welcomed by Wolves' supporters, What House ? also decided to change their brand from red to black for the new first team home shirt to better complement Wolves' iconic colours.

And that new kit was produced by top global Sportslifestyle giants PUMA, who now supply not only the replica kit but the club's technical and trainingwear as well.

Wayne Hennessey, Björn Sigurdarson, Danny Batth and Dorus De Vries are pictured above in the home goalkeepers, home, away and change goalkeepers' kits respectively, all of which are now available to purchase from the Club's Molineux Megastore and Dudley Street Superstore.

**Alternatively purchase online by clicking 'shop' at www.wolves.co.uk**

Also left are photos from the press conference which announced the new What House ? sponsorship, featuring Wolves' CEO Jez Moxey and What House ? Editorial Director Rupert Bates, while Kenny Jackett is pictured with Paul Cox, Managing Director of new back-of-shirt sponsor Reconomy.

# QUIZ & PUZZLE ANSWERS

**Wordsearch: Finders Keepers (pg 15)**

| | | | | | | | | | | | | | | | |
|---|---|---|---|---|---|---|---|---|---|---|---|---|---|---|---|
| M | A | L | C | O | L | M | F | I | N | L | A | Y | S | O | N |
| A | I | T | I | M | F | L | C | A | R | L | I | B | D | T | A |
| R | E | K | M | I | T | I | M | F | L | O | W | E | R | S | A |
| C | I | B | E | R | T | W | I | L | L | I | A | M | S | W | R |
| U | D | S | E | S | W | A | Y | N | E | H | Y | I | P | W | O |
| S | O | K | E | R | T | Y | L | M | T | H | N | C | E | A | N |
| H | J | J | O | N | T | O | E | H | P | H | E | H | C | H | M |
| A | A | R | O | N | O | K | W | L | H | P | H | A | R | S | C |
| H | E | N | E | T | I | J | F | E | I | R | E | E | E | D | C |
| N | K | K | T | L | W | M | L | O | L | A | N | L | I | A | A |
| E | I | A | R | O | I | A | B | U | P | L | N | O | P | R | R |
| M | M | A | T | T | M | U | R | R | A | Y | E | A | Y | B | E |
| A | C | S | T | L | J | A | C | K | R | P | S | K | R | L | Y |
| N | O | R | I | E | L | I | A | M | K | Z | E | E | A | U | V |
| N | E | H | C | K | H | E | N | N | E | S | Y | S | G | A | R |
| B | P | S | E | I | R | V | E | D | S | U | R | O | D | P | X |

**Quiz: Famous Faces (pg 43)**

**Photo IDs**
1. Denis Irwin
2. Rob Edwards
3. Isaac Okoronkwo
4. Norman Bell
5. Nathan Blake
6. Simon Osborn
7. Neil Emblen

**Anagram answer:**
**ROBBIE DENNISON**

**Quotes Quiz: Who's the boss? (pg 59)**

1. Graham Turner
2. Stan Cullis
3. Tommy Docherty
4. Bill McGarry
5. Mick McCarthy
6. Major Frank Buckley
7. Graham Taylor
8. Graham Hawkins
9. Dave Jones
10. John Barnwell

whathouse
.co.uk
whathouse
.co.uk
whathouse
.co.uk
whathouse
.co.uk
whathouse
.co.uk